THE MONSTER

AND THE LAST

BLOOD MATCH

THE MONSTER

AND THE LAST

BLOOD MATCH

NEW YORK TIMES BESTSELLING AUTHOR

K.A. LINDE

RED TOWER BOOKS™

Entangled Publishing, LLC
644 Shrewsbury Commons Ave., STE 181
Shrewsbury, PA 17361
rights@entangledpublishing.com

Edited by Sylvan Creekmore
Cover design by LJ Anderson and Bree Archer
Edge design by Bree Archer
Interior design by Britt Marczak

Paperback ISBN 978-1-64937-970-2
Ebook ISBN 978-1-64937-532-2

Manufactured in the United States of America
First Edition June 2025

10 9 8 7 6 5 4 3 2 1

RED TOWER BOOKS™

MORE FROM K.A. LINDE

To the girls who always wanted that vampire bite

The Monster and the Last Blood Match is a dark supernatural romance filled with vampires, the humans they rely on for survival, and the gritty underbelly of a society wrought with inner conflicts and dark secrets. However, the story includes elements that might not be suitable for all readers. Violence, gore, blood, emotional and physical abuse, control, possessiveness, owner/pet dynamics, threatened and attempted sexual and physical assault, and suffering caused by economic disparity are depicted in the novel. Readers who may be sensitive to these elements, please take note, guard your hearts, and step into the monster's tower...

CHAPTER ONE

"Number four hundred and ninety-two."

Reyna stared down at the crisp piece of paper she had been clutching the last three hours. She blinked in surprise and recognition: 4-9-2.

"That's me."

She raised her hand in the air. It was about time. She hadn't expected to be waiting here so long. Reyna stumbled to her feet, stretching out her sore muscles and stuffing her shaking hands into her worn-out jeans. She headed across the room to a woman standing at the front of the stark white hospital ward. The administrator had long blond hair that was straight to her shoulders and a white uniform that matched her surroundings. The only bit of color was the bloodred symbol on the pocket of her shirt—*Visage*.

The largest company in the world. It employed more people than anyone else in recorded history. Visage primarily specialized in what they called body employment services. It was just a fancy term for blood escorts. Whatever people wanted to call them—blood escort or bodily employment—they were still the main job for people desperate to get by in this terrible economy.

And Reyna was about to become one of them.

"Four-nine-two?" the woman asked.

"Yes," Reyna said, embarrassed that her voice shook. She still couldn't believe this was her life, that she was about to do this. Brian and Drew were going to kill her.

The woman ignored her discomfort.

"Right this way, four-nine-two." Her voice was flat and lifeless.

"It's Reyna," she told the lady curtly.

She had a name. She wasn't just some number.

The woman nodded minutely. Her big brown eyes stared through Reyna. She clearly didn't care what Reyna's name was. This was a job, and she was following orders. No more. No less. It was as much as Reyna had come to expect from everyone in this godforsaken place.

"Follow me," the woman said.

Reyna sighed and did as instructed. There was no point in fighting it. She had made up her mind to go through with the Visage testing. She'd snuck away without telling her brothers and applied. She had no degree and no job. All that did was force her brothers to take extra shifts to cover her. She needed to do something to put food on the table. She couldn't stand the sight of them wasting their lives away toiling in the factories, when she could be doing something to help their situation.

No, she was here of her own free will. If poverty and near-starvation could be considered part of her free will.

Not that that mattered to the administrator. Or likely to anyone at Visage. They didn't care who she was. She was just another subject in the system.

Since Visage had unveiled its plan to employ humans as blood donors for vampires ten years earlier, thousands had gone through testing. It had been a most fortuitous circumstance—for them, at least. Millions of people out of jobs in one fell swoop, and then out of the gloom and doom came a knight on a white horse to save them all.

An end to the fear of what lurked in the darkness.

An end to being hunted for their blood.

An end to the economic struggles entirely—so long as you gave up the very thing they had hunted humans for.

Ten years later and not much had really changed. The majority of people still lived below the poverty line, and now the populace was more tied to Visage than ever. But Reyna couldn't change that any more than she could quell the fear building in her stomach at the thought of becoming another mindless drone for the conglomerate.

Reyna fidgeted at the sight of the big white door looming ahead. The door that sealed her fate to Visage. *Can I really do this? Do I even have a choice?*

Unaware of or at least unconcerned with Reyna's fear, the administrator pushed the door open. Reyna swallowed hard. She could just make out the long stark white corridor beyond the door. Once she was through that door, there was no turning back.

But if there were another choice, then she would have already found it. Visage was the only option, the absolute last option.

Just the way they liked it.

"Are you ready, 492?" the woman snapped. At least there was *some* kind of reaction.

Reyna bit back a snide retort. "Yes."

Reyna walked through the door, and the admin escorted her down the long white corridor studded with white doors and past starkly dressed administrators standing like ducks in a row. They took a right, and the admin stopped in front of one of the plain white doors. She removed an identification card from her pocket with her name and picture on it and swiped it over a glass screen by the handle.

Reyna watched in awe as the door swiped open. The Warehouse District didn't have technology this advanced. Hell, machines everyone had taken for granted before the collapse—phones, laptops, cars—weren't even available to most people.

The interior of the room looked like any hospital room, though she didn't remember the last time she had been able to afford a real hospital visit. The administrator fiddled with a few tools on a wheeled cart. She glanced up at Reyna, realizing that she hadn't moved from her position in the doorway.

"Take a seat." She gestured to the bed.

Reyna took a deep breath, reminding herself of all the reasons she had decided to do this, then walked inside. The paper crinkled underneath her as she sat, and she cringed at the harsh lights. Everything smelled like plastic and disinfectant. Reyna had thought the waiting room was the most unwelcoming room she had ever been in. She'd been wrong.

When she was approved earlier that week, Visage had given her a packet explaining what was to come. The gist of it was—needles.

Lots and lots of needles.

Reyna barely suppressed a gag. She hated needles. Always had. She didn't even know where the fear stemmed from. If she'd had a traumatic experience as a child, no one who was still in her life knew about it. Considering what she was about to do, it was ridiculous to fear needles. They were going to be the least of her worries where vampires were concerned. She braced for the worst.

The woman strapped a band around Reyna's arm, clipped her finger in a large plastic clothespin-type device, and ran a giant thermometer over her forehead. She stuck a stethoscope under the band and squeezed a bag that inflated the band and constricted Reyna's arm. Reyna tried to relax, but she wasn't successful.

"Good," the administrator said. "Vitals all look good."

Reyna breathed a sigh of relief.

The woman spoke to herself as she entered information into the computer system. "Temperature—97.8 degrees Fahrenheit. Acceptable. Pulse—72 beats per minute. Acceptable. Blood Pressure—102 over 65. Acceptable/Low."

She turned away from her computer to face Reyna. "Family history?"

Reyna stilled her shaking hands. "My parents are, um…dead."

The words sounded hollow. It had been thirteen years since they died in the car accident. Since she and her brothers moved in with their uncle in the city. Since their uncle drank and gambled away their inheritance. Since the world went to utter shit.

"Any diseases or chronic illnesses?" the woman asked. Her voice was flat. No compassion in the Visage hospital ward.

"Breast cancer on my mother's side. That's all I know," she whispered.

"Are you often ill?"

"No."

"When was the last time you were admitted to the hospital?"

Reyna racked her brain. She couldn't even remember. "Probably when I was a baby."

The woman gave her a searching look. "Any other treatments or surgeries?"

"No."

As if anyone could afford a hospital stay. This woman had to know it. She wasn't going to act ashamed of her life.

The admin tapped out a few more notes and then withdrew a needle and a few small vials from a drawer. Reyna's stomach dropped out, and the color drained from her body. *Here we go.*

Reyna held her breath as the woman placed a tourniquet around her right arm, swabbed the crook of her elbow, and then without warning pricked the vein in her arm. She squeezed her eyes shut and tried to calm her rapidly accelerating heartbeat. She suddenly felt nauseated, weak, and clammy. Fear pricked at the back of her neck.

She glanced down at her arm and tried not to vomit. Bright red blood flowed out of the vein and into the little tube. Pain throbbed in her elbow, but she couldn't look past the blood. It made her stomach turn, and she had to physically look away until the administrator was finished.

After she removed the needle, the woman placed a bandage over the hole and then gave her a cup to pee in.

"Leave the cup in the compartment in the restroom." The woman pointed to a nearly invisible doorway to her right. "Come back here once you're through. The doctor will be with you soon."

"Thank you," Reyna said hollowly.

At least the worst was over.

Reyna tried not to think about the blood loss or needles. She needed to think about eating right, sending money to her brothers, and finally living a real life again. It wasn't as if this was permanent. She could get out at any time. She could work for a couple of months as a blood donor and then quit if she wanted. Just to get back on her feet or to help her find something else.

At least, she hoped that she would make enough to be able to send money to her brothers. If they had known she was here, they never would have approved. No one would approve of their little sister becoming a blood escort to a vampire.

She left her sample in the restroom and waited for the doctor. At least the bed was more comfortable than the chairs in the waiting room. Honestly, it was more comfortable than everything else they had at home, too.

A knock at the door, and the doctor strode inside with a clipboard. She was a tall, wiry woman with brown skin, black groomed hair held back in a ponytail, and dark, emotionless eyes. Like everyone else who worked there, she clearly didn't think smiling was part of bedside manners.

There was something about this woman that was other.

Vampire.

The word slithered up in Reyna's conscious and she recoiled away from the thought. It made no sense considering her current predicament, but she couldn't help it. Deeply ingrained fear stuck with her no matter her decision to work with them.

"Four hundred and ninety-two. Miss Reyna Carpenter. Five foot four inches. Brown eyes. Brown hair. White. O negative. Correct?"

"Yes," she confirmed.

"Good. I have to make sure that you fit all the parameters." She looked up at Reyna over the rim of her thick black-rimmed glasses.

"Negative for pregnancy. That's good."

Reyna breathed a sigh of relief. She hadn't thought it probable, but it had been possible. When she applied for the position at Visage, she had been in the off-again stage with her boyfriend, Steven. The problem was that Steven was charismatic as hell. Every time she walked away, somehow he would sweep her off her feet again. Which he had done a couple of weeks ago when he'd convinced her to meet him at the end of his shift. Two weeks of a whirlwind of romance and then a big "fuck you" at the end of it.

Steven had made her feel cheap and disposable. No better than the run-down trash that they lived in. When Visage had approved her for testing shortly afterward, she had felt like it made sense.

The door opened unexpectedly once again. "Excuse me. Dr. Trainer, you've been called to the east corridor. I was reassigned to number four hundred and ninety-two."

"Of course, Dr. Washington," Dr. Trainer said. "Here's her file."

They swapped information, and then Dr. Trainer left her alone with the new doctor. He was tall and pale with a slightly more disheveled appearance than the doctor she had been dealing with. Though what he lacked in proper grooming, he made up for with the severity of his features. He seemed excessively stern, and the haphazard state of his attire only gave off the impression of a mad scientist.

"Welcome, Miss Carpenter. I'm Dr. Roger Washington."

He extended his hand. Reyna looked down at it skeptically. No one had addressed her or acknowledged her as anything more than a subject to be tested and questioned. What was this, bad cop, good cop?

"Hi," she said softly. She shook his hand once. It was cold and made her shiver.

"After reviewing your profile, we've elected you to be a trial subject in our new program. Your blood type and specific history, build, and biology make you a great candidate for this venture. I'm the head of the team, and we're looking for interested participants.

You understand that anything we speak about here is completely classified, yes?"

"Sure."

A new program? Classified information? She didn't know what any of that meant, but she was willing to hear more about this. It sounded like they wanted her, and if they wanted her badly enough, then maybe she could get more money out of them.

"For some time, Visage has been considering going to a more streamlined system of employment for our human subjects," Dr. Washington explained.

"Streamlined…how?"

The man smiled, and her skin turned ashen. Sharp canines gleamed in the high contrast lighting. She tried to swallow but felt like her mouth was stuffed with cotton balls. She knew he was a vampire. She had known that both doctors were, but suddenly it felt different. This wasn't some person in the papers or on billboards, but a real live vampire that could reach out and touch her.

He assessed her discomfort and closed his mouth so that the stern expression was back in place. "You do realize, Miss Carpenter, that the company you wish to be employed by is run by vampires, and that if you are selected for this, you will live with vampires?"

"Yes, I'm well aware," she said, regaining her composure.

"Good." He nodded. "Now back to what I was saying. The current system places a subject with a Sponsor for one month. After that month, you are granted a week off to recuperate, and then you rotate to another blood match Sponsor. As an O negative subject, you would meet with a group of O negative Sponsors in your assigned region. The system then perpetually rotates. Everything is carefully monitored by Visage so that it is safe and orderly."

Reyna had read all about this on the pamphlet when she had originally applied. When vampires drank blood from just anyone, the blood fed them only on a completely basic and primal level, but it didn't provide anything more than that. It contaminated their systems, making them corrupt, lethal, and animalistic. When Visage came forward, they promised a new horizon for humans and vampires alike to coexist in a mutually beneficial atmosphere.

Thus came the blood type cure.

Vampires who drank blood that matched the blood type they had when they were human functioned at higher cognitive levels. Visage registered all the known vampires and offered humans money to become their blood donors.

"How is the new system different?" she asked.

The doctor smiled once more, and her fingers dug into the paper on the bed. "Now the Sponsor requests a blood type match and a certain profile, and the subject stays with the Sponsor...permanently."

Chapter Two

"Permanently?" Reyna gasped.

"Yes. The new system would place you with a vampire match. You would be placed in the home and share living quarters with your Sponsor."

"Forever?" she asked in disbelief.

"Well, not forever, as if there is no other option, Miss Carpenter. The system is supposed to fix some of the issues with the previous functions within Visage. It allows less fluctuation and gives the subjects a better lifestyle."

"So, we could never leave?"

"Of course not. If the subject or Sponsor deems that the relationship is no longer functional, then another Permanent would be located and your contract made void. We have no grounds to hold you against your will. We are merely trying to find a more suitable lifestyle for our Sponsors. And if it makes you feel any better, all Sponsors who are selected into this program are top-echelon candidates. You will be well taken care of."

A permanent placement with a vampire. She couldn't think of anything she would want to do less. It sounded like an easy way for vampires to take advantage of humans and eliminate the checks and balances of the previous system.

"It's a better situation for the Sponsors, but what about us?" she demanded. "How do we know that we'll truly be taken care of when there is no one to check in with once a month?"

"I can guarantee that every Sponsor has been carefully screened. They are very high-ranking officials within the organization. We would never place our employees in potentially dangerous situations."

"Of course not," she said dryly. "So, these Sponsors are bigger and better than the other ones. Does that mean the pay is better?"

He chuckled and then recovered his expression. "Straight to the point, I see. How does double the monthly salary sound for this Permanent position?"

Reyna's eyes were as big as saucers. Double? To stay at one vampire's house indefinitely?

That was incredible. She wouldn't have to work for Visage as long if she was able to make double the income they had originally reported. With double the pay, she could save up to go to college. With a shiny new degree, someone might even employ her. It all depended on how everything actually went once she was there. She could handle that. And it didn't matter what Brian or Drew said, she had to do this.

"Are you interested in this new program?" Dr. Washington asked her.

"I—"

She was about to say yes, but the doctor's eagerness stalled her. Why did he want this so bad? And what was it about the situation that put her on edge?

It wasn't the obvious things. She was surrounded by vampires and about to give her blood up to one on a regular basis. She had more or less come to terms with it, but something else bothered her.

"Why was I selected?" she asked instead.

He pursed his lips. "You fit the profile."

"And what profile is that?"

"Young, fit, and the proper match."

"You said something about my history in my file. *What* about my history?"

Dr. Washington narrowed his eyes and then pulled up her file on the computer.

"It says here that your parents are deceased. Car accident. You were only ten. Your brothers, Brian and Drew, were fourteen and twelve. Both are currently employed at Cartwright Warehouses. Your uncle is your only other living relative. He left you at age eleven and as far as our records show disappeared completely. No death has been reported. Your history, Miss Carpenter, shows that you are entirely alone other than two brothers who despair having another mouth to feed."

Reyna defiantly raised her chin. Hearing her bleak history spelled out before her in such terms made her heart constrict. "I know my own history well enough. But it doesn't explain how that makes me a good match for your Permanent program. Do you want someone without family? Someone that if things go south for you, there is no one who will be blowing up the papers in anger over my disappearance?"

He laughed. "I already told you that you will be perfectly safe. You're hesitant. I understand that, but you have the wrong impression of our organization."

"Do I?"

"We're not selecting you because we don't want any liabilities later. It's because you need it the most, Miss Carpenter. You have no one to help you, and you are a burden on your siblings," he said bluntly. "A permanent placement with Visage would provide all you've ever dreamed and more. We are looking for people who are truly interested in a permanent partnership with our Sponsors. If you'd rather a more temporary position for less pay, then this is not the service for you."

Reyna needed time to think. Brian and Drew wouldn't be happy that she had agreed to a month of work at Visage. She couldn't even imagine their reaction when they found out that she had agreed to a permanent spot in a vampire's home. She had never even considered working for Visage permanently. It was supposed to be a temporary fix for her family. Yet, even when she came home from working at Visage, she would still have to find a way to afford food long term, which meant she needed that degree.

She didn't know how long she would need to be a part of Visage before all of this could unfold and she and her brothers were living comfortably again. On the base salary, it would take much longer than the Permanent wage.

"I could still leave at any time if I need to, right?" she asked again for confirmation.

"Yes, of course," the doctor agreed. "If you find that the situation is not for you, then we would remove you from the program. But we have been very particular about our selections for you as well as the Sponsor and we do believe this will be a great match."

Reyna sighed. Here's to hoping that all her dreams really could come true. *How much worse could it be?*

"All right. What do I need to do?"

After Reyna had completed a mountain of paperwork, Dr. Washington returned to her room to collect all the documents. It felt a bit like she was signing her life away, but she made sure to read every line.

Dr. Washington scrutinized the many places she'd had to place her signature and then nodded. "This is satisfactory. Your Sponsor arrived to collect you."

Reyna jolted. "What? Now? Already?"

The doctor gave her a confused look. "You're not reconsidering, are you?"

Reyna tucked a lock of her brown hair behind her ear. "No. I'm not reconsidering. I was unaware that my employment began today and that I would be leaving with my Sponsor immediately."

"Well, employment does start as soon as the paperwork is signed. Plus, your Sponsor is a very busy man, and he won't have time to return to collect you another time."

"Oh. I see, but I need to speak with my brothers."

"I'm sure you will be able to get a message to them once you are settled into your new living quarters," the doctor said.

Reyna frowned. She couldn't believe she was about to divulge how utterly destitute they were, but there was no other option. They clearly had done their homework on her background already. It couldn't come as that much of a shock to them. "But we don't have a phone or anything."

"A letter?" he suggested.

Reyna's frown only deepened. "I really need to speak with them in person."

"I'm afraid that won't be possible at the moment. Your Sponsor is almost here. Unless you want to forfeit your position with Visage entirely, then you'll need to leave now."

"No, of course I don't want to forfeit my position. I signed all of that paperwork." She threw her hand out to the stack the doctor was still holding.

"Then you will have to speak to your Sponsor later about when you will have free time to visit your relatives. You're a Visage employee now and must work under Visage rules." His phone buzzed in his pocket. He retrieved the phone and then checked the device. The doctor's body tensed. "He's here."

"Already?" She pushed her shoulders back and tried to look taller sitting on the sterile hospital bed in her threadbare jeans. It was hard to do when her feet didn't quite hit the step below and her legs could swing back and forth with ease.

"Yes. He's on his way in right now."

"What's he like?" she asked with hesitancy. She wasn't entirely sure why she asked now. It might have been an important question to consider before agreeing to live with the vampire permanently for the next...ever. But in the end, it probably didn't matter. He was a vampire. How different could they all be?

"You'll see in a moment."

There was a knock at the door.

"Ah, here he is."

Reyna jumped to her feet. She had felt ridiculous sitting on that bed to begin with. She didn't want her first interaction with her new employer to be that of a scared little girl sitting on a hospital bed. She wanted to appear strong and confident. Ready to take on the world.

But when her Sponsor walked in the room, she shrank in on herself in terror. She had never felt so small before in her life.

The man filled the doorway. His mere presence made him seem to stand even taller than his immense height and strong build. It was as if she could feel the power vibrating beneath the surface. There was no other way to describe it. He held himself with such utter confidence that he took over the small room.

Her eyes lifted to meet his, and all she could do was stare into the endless dark depths. For a second, she saw something flicker in his eyes, something that spoke of need, but then it was gone. Replaced by nothingness. His features were chiseled out of stone. His cheekbones were sharp and defined, hollowing out his cheeks. His jaw was strong and pronounced. Even his dark hair was precisely cut and maintained. He wore a crisp black suit with a bloodred tie.

He was plainly terrifying to behold, but also gorgeous. Horrifyingly beautiful.

"Reyna, allow me to introduce you to your Sponsor," Dr. Washington said. "This is Beckham Anderson, senior vice president of Visage Incorporated."

She locked eyes with Beckham, and she refused to look away. If he was trying to intimidate her with his lethal stare, it was working, but she would never let him know that.

Here she was in tattered jeans, a plain gray T-shirt, black Converse sneakers, and a maroon baseball cap stuffed in her back pocket. Her hair was in a high ponytail. She wore not an ounce of makeup. And she was in a standoff against a man who was on all counts perfect. But she wouldn't look away. She wouldn't give him the satisfaction.

When she didn't say anything, Dr. Washington cleared his throat and continued. "Mr. Anderson, your new subject, Miss Reyna Carpenter."

No one spoke.

All the times she had thought about coming to Visage and becoming a blood escort, she had never truly known what to expect. She had never considered the vampire that she would have to live with. This man made her want to run as fast and as far away from him as possible. This man was a thing of nightmares. *How the hell am I supposed to live with him?*

"Well," Dr. Washington said uncomfortably, "what do you think?"

Beckham broke her gaze to turn to the doctor. "Yes. Fine. She'll do. I have a car waiting and a meeting to attend. Get her ready to leave immediately."

Reyna raised her eyebrows. That was nothing more than a short perusal. The paperwork had already been squared away, but she thought that he would want to ask her a few questions to get to know her. She *was*, after all, going to be living with him indefinitely. She guessed this was what an arranged marriage felt like.

"I believe she is ready to leave," the doctor said without acknowledging her. "We need your approval signature, and then she can be discharged."

The doctor handed over the last piece of paper she had signed, and Beckham scrawled his name across the line with a flourish.

"Great. She's mine. Can we go now?" Beckham asked sharply.

"Yes. Yes, of course. Reyna, come along."

Reyna forced herself to put one foot in front of the other. She could do this. She could leave behind everything she had ever known to go live with this strange man...vampire. To live with a strange vampire who was going to suck her blood on a regular basis. She swallowed hard and held her chin up. She was doing this for Brian and Drew, but also for herself. She wanted to make something of herself. One day, she would.

Every journey begins with one step. Hers began with this one.

She moved over to the doctor, feeling marginally more comfortable with him. Her Sponsor was already busy checking his phone. He wasn't paying attention to her at all.

"He's not going to hurt me, right?" she whispered, never taking her eyes off of Mr. Anderson.

Beckham's nostrils flared, and his eyes darted to hers. "I am not here to hurt you. You are my employee. I will treat you like an employee. And as my employee, we are in a bit of a hurry, so anything else you might wish to discuss with the doctor will have to wait. If everything is in order, we will leave."

Reyna stared up into the black pools of his eyes and realized she was drowning. She was floundering through an empty abyss with no way to escape. If she had once known how to swim, the ability had fled her mind. There was only her and this monster and her inability to say something to tamp down his ever-increasing anger. Very little was clear about what would follow once she walked through that door.

The only thing that was really *very* clear was that Beckham Anderson was a complete and total asshole.

CHAPTER THREE

Silence.

Apparently that was Beckham's MO. He was silent. He liked her silent. His phone was silent. Even the town car, the unbelievably sleek, beautiful, shouldn't-even-touch-it-was-so-shiny town car, was silent.

They drove out of the Visage facilities and then headed east toward the coastline. The town car zoomed at unbelievable speeds, driving away from her shitty home, away from her brothers, away from her life.

Reyna glanced over her shoulder and back through the rear window. Her pulse raced with regret at leaving everything she knew behind, and yet she wouldn't have changed her decision. They needed the money. This was the perfect opportunity. Though it wasn't what her brothers would have chosen for her. Few hard choices in life were ever what you wanted to take.

When she didn't show up at home tonight, Brian and Drew

were going to have a panic attack. She wished she had gotten to say goodbye. Since they didn't have a phone, she had no means of contacting them, and she couldn't reach their employer without risking backlash at the factory. Maybe she should have left a note letting them know where she was going. They probably would have been just as panicked when they found the note. No matter what, she would have to find a way to let her brothers know she was okay.

With a heavy sigh, she sat back in the seat, leaving her world behind her.

Then the city came into view. She had always found it hideous, cold and disgusting. When she had been forced to move in with her uncle for those few horrible years, she had learned to hate the city. Dirty and unforgiving. And filled with people neglectful and careless of their neighbors. Everyone trapped like rats.

With nothing to their name, her brothers had taken her and hitchhiked out of the city limits. They had moved from this hellhole and into a new one. She didn't mind trading one hell for another, since her brothers were able to get work in the warehouse district.

"So," Reyna said softly, "where exactly do you live?"

Beckham looked up at her over the top of his phone. His eyes were fierce and supremely disinterested. Black as night. He sent her a look that said, *Why the fuck are you talking to me?*

"You will see soon enough," he said, his tone dismissive.

She swallowed hard and averted her eyes. It was hard to look at him head-on. His eyes, though black and lifeless, were terrifying.

Her first instinct about him was absolutely accurate. He was a very powerful man, and he exuded that power in everything he did. Him just turning his head to look at her made her want to shrink in her seat. She didn't out of pride, but she wanted to. She couldn't imagine what it would be like to have seen a vampire like Beckham before the blood type cure had curbed their more gruesome baser instincts.

They drove into the heart of the city, and she plastered herself against the window to look at the tall buildings, masses of people, and strange sights and sounds. After she left with her brothers, she hadn't set foot in the city again. It wasn't a safe place for anyone alone, and her brothers would have never allowed it even if she had wanted to go. Which she didn't.

The next building took up an entire block. *Visage* was scrawled across the entrance in big, bold red letters. She had never seen their downtown offices. It was all glass and impossibly tall. Even craning her neck, she couldn't see the top.

"Do you work there? In *that*?" she asked before she could stop herself.

He sighed rather heavily. "Yes. Now would you please be quiet, sit still, and stop gawking? I have business to attend to, and I can't concentrate with you breathing on the windows."

Reyna snapped back into her seat and glared in his direction. What an asshole. She was just curious about this new life she was about to lead. The least he could do was answer a few questions. He obviously didn't know this was her first time in the city in ten years. He obviously didn't care, either.

She let her gaze drift back out the window in frustration. It all looked the same anyway. Dark and bleak. Just like Beckham's attitude.

A few tense minutes later, they slowed in front of another enormous building. Beckham's driver pulled up into the circular loading zone, and a valet rushed over to open the door. Beckham exited first without a backward glance in her direction. With another agitated sigh, she scooted across the seat to follow him.

Reyna trotted across the empty space to catch up with Beckham. Spotless sliding glass doors zipped open at their approach, and they entered into a colossal lobby entranceway. As she stared around at her lush surroundings, her mouth dropped open. The room went up as far as the eye could see. A clear glass elevator shot quickly up its track to the highest reaches of the building. She trekked across a polished marble floor, past furniture so luxurious she couldn't even name the fabrics they were made out of, and all the people...

She couldn't even fathom it. They were all *beautiful*. Beyond beautiful. Wearing expensive clothing, with impeccable skin and perfect hair.

Her eyes fell down to her outfit, and she picked at the jagged hem of her favorite T-shirt. Her jeans were old and nearly worn through at the knee. Her sneakers were an old pair of Converse someone else had grown out of. She and her brothers couldn't afford brand-new shoes. They'd always had to make do with what they had. She clearly didn't fit in here *at all*.

As she passed, people blatantly stared at her. She ducked her head to her chin and ignored the stares. It was worse that she couldn't help staring at the incredible room. She wished for once that she could be as invisible as she was back at home.

Beckham swiped a card over a black box, and the elevator door opened. He used another swipe card once they walked into the glass elevator and pressed a button to take them up to the top floor: PENTHOUSE.

Her heart sputtered.

"You live in the penthouse?" she gasped. "Who does that?"

"I do."

That was it. Nothing more from him. He was clearly a man of few words.

The elevator shot them up so fast Reyna felt like she left her stomach behind on the first floor. Once she had finally righted herself, it slowed to a stop so high up that the people below looked like ants. The door dinged open on the top floor, directly into Beckham's penthouse. She took one step forward out of the elevator and into an enormous room.

And what a room it was.

Reyna stumbled forward in a daze of luxury she couldn't process. He owned an expansive living room with a huge sectional couch and a television large enough to fill an entire wall. Gorgeous black-and-white photographs on canvas covered the otherwise empty walls. A massive stainless steel kitchen was off to the right. It appeared too clean for her to even walk into, let alone anyone to cook in. Her eyes were drawn back to the living room and the panoramic view of the city looking out at Visage's downtown building. It even had a balcony with an infinity pool and Jacuzzi.

Who would have guessed living with a vampire was like being surrounded by a slice of Heaven?

"Wow," she breathed. "Your kitchen is bigger than my whole apartment."

Then she cringed. She hadn't meant to mention her home. She didn't want Beckham to know anything about where she came from. Not that he seemed like the type to ask. But if this was her job, then she had no intention of mixing business and pleasure.

She covered her embarrassment by wandering farther into the living room. Her eyes were drawn to the photographs on the walls of the apartment. They showcased dark city landscapes; an up-close shot of a pretty woman drinking coffee at a café; a cloudy skyline; a view of a square block from on high; a collection of people walking down the streets, their faces and movements blurred; and on and on. All of them were mesmerizing. Such a dark and gloomy version of the city. Yet still striking in its own way.

"I love these," she said, her fingers running along one of the black frames.

When Beckham didn't say anything, she turned back to him. He was staring down at his phone and completely ignoring her. She waited another minute for him to say something. Anything, really.

Finally, he finished whatever he was doing and tucked his phone into the pocket of his suit. She felt his eyes on her and balled her hands into fists at her sides, determined not to look away again. She didn't want to fear him.

"Well, this is my place. You'll be staying here indefinitely. So, get used to it."

She wanted to laugh. Get used to it? Was he for real?

"I have some ground rules that I would like you to adhere to while you are living here."

"Okay," she said apprehensively.

"First, no outside guests of any kind at any time."

"Wait, what? Really?" she asked. She couldn't ever bring anyone to the new place she was living? That seemed unrealistic if she had to live here basically forever.

He glared at her. "Was I unclear?"

"No, but why can't I bring anyone over?"

"I wasn't aware that I needed to explain myself to you, Miss Carpenter. As your employer, you will follow my rules or you will leave empty-handed. Am I understood?"

She swallowed down her anger. Not that she had ever intended on bringing anyone else here. The only other people she knew were an hour drive from the city and didn't have cars. But it would have been nice to have the option in case she made friends. Hopefully she'd make some friends.

"Yes. You're understood," Reyna said.

"Fantastic. Second, you must stay here every single night."

Reyna furrowed her brows. "Where else would I stay?"

He crossed his arms stiffly and stared at her with an all-knowing look on his face. She blushed at the insinuation in that look. *Oh, sex. Right.*

"Do I have a curfew, too?" she asked sarcastically.

He didn't even justify that with an answer.

"Third, I want to be able to get ahold of you at all times. So, you will need this." He produced a phone from his pocket and handed it over to her. It had a long shiny display and felt odd and clunky in her small hand. She'd never had one of these. Never even held one before.

"Um…how does it work?"

He sighed, exasperated, and showed her the basic mechanics of the phone. After a short introduction, she knew how to turn it on, make a phone call, send a text message, and go online. What the hell she would do with all of these new functions was beyond her.

"You need to have this with you at all times. If I try to reach you and cannot get ahold of you, I will be *very* displeased," he said.

By the look on his face, she gathered that *displeased* meant that once he found her, he would tear her apart limb from limb.

"Okay. Got it." She slid the phone into her jean pocket. She hoped she remembered all of that.

"A few final things—your room is down the hall to the right."

He pointed behind her.

"And where is yours?" she asked.

As soon as the words left her mouth, she wished she could take them back. She couldn't believe she had asked that. It made it seem like she was interested in being in his bedroom, which was *not* the case. Some of the people who worked for Visage gave up more than their blood, but she wasn't here to have sex with anyone. She was here to give her blood and make some money.

That was it.

"My room is none of your concern, Miss Carpenter."

"Of course," she mumbled, looking away. "I didn't mean... I just... Never mind."

"As I was saying, your room is down the hall. The refrigerator is completely stocked, but if there is something specific you like, you have access to my butler, who will get you anything you like."

"I'm sorry, did you say *butler*?"

"His line is programmed in your phone," Beckham explained.

"So, really *anything*?"

"Within reason, of course. Now, that is all the time I have for you today. I must get back to work." He turned and began walking away from her.

"Wait," she called, reaching her hand out. When he turned and looked at her as if she were the biggest nuisance he had ever seen, she let her hand drop. "I want to make sure I understand the rules. I can leave?"

Beckham raised an eyebrow. "So, eager to leave already?"

"No," she said, taking a step backward at his look. "I wanted to know if I was permitted to leave."

She needed to see her brothers as soon as possible but didn't want to break any rules on the first day of her new job.

"You are not my prisoner. You may come and go as you please, but as my houseguest I do like to know where you are at all times. Text me when you come and go."

"Oh." She breathed out softly.

"I'm paying a lot of money for you to be here. I don't want to waste my investment," he said plainly.

She shuddered at the word. She was here as a feeder and nothing more. He didn't even have the decency to hide the underlying humiliation of her purpose.

"Investment," she repeated hollowly.

"Yes, Miss Carpenter. You are a very very expensive investment," he repeated harshly.

"I see. So, are we going to do this, then?" she spat.

Her anger flared and intensified immediately. She yanked her shirt aside at her throat and bared her neck. This was what she was here for, right? Forget the fancy penthouse, new phone, a refrigerator with enough food to feed her entire apartment complex back in the warehouses, her own room, or a butler. Plain and simple. She was food. She sustained him. If she was here to do a job, then she wanted to remind herself exactly why she was here. She couldn't let the fancy place she had walked into glamour her thoughts. None of this was hers. She was here at the mercy of a vampire who could send her away for a replacement as easily as he could drain her dry. She refused to forget that again.

Her hands trembled as fear pricked at her. And she waited, refusing to back down, even when Beckham made no move toward her.

Beckham cocked his head to the side, simply watching her. "I'm not hungry, and you should—" He looked her up and down. "Freshen up."

And with that he walked down the hall, into a room, and slammed the door.

She righted herself slowly. Her breathing was uneven, and she couldn't believe what had just happened. He had rejected her. Completely and utterly rejected her.

Somehow that damn man made her feel even more insulted in his absence.

CHAPTER FOUR

Reyna jolted out of sleep and bolted upright in bed. She slapped her hand to her heaving chest. Her heart rate was through the roof, and for a moment she couldn't remember where she was or why she was there. She breathed out twice heavily as she took in her surroundings.

Visage.

Beckham.

Penthouse.

Large fluffy white bed, white plush carpet, long hanging curtains in the softest green. She had an empty walk-in closet that she was sure she would never have occasion to fill, and her own bathroom with a Jacuzzi tub and a large waterfall shower.

She had spent more than a half hour last night under the showerhead, scrubbing every inch of her body in the boiling water. She hadn't even realized how dirty she was. It was as if she had entirely new skin. And her dark hair, which had always been dull and flat, had fallen in soft, shiny tresses down her back due to the expensive shampoo and conditioner treatment.

But now she had to get back to reality. It was her first real day on the job. She was sure that Beckham was going to want to feed. She needed to prepare herself for when that time came, which meant breakfast. A big hearty breakfast to keep her from feeling lightheaded due to the blood loss.

She shuddered. *Blood loss.*

Reyna hopped out of bed and looked around for her clothes. She'd gone to bed in an oversize white T-shirt she had found in one of her drawers. It had been a better alternative to getting back in her dirty clothes last night.

But now that she was ready to face the day, she needed her old clothes. And they were nowhere to be found.

She walked into the closet, and her mouth dropped wide open. A quarter of the space was already stocked full of clothes. Dresses upon gorgeous dresses in every color imaginable. Hanging skirts, sheer tops, slick slacks that would surely hug her figure. So many clothes. More than she could have ever dreamed of back at home. She ran her fingers over the expensive materials—satin, lace, silk—and then quickly pulled herself back. *What are they* doing *here?*

She checked the tags and saw they were all brand new and in her size. *But how does anyone know my size?*

Though the clothes were beautiful, they didn't feel like *her* clothes. They felt like playing dress-up with a doll. As if someone had picked out clothes haphazardly with no care for the person in mind.

She turned away from the display of clothing and looked through the rest of the room. Drawers were full of undergarments so small and lacy she wasn't sure they would cover an inch of her body. She closed them hastily.

Her closet had been empty last night. She didn't understand how anything had gotten inside without her knowing. She didn't like that anyone had access to her room, even though she hadn't had one to herself in ten years. She was turning to leave when she noticed her old clothes were piled in the trash can.

"What the—"

She yanked them out of the trash.

"I can't *believe* someone would throw away my clothes."

Reyna tugged her ratty T-shirt back onto her clean body and shimmied into her well-worn jeans. She wasn't going to wear all that prim and proper clothing. If Beckham had ordered this, then he needed to think again. She wasn't some doll he could dress up. She would wear whatever she wanted.

Once she had her clothes back on, she rushed out into the living room, only to find it empty. She muttered furiously under her breath and went into the kitchen to make breakfast. She was gathering ingredients for an omelet when Beckham strode out of the back hallway. He looked as imposing as ever, in a black three-piece suit and a dark-purple patterned tie.

He was checking his phone as always and didn't look up until he heard the first crack of an egg. His eyes found her. Her returning look was steely. He appraised her, and she quickly looked away. Even though she was angry, it was hard to keep eye contact with him. Half of the time he looked like he wanted to have her for breakfast, and the other half he looked like he wanted to break her neck and throw her out the window.

"Why in the world are you still in those hideous clothes?" he demanded tersely.

"Why in the world did you try to throw out my clothes?"

"They're disgusting."

"Well, the other clothes didn't feel like me," she snapped, cracking another egg and whisking the contents vigorously.

"They are all brand new."

She shrugged her shoulders nonchalantly. She didn't even look up at him.

"And very expensive."

Reyna sighed and made eye contact. "They look like they're made for a baby doll." She made a disgusted face. "I don't know anyone who would wear clothes like that to sit around the house."

Beckham glared at her. "You don't know anyone. Of course you wouldn't know anyone who could wear those clothes."

She cringed.

"Well, I want something that's more *me*," she said, holding her ground.

"What you are wearing right now is no longer *you*." His voice was dangerously low. "Trash it."

"Excuse me?"

Now her eyes were threatening. He couldn't order her around like this.

"I said trash it."

"I work for you, but that doesn't mean you can dictate everything in my life."

Beckham tilted his head down and stared at her as if she were a three-year-old throwing a tantrum. He slowly walked toward her. "I said trash your clothes. Now. Purchase new clothes if you don't like the ones ordered for you, but I can't be seen with anyone dressed the way you are right now. You already made a spectacle of yourself last night in the lobby. Would you like to continue to embarrass yourself?"

His words brokered no argument, and Reyna wordlessly shook her head. With him standing so near her, she was trembling from head to toe.

"Good. Then go change."

Reyna dropped the whisk in the bowl, maneuvered around him, and then disappeared back into her room. She couldn't believe she was letting him order her around and dress her as if she were a child, but how could she say no?

She located the least extravagant outfit she could find—a white chiffon button-up blouse tucked into a rose gold sequined skirt—and tried not to feel ridiculous walking around in the ensemble.

Beckham's nod of approval did nothing to make her feel less awkward. Though it did make her feel a slight glimmer of relief that she had done something to garner that approval even if she had just fought him on it.

"Here," he said. He slid a black card across the counter to her.

"What is it?"

"The company has set up an account for you with access to your payments. It's all in your savings. You can charge anything else to this card. It doubles as a key pass for the penthouse. Your first payment has already been deposited."

She took the key in her hand and stared at it in awe. She was holding a small fortune in her hand. It was so surreal.

"Thank you."

"Don't lose it. Those are not easy to get ahold of."

She nodded and then went back to her breakfast. She finished her omelet and sat down to eat it, shifting her skirt so that her ass wouldn't hang out. When she sat down next to Beckham, he looked up from his phone. He seemed surprised she was still there. He appeared to be so used to being alone that having another person in his house was throwing him off.

"Yes, well then…" he said as a way of farewell and then headed for the door.

"Where are you going?" she called.

He stiffened at the question. "Work."

"When will you be back?"

"I downloaded my schedule to your phone. Access the calendar feature, and you will have the updated information."

"Oh. Calendar feature. Right," she said. Of course he had a schedule for all his work-related things.

Without further ado, Beckham walked out of the penthouse, leaving her all alone. And she had no better idea as to what the hell she was supposed to do in the first place. They hadn't discussed when he was going to feed, and he hadn't asked to drink from her once. Vampires needed to eat every couple of days but could go as long as a week without sustenance. Yet all of the information at Visage had made it seem like her Sponsor would wish to drink from her every day.

Isn't that what he's paying me for?

CHAPTER FIVE

Reyna paced the apartment.

She had finally managed to check Beckham's schedule on her phone. He was supposed to be gone most of the day with work appointments. She had double-checked to see if he had scheduled time in his extremely busy calendar to eat but had no luck. She wasn't on there at all, and as far as she could tell, unless she was reading things wrong, he never took a break. He never slowed down. He didn't seem to do *anything* except work.

Which was just fine by her.

With him gone for the day, she could go see her brothers. It would be a quick trip. No more than three or four hours. She would be back before Beckham even knew she had left the city.

Not that he had said that she couldn't leave. In fact, he had specifically said that she could. However, it didn't make her any less frightened about what he would do if she did something else that displeased him. Wearing her old clothes had almost set him off. He was a ticking time bomb, and she was worried that she would end up on the wrong end of his explosion.

Still, she *had* to see her brothers. She would make sure she didn't break any of his rules, and she would be golden.

She jotted out a text to Beckham. The buttons were hard to manage, and she had to backtrack a dozen times before she got the message right.

> *Going out. Won't be gone long. Bringing*
> *phone and card.*

A message returned from him almost immediately. *How the hell did he type that fast?*

> *Call my driver, Gerard. He will take*
> *you anywhere in the city. If you go*
> *shopping for new clothes, charge*
> *them to the card. I don't want you in*
> *anything cheap. Do you understand?*

> *Yes.*

> *Good. Don't be late tonight. We need*
> *to talk.*

She gulped. *Talk.* That couldn't be good. *Is he already upset with me? Or is that some kind of code for him wanting to eat?* Either way, she would find out tonight. He wouldn't be back until later, which gave her plenty of time to see her brothers and get back for their talk.

Finding a black crossbody purse in her closet, she placed her phone and the precious black card in the bag. The only shoes in the whole closet that weren't four- to six-inch stiletto high heels were nude wedges. They would have to do. She placed them on her feet and then went downstairs. She should call Beckham's driver, but Beckham had said that the driver would take her anywhere *in* the city. Where she wanted to go was out of the city. If she had enough money to buy expensive clothes, then she had enough to take a cab in and out of the city.

With that settled, she took the elevator downstairs. Judging by the looks from the people around her, it was clear that no one recognized her as the woman Beckham had brought back with him last night. Somehow in the course of an evening she managed to meet their high standards. A woman even looked envious of her ridiculous wedge heels. What she wouldn't do for a pair of tennis shoes right now.

The valet snapped to attention when he saw her. "May I help you, ma'am?"

Ma'am. Holy shit!

"Um…I need a cab?"

The valet whistled, and a black town car pulled up in front of the building.

"Is that a cab?" she asked him hesitantly. "I thought they were yellow."

He eyed her curiously. "Only the best for our Visage clients."

"Oh. Well, do you mind me asking you how much it is?"

She blushed when she asked, but she wasn't sure she could afford a town car for such a long drive in and out of the city.

"You're new here, aren't you?" he asked, smiling politely. It was nice to have someone treat her kindly after tiptoeing around Beckham.

"Yes," she breathed. "Is it that obvious?"

"Just a bit. I'm Everett."

"Reyna." They shook hands, and she breathed a sigh of relief for finding an ounce of humanity in this situation.

"Well, don't worry about the cab. It's all billed to your room. You have a card?" She produced the black card, and he whistled low. "What?"

"What?"

"Those are unlimited cards."

"I'm sorry, what?"

He frowned at her apologetically. "A black card. It means you have unlimited funds."

Her eyes widened, and she blinked rapidly a few times. That couldn't be right. No way. She was getting paid for this. She wasn't being given access to Beckham's immense wealth.

"I think you're mistaken."

His smile returned. "You're probably right."

But she knew he was lying.

"After you." He opened the door for her, and she yanked her skirt down as she slid into the leather interior.

"Thanks."

He smiled again. "Nice to meet you, Reyna."

"You too, Everett."

"Where to, miss?" the driver asked.

"Warehouse District, 54 Boulevard East."

His eyebrows rose at the address. He was obviously wondering why a woman leaving this residence, dressed to the nines, was going to a run-down suburb.

"Just tap your card on the screen and we'll begin."

She removed the black card, wondering all the while if what Everett had said was true. She stared at the computer display in the back of the town car, then did as instructed. Once her card hit the monitor, it lit up.

```
Beckham Anderson
Reyna Carpenter
Visage Incorporated
Unlimited
```

Her jaw went slack.

And then the numbers ticked up. She watched as the cost for the ride increased dramatically. More money than she or her brothers had seen in a lifetime was now being used for one car ride out of the city. Unbelievable.

She couldn't tear her eyes away from the screen as the city disappeared behind them and they rolled up to her neighborhood. It had only been a day, and already it felt like a lifetime. The driver pulled up to the Warehouse District slowly, almost cautiously. Being away in Beckham's immaculately clean apartment made a stark contrast to her home.

It was filthy.

Filthy was an understatement. It was black. Soot. Pollution.

It was the opposite of Visage.

Ironic that her home would be darker and more eerie than a place filled with vampires who had been known to crave the night, thrive in the night.

"Fifty-four Boulevard East. What building?" the driver asked.

She pointed to a ramshackle apartment building five stories high. Half of the roof had blown off a couple of years back during a bad storm, and so it looked even more dilapidated than the surrounding buildings. Her brothers lived on the third floor in a drafty little hole in the wall.

"I'm going to see if anyone is home. Will you wait?" she asked.

"Miss, I wouldn't recommend someone like yourself going up there alone."

One day away from home, and already I don't belong.

"I'll be fine. Just wait for me right here."

As she opened the door, she shivered slightly. Her nude wedges touched the sooty earth. For some reason, the first thought in her mind was that Beckham would never let her keep these shoes now.

She made it up to the third-floor landing uninterrupted. Not even Mrs. Lowry was sitting with her door open, ready to yell at anyone who passed. The door to her apartment was never locked, because there was nothing to steal, and she walked right inside.

"Brian! Drew!" she called.

No reply came. She walked into the one bedroom and found it empty, just three sad pallets on the floor. Her brothers must be at work. She should have gone there first, but she'd wanted to check the apartment.

Hurrying down the stairs, she nearly ran into Gary Forman, the resident pervert. He grabbed her arm roughly. "Can you spare some change? A pretty young thing like yourself is sure to have a little something extra for a poor man like myself."

"Gary, it's me, Reyna. Let me go."

"Reyna?" His eyes bulged, but he didn't let go of her arm. "Nah. Reyna left yesterday. Her brothers are looking all over for her."

"Well, I came back," she snapped. "Will you tell them I'm going to the warehouses if they come looking for me here?"

She yanked her arm free and scurried away as fast as she could. When she sank down mercifully into the back seat again, her stomach was in knots. And she realized with a sigh that she had a grimy handprint on her otherwise clean skin. No wonder she had never felt clean before.

She directed the driver to the warehouse where her brothers worked and made him park around the corner so the cab wasn't visible. He offered to come in with her, but she worried more about someone stealing his car than anything happening to her.

Reyna rounded the corner to the front of the warehouse as a shift was getting out. Her heart stopped as at least a dozen hungry men stared at her. Never in her life had she been afraid of men in this neighborhood, but she didn't look like a woman from the warehouses. She looked like a high-class city girl. Even she wouldn't recognize herself here.

Then one of them stepped forward. Steven. She ground her teeth in frustration. This was not a good time for her to see her ex. She hadn't spoken with him since he had left her to be with another woman, and she didn't really want to talk to him right now. But she had to if she was going to find her brothers in a reasonable amount of time. The clock was ticking.

"Hey, Steven," she said, beelining toward him. The other guys dispersed when they saw that she was taken, but a few glanced over at her curiously as they passed.

"Hey, baby. What can I do for you?" His eyes crawled down her body.

"I'm looking for my brothers," she said impatiently.

"Do I know them?"

She gave him a disbelieving look. *Holy shit!* They had dated for over a year, and he couldn't even recognize her in a change of clothes after a good long shower.

She snapped her fingers in his face, drawing his eyes up from her tits. "Steven, it's me, Reyna."

His eyes nearly popped out of his face. "Reyna Carpenter? Shit, woman!"

"Yeah. It's different," she said tonelessly. "Have you seen Brian or Drew?"

"Different? You look fucking amazing."

"Thanks, but have you seen my brothers?" she asked. She couldn't keep the impatience from her voice.

"They were out looking for you yesterday." Steven whistled and ran his hand down her side boldly. "Little Reyna Carpenter all grown up and a woman underneath those jeans and T-shirt."

"Cut it out, Steven." She slapped his hand away. "You already know what I look like. I'm not here for you. I need to see my brothers."

"Don't worry about them," he said persuasively. He walked her backward with this hungry look in his eye that she had seen before. It meant trouble.

"Steven," she warned.

"Come on, baby. Don't you want another round?"

"You're the one who left me, remember? You wanted to get it elsewhere."

"That's not how I remember it," he said dismissively.

Her back hit the wall of the warehouse, and she gasped. His eyes lit up. It was clear that he had the upper hand, and he liked it. In this neighborhood, no one would stop him from coming on to her. She should have listened to her driver and thought about her safety. She hadn't thought she needed it from anyone here, least of all Steven.

"Where did you get these new threads?" he asked, plucking the fabric.

"It doesn't matter."

"Reyna, you can tell me." His hand ran down her waist, and she pushed him away. Any advantage she'd had, she lost when her back hit the wall.

"I'm not interested."

"Explain to me how a girl with nothing can go from that to this overnight. Huh?" He eyed her up and down suggestively. "Either she's a whore or she's a blood whore. You been to Visage, Reyna?"

She looked away, unable to see the accusation in his eyes.

"Leave me alone." But it sounded weak even to her ears.

"So you have. Let me see that neck." He tilted her head, searching out the customary bite marks that signified someone was working for a vampire. She slapped his hand away, but he grasped it and pinned it to her side.

"You can be a whore for a vamp. You can be a whore for me."

His lips lowered to her neck. His large body pinned her roughly against the wall. No matter how much she moved or squirmed or kicked to try to loosen herself, she couldn't get away.

Tears flowed down her face. She had decided to go to Visage to help her family. She had worried the whole time that she would be used and taken advantage of by the vampire who took her in. But so far Beckham had done none of those things. He'd given her a place to live, a new wardrobe, and access to unlimited funds. He hadn't even bitten her yet. Instead, her worst nightmares were coming true from someone she had known at home.

Her world had just flipped upside down.

CHAPTER SIX

"Get off her," someone cried behind Reyna.

She closed her eyes and tried to make it go away. This had been a mistake. She shouldn't have come here. Not looking like this. But she had never anticipated that she wouldn't even be recognizable. She looked different, but she was the same Reyna.

Steven was hauled off of Reyna, and she stumbled away from him, gasping. She covered her mouth and watched as he was pushed backward.

"Brian! Drew!" she cried. Her brothers had saved her.

But they weren't paying attention now. They were focused on Steven. He was outnumbered two to one, and while they had been friends at work, her brothers didn't take kindly to anyone disrespecting a woman. She had seen them come home bloody more nights than she could count. They were the only people around here that stood up for anyone. They had always stood up for her.

Steven threw a punch, but Brian grabbed his arm, twisted him around, and bent it behind his back. Drew landed a solid punch to his kidney and then another to his face. Then he swept Steven's feet out from under him. Steven landed in a heap on the hard gravel. As he sputtered and tried to straighten himself, Brian kicked him hard in his ribs, and Drew got in a swift kick to the temple. Steven went slack, passing out.

"Oh my God, I've never been happier to see you," Reyna cried.

They turned and stared at her. Drew's eyes widened in recognition first. "Reyna?" he asked, confused.

Dear God, do I look so different in these clothes that even my own brothers don't recognize me?

She rushed into Drew's arms and buried her face in his shoulder. He wrapped an arm around her and patted her twice on the back. "It's all right. You're safe now."

She swallowed hard and nodded. "I can't believe he would do that."

"We can't, either. Guy is a jerk. Forget about it. Just tell us where you've been. We've been looking for you everywhere."

Brian touched her arm gently and pulled her back from Drew. "What the hell happened to you?"

Both of their eyes went wide when they got a good look at her. She couldn't imagine what she looked like to them right now. She wasn't in the fanciest clothes in her new closet, but it was nicer than anything they had ever seen before. Her skin was practically flawless. Her hair was shiny and smelled like lavender and honey.

"Let's go home, and I'll tell you all about it," she promised.

Brian shook his head and crossed his arms. He was the older of the two, and he always played parent. He had worry lines in his forehead, and his mouth was set in a stern frown. It was clear that her absence had done a number on him. He looked too fatigued for someone so young.

"We need to talk now, Reyna. You scared the shit out of us. We had to miss work. We'll never make that money up. There needs to be some real explaining."

"I know. I know. I'm sorry. I can explain."

"Then explain," Drew said, trying to mold into the same stance as his brother. He had always idolized Brian, but he was so much softer and more artistic. If anyone in her family needed to get away from the warehouses, it was Drew. He was too smart and too creative to be stuck in a factory.

"Come on. I have a car waiting for us around the block."

She glanced around anxiously at the people who were walking out of the factory. They kept looking down at Steven's body and then up at her new clothes. Rich people were not welcome in this area. They were more likely to get mugged or killed. She should have thought better about this. But how could she have possibly known that she would be unrecognizable in the only home she'd ever known?

"We're drawing a crowd," she whispered.

Brian and Drew clued in on what she was saying and gestured for her to lead the way.

Drew rushed forward to walk next to her. He leaned over and whispered into her ear. "A *car*, Rey?"

"I'll explain at home," she said sheepishly.

Luckily when they made it back to the car, it was still perfectly intact, the driver still seated inside, not a dent or scratch on the shiny black exterior. Something she couldn't say about her own appearance. Brian and Drew looked beyond shocked.

"That's not a car, Reyna," Brian said. "That's a very very expensive car. You're freaking me out."

When the driver saw them approaching, he hopped out of the front. "Here you are, Miss Carpenter." He opened the door for her. She smiled at him and avoided the looks her brothers were giving her. This wasn't going to be fun.

"Reyna, start talking," Brian demanded once they were inside the car and on the way back to their apartment.

She nodded at the driver. "We'll talk when we're alone."

The short drive was tense.

Drew kept a close hold on her as if she might disappear again, but Brian was seething. He probably realized more than Drew had that something had gone very wrong. And as the patriarch of their family, he was responsible for making sure that didn't happen. She wanted to reassure him, but the truth was that something *had* gone very wrong.

Once the driver pulled up in front of their apartment once more, they piled out of the car. When she saw the total cost for her drive, her body froze. No way was there enough money to cover that. Rising fuel prices had made public transportation a necessity, and in most places people walked. She had walked all the way to the Visage hospital, after all.

"Would you like me to wait, Miss Carpenter?"

"Is it going to cost me a small fortune for you to do so?"

He laughed. "I'm afraid so, but I doubt Mr. Anderson would mind."

She sighed. She couldn't live off of his charity like that. She would find another way back. "No. I'll call for another cab."

"Are you certain? I don't mind staying."

"No, it's okay."

Shutting the door behind her, she followed her brothers up to the third floor of their building and then into their tiny one bedroom again. When she was in here in a hurry earlier, she hadn't truly noticed the extent of the difference between her home and Beckham's penthouse. One day and it already felt too small, cramped.

But at the same time, it felt homey. Lived-in.

Beckham's place, in comparison, was stale. There was no love there. All the money in the world couldn't make a house feel like a home.

"We're here," Brian said. "Now talk. Where have you been? Why are you dressed like that? How did you get a car like that?"

Drew frowned and looked away from her. It was as if he already knew the answer. Brian didn't want to believe it. He had to hear it from her before it could be true.

"I went to Visage yesterday."

"What?" Brian cried. "No."

"I put in an application weeks ago. My number was called. I went to the hospital, went through testing, and was placed with a Sponsor."

Her brothers looked horrified. Utterly horrified.

"You didn't," Brian said softly.

"I did."

Seeing his pain made her confidence waver, but she couldn't go back on it now.

"I was placed with a high-ranking Visage official, Beckham Anderson."

"We don't care what his name is," Drew spat. "We care that he's drinking blood from our sister."

Reyna flinched. "He hasn't… Well, I guess not yet."

"How could you do this?" Brian asked.

"Stop looking at me like that," Reyna said, pointing her finger at her brothers. "You two work day in and day out to make scraps, and for what? This one-bedroom apartment? Barely enough food to feed ourselves? Half the time, we don't have electricity or running water. You work too hard for too little, and I couldn't sit around and let it happen any longer."

"So, you decided to feed those bloodsucking bastards?" Brian yelled.

"I looked for work. You both *know* I looked everywhere for work. But no one would hire me." She threw her arms out wide. "I'm nobody. I'm nothing. I've no education. No skills. There was no other choice."

"There's always a choice. And you knew it was the wrong one, which is why you didn't tell us," Brian said.

"Don't judge me, Brian." She had made her decision, and she was sticking to it. "I did what I had to do. And better yet, I got put into a system where I make double the average employee."

"Call it what it is, Rey. Blood escort," Drew said.

She couldn't look him in the eye. She was too ashamed of that word.

"Why are you making double?" Brian demanded. His arms were crossed, and he looked pissed. This wasn't the happy reunion she had been hoping for.

This was the part she had been dreading. Most Visage employees rotated monthly, with time off with family when they weren't needed. Her situation was different, and her brothers were going to hate it.

"Because I signed up for a new position. One of the doctors has been developing a new match system," she said carefully.

"Isn't it done by blood type? How can it be new?" Brian asked.

"Well, they're trying to find individuals who are interested in a longer-term position."

Brian furrowed his brow. "How much longer?"

"Um...indefinitely."

Drew stalked away from her. "You've got to be kidding me."

"They want to keep you as a feeder forever?"

"No, it's just a permanent living situation. Once I have enough money, I'll come back home. We'll be able to afford a better place. I could go to college. We could make something of ourselves."

"You think those bloodsuckers are going to let you leave once they have you trapped in their system?" Brian asked. His eyes were steely.

"You don't have any idea what you're talking about. That's not what they're doing."

"You can't do this, Rey," Drew said.

"It's already done," she told them. She took a step back. They weren't making her budge on this. She had already weighed the pros against the cons. There was nothing they could say to change her mind. "I'm living in the city now. I'm staying with my Sponsor. He gave me all these new clothes and access to a driver. I can't leave."

"He bought you," Brian said softly. "Our little sister is enslaved to a vampire."

"Oh my God, I am not enslaved."

"He gives you money, buys you new clothes so that you're completely unrecognizable, and lets you stay in his place. He is making you completely indebted to him. So when he takes your blood, you feel like you owe it to him. You feel like your place is beside a monster, when your place is here." Brian grabbed her hands in his. "With us, Reyna."

"You don't have to do this," Drew said. "Come back. Let us take care of you. We were doing fine."

She pulled her hands away from her brothers. "Fine? This is your idea of fine? We deserve better than a shitty apartment. We deserve better than a moldy, drafty bedroom that makes us sick. We deserve jobs that pay us fairly and that don't work us to death. We deserve real food, a livable wage, access to health care, and so much more. You can't sit here and tell me that we're fine. Because we are *far* from fine."

Her brothers looked away from her. They couldn't deny the things that she had said. They really needed the money.

"This is my choice. You guys took care of me my whole life. Let me take care of you now. I'm going to send the money back to you so you can start living better."

"Rey, please," Drew said.

"We can't let you end up like this," Brian said. "After everything we did to raise you—"

"I love you guys, but I couldn't ask for a better position. I'm not changing my mind."

Drew came over to her first. He wrapped his arms around her and pulled her in for a big hug. As solid as she had been when she had told them about her situation, she was still so frightened. She couldn't even tell them about Beckham. They would freak out if they knew what he was really like.

"Get over here," Drew said.

And then Brian's arms fell around them both. She tried not to get choked up, but the truth was, she didn't know when she would be seeing them again.

If she would be seeing them again.

Chapter Seven

"Oh my God, what is the time?"

Brian pulled out their dad's old pocket watch. "Quarter to five. Did you want to get dinner?"

Reyna jumped to her feet. "Quarter to five! I need to leave. I have to be back in the city. How did it get so late?"

When she lived here, she'd rarely had time to hang out with her brothers. They were always exhausted from working fourteen-hour days. Time had slipped away from them. She had only meant to stay a short while and be back before Beckham even noticed. Now she was worried that she was going to be massively late, and they were supposed to talk tonight.

"Shit!"

She reached for her purse and pulled out her phone. She hadn't checked the thing all day. In fact, she had completely forgotten about it after she had sent Beckham those text messages this morning.

"Is that a phone?" Drew asked in awe.

"Yeah. Beckham gave it to me."

Brian pursed his lips, clearly displeased with how much wealth the man was displaying, but there was really nothing he could do about it at the moment.

She fiddled with the display until it lit up, and then her heart plummeted. Two missed calls and two text messages from Beckham. Also one voice mail, which she didn't know how to access. She clicked on the first text message.

Leaving early from work so we can talk.
Have you eaten?

Her breath caught in her throat. He was inquiring about her eating? Did that mean he wanted to make sure she had eaten so he could eat? Or was he simply curious about her eating habits? Or did he want to take her out to eat in one of those ridiculous outfits?

She remembered the second message and returned to the screen to open the second.

Where are you? I'm home. I've tried
to reach you. I told you to have your
phone on you at all times. Call me
immediately upon receipt of this
message.

"What's wrong?" Brian asked. "You're white as a ghost."

"I...I should have been back already. He needs me to leave."

"You can't stay for a little longer?"

"No," she said flatly.

Brian pursed his lips. "I don't like this, Reyna."

"Well, we all have to make sacrifices." She bit her lip and then stared down at her phone forlornly. "I have to call him back."

"You look terrified, Rey," Drew said softly.

She locked eyes with him. "I am."

Then she entered the bedroom for a semblance of privacy.

She had planned her entire day around getting back to Beckham in time. And she couldn't even manage that. Even in their short interactions, Beckham had a temper, was volatile and erratic. The last thing she wanted to do was upset him.

Gulping dramatically, she pressed the number to call him back and held the phone awkwardly to her face. It rang only once before his deep voice cut through the line.

"Reyna," he growled.

"Hey," she said awkwardly. "Sorry. I guess I didn't hear my phone."

"Where the hell are you?"

"I went out," she said defiantly. "I texted you."

"That was hours ago, and you didn't even say *where* you were going."

"I didn't know I had to."

He grumbled under his breath. She was irritating him with her comebacks, but she hadn't actually broken any rules except that she hadn't answered her phone right away.

"Well, where the hell are you, then?"

"I'm visiting some friends. You said I could leave," she reminded him again.

"I bloody well know what I said, Reyna. Stop avoiding my question. Where? Where are you? And why the hell are you not in my penthouse?"

Reyna closed her eyes and cleared her throat. *Here goes nothing.* "The Warehouse District."

Beckham cursed under his breath. "That's an hour away."

"I know," she whispered.

"This is unacceptable. I said you could have anything within reason. *Within reason* does not mean driving an hour out of the city and spending the day in the slums."

"You didn't specify."

"Well, now I am. Get back here *now*, and we'll discuss exactly what *within reason* means to me."

The line went dead in her hand.

Her lower lip wobbled as she fought to hold the tears in. She wouldn't cry. Not over Beckham. This was her first job, and already she feared she was going to be fired. This Permanent position wouldn't be that permanent if he got this angry with her on day one.

She waited a few minutes to compose herself. Another message came in from Beckham.

I'm sending a cab to retrieve you. Respond with your address immediately.

She typed out the address to her brothers' home. She hated that he would now have access to it. Though it was probably in her file if he wanted to retrieve it himself. She almost apologized through the message but stopped herself at the last moment.

"What happened?" Drew asked when she walked back into the living room.

"I have to leave. He's sending a car to pick me up."

"Rey," Brian said, his voice strained. "Are you sure about this?"

"There's no other choice, Brian."

"We can't protect you out there. How do you know that he's not going to kill you on a whim? He's a monster, after all."

"I guess I don't. But he's paying a lot of money just to kill me. I need to trust that things will work out."

The words were difficult to get out. She didn't trust that things would work out. She trusted that Beckham was going to fire her for insubordination and find some way to fine her for the exorbitant cab ride she had taken. But she had to put on a brave face for her brothers. They needed the reassurance more than she did.

Fifteen minutes later, a large black SUV parked outside of their apartment. It couldn't have looked more out of place.

"Here," she said, handing them a piece of paper. "I know you don't have a phone, but if there's ever an emergency, you can get ahold of me at that number."

"How will you reach us?"

She sniffled and looked away. "I don't know."

"When will we see you again?" Drew asked.

She shook her head. She didn't know that, either.

"I'll miss you," she whispered. Then she pulled them both into a fierce hug and quickly disappeared into the tinted car. She'd wanted to prolong her goodbye, but it hurt too much. It hurt to leave them behind.

As they drove away from the Warehouse District, Reyna twisted in her seat and watched her brothers' bodies slowly fade into the distance. When she could no longer see them, she turned back to the front of the car and tried not to cry. She needed to put on a good face for Beckham. She had almost an hour to practice.

· · ·

It took less time to get back than it had to get to the warehouses. She figured Beckham had put the fear of God into the driver.

If he even believed in God.

If God even believed in him.

Her one friendly face wasn't working valet, and she walked briskly across the entrance to the elevators. She didn't look presentable. All the people who had stared at her so enviously this morning now looked on with disdain. She didn't even want to see what she looked like.

She slipped her black card into the slot in the elevator, and it rose up effortlessly. It dinged open to Beckham's spotless penthouse. She took a deep breath and then walked uneasily on her wedge heels.

Beckham wasn't in the living room or the kitchen when she arrived. She glanced over at the door that always remained closed. She wondered if it was to his bedroom or if it was another corridor. Either way, she wasn't planning to find out when he was already pissed off at her.

She tiptoed toward her room, hoping to change into something more presentable before she had to face him down.

"Reyna."

Her feet stilled on the carpeted floor. Her eyes closed for a moment as she reined in her fear. She couldn't face him like a scared puppy. She would get through this.

She slowly turned to face him. "Hi."

"How was your trip?" Beckham's voice was like ice.

"Fine." She swallowed and held her hands at her sides. "How was work?"

"Fine." He moved toward her with such ease and grace that he was almost floating. She tried not to shudder at his approach. She would not fear him openly, but she was sure that he could practically smell it.

"Reyna," he said, stopping directly in front of her. "You are the most insubordinate employee I have ever had, and you've only been working for me for twenty-four hours."

"You must have a very predictable work environment."

She couldn't believe she had just said that. Provoking him was at the bottom of her list of things she wanted to do.

"I like my work that way. I like my *life* that way. You, however, are not fitting into my life."

"You haven't given me much time. I had to leave. It was really important."

"I shouldn't have to give you time," he growled. "Tell me why you went down to the warehouses."

She swallowed hard. She didn't want to talk about her brothers. The more he knew about her, the more he could use against her. This was a professional relationship, and she didn't have to share anything about her life with him.

"Well?"

"Look, if you're going to fire me, get on with it."

Beckham tilted his head. She stared up into the depths of his eyes, which appeared almost as black as onyx. When he looked at her like that, she would give almost anything to know what was running through his mind.

"Fire you? Is that what you think?"

"What am I supposed to think?" she asked helplessly.

"I want answers. You work for me. You missed an important meeting. I deserve to know where you were."

Reyna looked away for the first time. She couldn't stand there and lie to him, but she couldn't say anything about her brothers, either. She didn't think he was going to let her off the hook. She couldn't believe he hadn't immediately fired her. So, things were already looking up.

"I went to visit my brothers. I didn't tell them I was going to Visage, and so they didn't know where I was once I got the position with you."

Beckham visibly relaxed at the news. "Your brothers."

She sagged. "Yes. I needed to tell them where I was. I didn't want them to worry."

"And that's all you did? You look like you've been rolling around in the dirt."

"I...well"—she cringed—"I did run into my ex."

All the tension returned to his shoulders. "You look like you literally ran into him."

"It was nothing. He just—" Reyna couldn't even bear to say it. How could she explain to a vampire that she was getting judged for living with him? Simply for doing what was right for her family.

"He just what?" Beckham spoke in such a forceful command.

"Nothing. People don't always have high opinions of women who work for Visage."

"Was he rude to you?"

Reyna actually laughed. *Rude.* "Now that I think about it, he's always been rude to me. Or more like he's never been rude, he's always been a jackass."

"And yet you went to see him?" Beckham asked.

What was with the third degree? And why was she answering his questions anyway? He looked so interested. In fact, it was kind of hard to tear herself away from his eyes. They were so captivating. She should have been shaking in her heels while talking to him about this, but he seemed tense, not enraged. It gave her the courage to continue.

"No, I didn't. He works at the warehouse. I ran into him when I went there looking for my brothers," she explained.

"And what is his name?" Beckham demanded.

"What? Why?" she asked, snapping out of her trance.

"I won't have anyone threatening you. You are very valuable."

Valuable. Like a diamond or a piece of art. An object. Not a human at all.

She turned away from him, the words stinging. "It doesn't matter."

"Don't turn away from me."

Her body stiffened at the command. She swallowed hard, worried that the fierce predator would return and he'd start looking at her as if he was going to break her in half.

"We're not finished here," he told her, forcing her to look back up at him. "We have to lay some more ground rules. I can't let you leave the building unless you are with my driver at all times. Additionally, I want to be informed of *where* you are going, not just that you are leaving."

"I don't need a minder."

"You've proven that to be false."

Reyna sighed. Though she wanted to be angry that she had these additional restrictions placed on her, she couldn't manage it. He had seemed so concerned, in his own way, with her safety. She almost felt a little guilty for scaring him. She could have laughed at the absurdity of it all.

She had scared a vampire.

"I'm sorry," she finally whispered.

She hadn't been before. She had been angry. Now she felt bad about her actions. She had needed to see her brothers, but she hadn't thought it was possible to upset Beckham. Not that he looked upset, exactly. It was just a feeling she got from him.

"I accept your apology. That's all."

He strode back toward the hall as if that was the end of everything for the evening.

"Excuse me," she whispered. "Didn't you want to speak with me about something? Or was that all?"

He stopped walking but didn't turn toward her. "Actually, yes. We have plans tomorrow morning. Be ready to go by eight."

"Plans?" She lifted an eyebrow in question.

"There have been some developments."

He finally looked at her across the distance, and she tried not to get lost all over again. How were his eyes so hypnotic? Was that some kind of vampire sense? He still made her nervous, yet she couldn't look away.

"You'll be informed in the morning now that I know that you're safe," Beckham said.

She opened her mouth to ask another question, then quickly snapped it shut. Some other time.

"Was there something else?" he asked.

The few feet of distance between them felt like an eternity. He was so close and yet so far, and she felt reluctant to ask the one question she had regarding their situation. The one question she dreaded.

"I read through your schedule and didn't see anything on there about eating," she whispered. "I didn't know if it was a mistake or when…" Her voice trailed off as she watched the hungry glint in his eye reappear. Why the hell had she brought this up again?

"Why?" he asked, taking unhurried steps toward her. "Are you so ready to give your blood to me, Little One?"

Reyna stood stark still, uncertain how to respond. She wasn't eager. She just wanted to be prepared. But the way he was looking at her set her blood to boil. She had never been looked at like that before.

"Well?"

He was directly in front of her now, and she couldn't hide her racing heartbeat. She had unlocked Pandora's box. Any minute now, she would feel what it was like to have a vampire take from her. She felt shaky and afraid and like she couldn't breathe, all at once.

Beckham raised his hand and slid it through her hair. Her eyes automatically closed at the feel of his large hands taking control of her. She realized it was the first time he had actually touched her, and it made her so very aware of how powerful he truly was. This was what she always saw brimming under the surface. With the weight of it directed at her, she felt as weak as a lamb beneath his fingertips.

Slowly, he ran down the curve of her neck to the vein beating fiercely against her skin. She opened her eyes and was certain fear reflected back into them. Here were her fears magnified tenfold.

His head dipped down to the soft skin. She inhaled deeply as his lips caressed the tender skin. Her eyes fluttered closed again, and all thoughts fled her mind.

This wasn't what she had expected. Terror, stark terror. That was all she had anticipated. Not this. Not whatever was fluttering around in her stomach and heating her lower body at his nearness. Some part of her mind told her to pull away, that this was the last thing she wanted. She would give her blood out of necessity. She wouldn't like it. But it was quickly silenced by the soft kisses across her collarbone.

Then she felt it: a sharp prick on her neck. Her entire body shivered in anticipation of what was to come.

And then she was roughly shoved away from Beckham.

Her body collided with the wall five feet from where she had been standing. Her head cracked back against it. It wasn't all that hard, but she could already feel a headache blossoming, and her vision went blurry for a second. Her hand went to her neck where there was the faintest trace of blood.

"What? What happened?" she asked. Fear crept back in, obliterating everything else that had just shot through her.

He was breathing heavily and refused to look at her.

"Beckham?" she whispered, using his name for the first time.

His eyes snapped to hers. "Nothing. Nothing happened," he growled, and then he stormed from the room without another word.

She was so terribly confused.

Why hadn't he followed through? Why did she wish he had?

CHAPTER EIGHT

Reyna wasn't used to the new clothes.

She wondered if she would ever get used to the new clothes.

There was nothing in her closet that was less extravagant than her ensemble from yesterday, and her wedges had disappeared. Beckham had probably had someone trash them, since they had set foot on warehouse soil.

She almost wanted to wear something over the top, but she still didn't know where she was going. And fear of what had happened last night and Beckham's uncontrolled anger kept her from acting out. She slipped into a plain black dress that was surprisingly comfortable. The material felt light as air. She wished for her Converse in that moment, but ended up in a pair of four-inch black heels. They squished her toes a little bit but otherwise had a good bit of cushion in them.

She teetered over to the mirror to take a look. Though she felt ridiculous, she had to admit that she looked good. Not great. But passable.

Beckham was waiting for her when she exited her room. He was dangerously good-looking in a stark black suit with a black shirt and tie. The way he drank her in was enough to say that she had done well. He stared at her a full ten seconds longer than normal before returning his gaze to his phone.

"Acceptable?" she asked, turning in place. Now she really did feel like a baby doll.

"You look fine."

Fine. Right.

"Let's go." He headed toward the elevator. She hurried to keep up, but in her ridiculous heels, it was a struggle. The doors nearly closed on her, and she tripped forward and threw her arm out to catch it. It opened right back up.

She grappled for proper footing but couldn't catch herself. She stumbled right into Beckham, her arms grabbed onto his suit, and her body collided with his chest.

"Oh God," she groaned, trying to right herself and only slipping farther.

Beckham's hand reached out, touched her waist, and held her securely in an upright position. But she was still pushed against him, staring into those bottomless pools of darkness.

"Um…sorry," she whispered.

She swallowed and tried not to look up at his lips. The lips that had been kissing her neck last night. No, she wouldn't think about last night at all. Not about the kiss or the bite or how much she had wanted it to happen when he had touched her. Like right now with his hand on her waist.

Reyna stumbled back a step. She cleared her throat. "Sorry."

"Be more careful," he said gruffly.

"Noted." Reyna shivered under his gaze, feeling the full weight of his power. How could she be thinking about his lips? The only thing he wanted to do was rip her throat out. And he could do it with ease.

Except he hadn't.

At least, not yet. She swallowed hard and tried to keep her unease at bay as the elevator whooshed down to the bottom floor. As they exited, Beckham received a phone call.

"I have to take this," he said. "Go get in the car. I'll be there in a minute."

"Okay."

She wondered who was calling him so early. Then again, she had never even had a phone call, so what did she know? It must be important.

She hurried across the marble floor as best she could without slipping. It was probably the least sexy thing she had ever done in her life. Her walk was more of a waddle. Her feet were pinched, and her dress kept riding up. When her feet touched down on the carpet before the sliding glass doors, she hastened her steps.

"Everett," she cried. Then she covered her mouth. She hadn't meant to be so loud or enthusiastic, but he was the only person who had been nice to her.

His smile brightened when he saw her. "Hello, Reyna. Did you have a good day yesterday?"

Her own smile faltered. "It was eventful."

"I'm sure it was. Do you need a cab?"

"Actually, I'm supposed to get in Beck…erm, Mr. Anderson's vehicle."

Everett nodded and quickly looked away from her. He snapped his fingers at a man across the parking lot, and soon a sleek black town car drove up in front of the valet.

"Here you are," he said, his voice switching to a formality. She didn't understand what she had done wrong.

She reached for his arm to stop him. "Is everything all right?"

"Of course."

The car parked in the front.

"Allow me." He escorted her over to the vehicle and popped open the back door.

"Everett?"

"Reyna, you are here with our most distinguished guest. I thought… Well, it doesn't matter." He smiled.

"You thought what? That I could use a friend? Because that would be accurate."

He laughed. "A friend. You're not from the city, are you?"

"No," she answered truthfully.

"I can tell." Everett sighed and then pulled a card from his suit pocket. As he helped her into the car, he slipped the piece of paper into her purse. "A few of us are going out this weekend to a club nearby. Give me a call if you want to join."

"Okay," she answered a little too earnestly. She coughed and then backpedaled. "I mean, yes. Uh…if I can get away."

"If not, then there's always another time."

She nodded. "Thank you."

"No, thank you."

She sank into the back seat, and Everett shut the door. She reached into her purse and withdrew the plain white card. She ran her fingers over the letters. Everett Taylor. She almost jumped with joy that she had plans this weekend. Real plans. With humans.

The car door opened again, and Reyna quickly stuffed the card back into her bag. She scooted over to the far seat as Beckham sat down.

"Let's go."

Beckham immediately pulled his phone out again and directed all of his attention to it. She was certain he was addicted to the thing. How could one person spend an endless amount of time glued to a screen? He missed everything with his face buried in his phone. She didn't care if he had lived in the city for the last two hundred years. Well, she didn't know how old he was. There was still so much to see.

With her eyes still directed out the window, she asked, "Where are we going, anyway?"

"Work."

Reyna cringed at the thought of going to Visage headquarters with so many vampires all in one place. "Oh. Just work? That's all? I got all dressed up for us to go to your work?"

"You consider *that* dressed up?"

She ran her fingers down the silky material. "Yes. Very."

He laughed humorlessly. "Work. That's all. We're having a special presentation this morning. You'll be involved."

"Me?" she squeaked. "Involved how?"

"You'll be part of the presentation. Maybe say a few words. Just do whatever I tell you," he said distractedly.

"Sorry," she said, shaking her head. "There are two things I don't do: needles and public speaking."

His head popped up from his phone. "You're afraid of needles?"

She shuddered. At least she had gotten his attention. "They give me the creeps."

He gave her the funniest look, as if he couldn't believe that anyone could be afraid of needles.

"Look, it's a common fear." She fidgeted in her seat uncomfortably.

"Do you miss the irony in being afraid of needles when you're working as a subject for a vampire?"

She cut her eyes over to him and forced herself not to touch the spot on her neck where he had nicked her last night. "I think a vampire would have to bite me for it to be ironic."

"Don't tempt me, Little One," he growled.

Reyna straightened quickly. That wasn't what she had meant.

"So, is that my new nickname or something? Is *Reyna* too long?" she asked, trying to lighten the mood and stop thinking about the powerful man sitting only inches from her. If she kept pushing him to feed on her, he might actually do it. Then she'd really test her fears.

"*Reyna* is perfectly adequate."

He returned to his phone, and that was the end of the conversation. Her gaze went back out the window to the bleak city all cast in the early morning glow. It was eerily beautiful in its own way.

Then his hand brushed her dark hair off her shoulder and all thoughts of the city evaporated. Goosebumps erupted on her skin. With her hair out of the way, he touched the tender spot where his fangs had pierced.

"Yes."

Reyna didn't move. She didn't even breathe. She felt the power of his touch vibrate through her body. His fingers moved from her neck up to her chin, and he forced her to look at him.

"Look at how you tremble."

A smug expression crossed his face. He seemed pleased that his touch frightened her. But she couldn't keep from feeling that way. He tilted his head in assessment and then seemed to find what he was looking for.

"Yes, Reyna, you are my Little One."

All that was before her was Beckham.

A predator luring his prey.

And she was trapped.

As thoroughly as a rabbit in a snare.

Beckham abruptly dropped his hand. For a moment, she had completely forgotten where she was and what she was doing. She shifted in her seat and tried to get herself back under control.

The car stopped in front of Visage, and the driver, Gerard, hurried around the car and opened the door for Beckham. Gerard then offered her his hand, assisting her from the vehicle. She tottered for a moment, then regained her balance. Her head tilted up at the enormous Visage building in utter awe of the sheer magnitude of the all-glass facade.

When she saw that Beckham hadn't waited for her, hadn't even looked back to see if she was coming, she jumped and made a dash to catch up. Luckily, her high heels held traction on the concrete steps, and then she was breezing into Visage Incorporated right behind Beckham. As she walked into the tallest building in the city, her feet stilled again.

The entryway was a sight to behold. Glass upon glass upon more glass. And everything else was beautifully clean white marble and porcelain and polished granite.

"Reyna," Beckham said sharply.

"Sorry." She hurried to his side. "It's just incredible."

"Follow me through the security screening."

"The what?"

He sighed. "Pass through the body scanner."

She looked at the glass box that she hadn't noticed in her distraction. "What are they looking for?"

"Anyone and anything that doesn't belong. I've already had you signed in."

"Okay."

She walked forward uncertainly. As she passed into the scanner, a red light blinked and then passed over her body. A duplicate image materialized before her. The light blinked blue and then posted a message: Human subject Reyna Carpenter. Identity confirmed. Approved.

She continued forward and shuddered as her body image disappeared. Beckham was waiting for her on the other side.

"What the hell was that?"

"A security measure."

"What happens if you aren't approved?"

"Don't ever find out."

Reyna rolled her eyes at his nonanswer and then looked around at the Visage building. Everyone in attendance was dressed in a black suit. Even the women were in black skirt suits, with stark white blouses. Everything was crisp and orderly. Not a thing out of place.

Reyna followed Beckham to the elevator. "Is everyone who works here a vampire?"

"Of course not. *You* work here."

"You know what I mean, Becks."

His hand stopped before pressing the button, and he looked down at her. "*Becks?* Is this my new nickname? Is *Beckham* too long?"

Reyna shrugged. But she had a small measure of victory at throwing him off for a moment.

When the empty elevator opened before them, they stepped inside and Beckham selected his floor.

"Do any humans work on your level?"

"Why do you always ask so many questions?" he growled.

She shrank a little in on herself but still said, "Because you don't give me any answers."

He reached instinctively for his phone in his pocket. "You have all the answers you need."

"Fine."

Beckham ignored her by focusing on whatever was going on on his phone. The elevator stopped on his floor, but before she could exit, Beckham reached out and stopped the doors from opening.

"What?" she asked, exasperated.

"Try not to bother anyone." Reyna narrowed her eyes. "Not everyone is as…kind as I am."

"Kind?" She couldn't keep the sarcasm from her voice.

His eyes hardened darkly. "Yes. And do be sure to remember that."

Unceremoniously, he opened the doors once more and left the elevator. She grumbled under her breath but followed him. There was clearly a reason for him to give her that warning. Perhaps she needed to be more careful at his work, surrounded by a sea of vampires. She stuck close to his side as they made their way to his office.

"Becks?" she whispered when she felt eyes on her from all directions. "Does everyone know?"

"Know what?"

"You know…"

"That you are human?" he asked. "Yes, I think that's quite obvious."

Of course, that wasn't what she had meant. She wondered if they all knew that Beckham was her Sponsor. Did they all look down on her for becoming a human employee? They needed people like her to make any money and keep the company afloat. But that didn't mean they didn't judge the humans who worked for them. She had seen worse behavior from her own kind. She couldn't imagine how much she would be shunned by the vampires.

But she didn't voice any of her concerns as they walked through the corridor.

Unsurprisingly, Beckham had a corner office on the top floor. The heights were dizzying, and she quickly looked away from the window. She wasn't afraid of heights, but it was still intimidating.

Beckham walked to a big black desk facing a giant wall of screens. He tapped a few things on his computer and zoned out to his work.

"Anderson," someone called from the doorway.

Reyna whipped around and saw a man walk in. He was tall, fair, and not exactly handsome, but he carried himself with authority. She couldn't imagine anyone else barging into Beckham's office otherwise.

"Batiste," Beckham said casually. She could hear an edge to his voice, though. This must be one of the vampires to be wary of.

"Is this her?" His eyes crawled over her skin, and she suddenly felt completely exposed in her small black dress.

"Yes. Reyna, this is Roland Batiste."

Roland stalked across the room and held his hand out. She slowly placed hers in his.

"Hi," she said uncertainly.

"Pleasure is all mine, mademoiselle. You are simply *magnifique*." He kissed her hand dramatically. "William was right. The absolute *best*."

"Do you mind, Roland?" Beckham said, suddenly standing right next to her and touching her elbow.

She shouldn't gain warmth from his nearness, but she did. Roland made her skin crawl. There was something about him that sent off bad vibes. She suddenly understood what Beckham had meant in the elevator. Roland was dangerous. She could feel it in her very being. It scared her that Beckham was somehow the good guy in this situation. Everything about it terrified her.

"Mais bien sûr."

Reyna looked up at Beckham quizzically. She didn't understand what he was saying. "Is that French?" she asked.

Roland laughed. "Indeed it is. I said *but of course*. Where are my manners?"

"Lacking as usual," Beckham said dryly.

Roland continued to chuckle as if Beckham had honestly said something funny. Reyna could see he was quite serious. He didn't want anyone, especially not this Roland, to touch her.

"William wants us in the meeting room in five. I'm going to bring my pet as well. Wait until you see her. She's what you Americans call a knockout."

Beckham waved him off irritably, and Roland left the room. Reyna released a breath at his departure.

"Is that the kind of person you meant when you said you were nice?"

He was still looking at the door, but he hadn't let her go. His voice was stern when he spoke next. "Yes. That is exactly what I meant."

CHAPTER NINE

"Do exactly what I say," Beckham said as they approached the open conference room door.

She nodded her head minutely. After her encounter with Roland, she wasn't looking forward to this meeting. She was about to enter a room full of very powerful vampires, and if nothing else, that alone had frightened her into silence.

She wished she knew what the hell she was doing here.

As Beckham entered the large conference room, Reyna tiptoed after him with her head down. The room was already full and buzzing with excitement. She prayed that she was invisible, even as she stuck out like a sore thumb.

Beckham took a seat near the back of the large rectangular table.

"Sit here," he said, pointing to the seat next to him. The chair dwarfed her figure, but she was in no position to argue.

A few minutes later, the room quieted, and a man walked inside. He was hunched over and relying heavily on his cane. His hair was thin, his skin pasty, and he seemed even paler than the other vampires. If she hadn't known he was one, she would have thought he was just a dying old man. But all of the men and women in the room were very clearly vampires with their perfect complexions, perfect outfits, and perfectly beautiful young bodies. And they all very clearly were deferential to this man.

He walked to the head of the table and then eased into his chair. With how frail and sickly he looked, someone should have rushed to his aide to help him sit, but no one moved. She also expected him to be completely not threatening, but when his eyes swept across the table and found her seated next to Beckham, she knew he was lethal.

A shiver ran up her spine, and she quickly averted her eyes. This was not a man to be trifled with. Not even in his condition.

"Welcome," he said. His voice boomed despite the apparent illness. "For those of you who don't know who I am, I am William Harrington, founder and CEO of Visage Incorporated, and today is a great day for the company."

The room was silent, and she could feel the anticipation growing.

"You have all contributed immensely to what has happened on this day. I have been working toward this outcome for us for over twenty years, and today we have our victory."

Reyna swallowed. This didn't sound good.

"As you all well know, since the White House has made the announcement, the Blood Census was passed through Congress and signed into law by the president."

Everyone seated at the table applauded, but she looked around in confusion. A *Blood Census*? What the hell was that?

The man held his hand up, and the room immediately fell silent. "Our version of the legislation went through, and the president has agreed to work directly with Visage to complete all the blood type testing included in the Census sample. Once the sample is complete, we will officially have a full list of all the blood types of the human population in this country."

Reyna's face paled. Why would they need a full list of blood types? Didn't they already have a voluntary program with more people employed than any other company in the world? Why would they need or even want a full registry of humans' blood types?

The room erupted into applause again, but Reyna leaned over to Beckham. "Do I have to enter the Blood Census?" she whispered.

"No."

"Why not?"

"Only people who haven't been tested by Visage in the last ten years have to complete the blood test aspect of the Census."

"Why?"

"Why what?" he growled low.

"Why only the last ten years?"

"New technology."

Reyna wrinkled her nose. "What's the difference if they're just testing for your blood type? They've been able to do that for decades."

"Leave it alone, Reyna. We're in the middle of a meeting," he snapped.

She sat back roughly into her chair. She hated the dismissal. Surely she wasn't the only person who thought it was strange to include a blood test in a census.

She tuned out the next half hour as they discussed implementation and the business aspects of Visage's involvement in the Census. They must have switched topics at some point, because Beckham nudged her chair to get her attention. Her eyes snapped to the front of the room, where the man was still speaking.

"As we have discussed in previous meetings, the Permanent Sponsor positions have officially gone into effect."

Oh. That's me.

"Three of our highest-ranking officials have brought their subjects with them today to discuss the new program. Roland Batiste, Cassandra Dresla, and Beckham Anderson. Please come forward with your subjects."

Beckham's chair scraped back against the floor, and he helped Reyna out of her seat. Her legs shook as she moved to the front of the room. Roland followed next, and behind him was a tall, model-thin woman in a skintight white dress with long, flowing blond hair. Behind them came a woman with wavy red hair pinned up at the base of her neck who was a million degrees of beautiful. She looked fierce but seductive.

She reached Roland first. "Roland, my love."

His smile was magnetic as he kissed her cheeks. "Cassandra."

She smiled at Beckham and came to stand next to him. "Beckham, darling." She kissed both of his cheeks in greeting.

"Cassie," Beckham said cordially.

Behind Cassandra appeared a man. He was pretty for a guy with fair hair and pouty lips. His eyes never strayed from Cassandra's face, and he seemed completely enthralled.

Roland stepped forward first. "I'm satisfied with my experience with a Permanent subject. We've been together for about two weeks, and already it is better than the rotation program. I am able to get to know her," he said, eyeing the woman blatantly, "on a more personal level. Because I know she's not about to leave. This is my Sophie."

Sophie strutted forward, placed her hand on her hip, and sank into the position. She didn't look frightened at all. She reveled in the attention. "I'm so happy to be here. I was in the rotation program before this, and finding out about a Permanent position was the dream of a lifetime. I honestly couldn't have asked for anything or anyone better."

Reyna refrained from rolling her eyes. What a load of shit!

Cassandra smiled and ran her hand down her subject's arm. "This is Felix. He was placed in my care a month ago. I'll admit I was skeptical. A Permanent human entering my life, living in my home, dealing with my busy schedule sounded unpleasant, to say the least. But having someone always there and not having to worry about fitting them into the schedule. Well, Felix has changed my mind. He's delicious."

Reyna couldn't keep from cringing. Bad choice in words.

Felix tore his eyes from Cassandra only long enough to speak to the crowd. "Before being included in Visage, I had gone through three years of college, was nearly a hundred thousand dollars in debt, and had nothing to show for it. When the economy collapsed, I couldn't get a job. There was nowhere for me to go. I had to enter the program, and in the couple of years I've had to work at Visage, nothing has been better than being in a permanent and secure position with Cassandra." He turned back to stare at her lovingly. Enamored. Practically hypnotized.

Now it was Beckham's turn. Oh God! And then her turn. What the hell was she supposed to say? She couldn't speak to this group. She had only been here a couple of days and fucked up more than she had thought possible. Not to mention that she had no prior experiences with Visage to draw from. This was all so new to her.

Beckham stared straight ahead. He never even looked at her. "I'm happy to participate in the Permanent program. My subject is Reyna. She is obedient and the model of a perfect subject."

Reyna's mouth nearly dropped open. What the fuck? Since when? She dropped her chin to her chest and stared at the floor, hoping to cover her disbelief with discomfort.

"Many of you know that I was outspoken against the Permanent position from the get-go—"

She hadn't known that.

"Having Reyna in my home even for the past couple of days has completely reversed that position. This is the future of Visage."

Reyna tried to hide the shock from her face. What was he talking about? He hated having her in his house. He hated having her around. He hated looking out for her. Why was Beckham saying all of this?

Her eyes turned to their leader, and she saw the triumphant look on his face. What had she walked into?

"Reyna," Beckham said, gesturing her forward.

She put one foot in front of the other and felt her body seize. Everyone was staring at her. Everyone was waiting for her to say something. Her hands were clammy, her skin cold, and she felt like she might faint. She opened her mouth to speak, but nothing came out.

She put a hand to her heart, and her chest was pumping up and down with her erratic breathing. What was she supposed to say? What did they expect of her? Oh God! The expectations.

No. She couldn't do this.

"Reyna," Beckham said softly. He touched the small of her back, and she sank into his touch. He pulled her toward him. "I apologize. She doesn't like public speaking."

"Sick. Going to be sick," she whispered.

"I'm going to take her out of here," he said immediately. She wasn't sure if he was really concerned at the moment or just embarrassed, but she couldn't care. She felt like she couldn't breathe, and she was going to hyperventilate.

"Yes. Make sure she is all right, Beckham," Mr. Harrington said. Beckham walked her toward the back door. "Humans. Such fragile things. Well, the Permanent positions will begin rolling out for all top Visage employees as soon as we find suitable choices."

The door shut behind them, and Beckham placed a hand on her shoulder. "Reyna, calm down. You're fine. Everyone is gone."

"S-sorry," she stuttered. She put a hand to her forehead, and the other was holding his jacket.

"When you said you didn't enjoy public speaking, I thought you meant that you weren't fond of it. I didn't think you meant that you would freeze up and almost pass out."

"Oh hey, public speaking makes me almost pass out," she quipped.

"Do you always do that?"

"What?"

"Use sarcasm as a defense mechanism."

"You think?" she asked. Her breathing was slowly getting under control. She leaned heavily against the door and threw her head back.

His eyes widened as he stared down at her exposed throat. She felt him inch toward her. Her own body stilled at his approach. For a moment, it was as if the world revolved around them. As if she had been waiting her whole life for him to get close to her. Then he took a step back and cleared his throat. "I should probably return."

She closed her eyes, not sure if it was in fear or in embarrassment at what he must have seen in them. "Fine. Go."

"Your heart is racing," he growled softly, so close to her she could practically feel him on her.

"Yes," she murmured. His hand brushed her neck gently, and she almost stopped breathing altogether. "Becks?"

She opened her eyes when the pressure disappeared, and he was gone. She straightened. She looked through the glass, back into the room, but he was nowhere to be seen. What the hell? Where had he gone, and why had he disappeared so suddenly when he had touched her?

Beckham was an enigma wrapped in a mystery.

CHAPTER TEN

Reyna stayed leaning back against the door until she finally calmed down, her pulse returned to normal, and her breathing wasn't ragged. Though she was confused about what had happened with Beckham, her mind was back to functioning on a normal level.

She didn't know what had scared him off, and asking him would do no good. She hadn't been with him all that long, and it was clear that he didn't like to answer questions or for her to ask them.

A few minutes later, the staff meeting dispersed and all the vampires exited the room. She plastered herself against the wall, suddenly feeling very vulnerable without Beckham there next to her. But people barely glanced at her as they left. The flow had reduced to a trickle when Roland and Cassandra appeared with their subjects and Mr. Harrington.

"Ah, there you are, Miss Carpenter," he said. "I don't believe we were officially introduced. William Harrington."

He extended his hand out to her, and she placed hers in his.

"Um…you can call me Reyna."

"Reyna, of course. Sorry to see your discomfort earlier. Are you feeling better?"

"Yes. Much better," she said quickly. She drew into herself at the present company. God, where was Beckham? He might make her uneasy, but he was her vampire, at least.

"Good." Mr. Harrington gave her a toothy grin, and she could see his fangs. She tried to keep from shuddering. "How are you liking the program so far?"

His eyes were as sharp as his fangs when he asked her. She didn't know what he was fishing for, but she wasn't going to give him any more information than he needed. "Good. I'm very satisfied."

"I bet you are," Roland said.

She ignored that comment. "Thank you for asking, Mr. Harrington."

"Where did Beckham get to, anyway?"

Roland shrugged. "Do you want to wait for him? I can take care of his pet until he shows up," he said, placing his hand on Reyna's shoulder.

Her heart kicked into overdrive. No. She wasn't supposed to be alone with Roland. That much had been very clear from Beckham, but where the hell was he?

Sophie reached out and took his hand. "Why? Do you want her, too?"

"Oh baby, don't worry," he said, petting her hair like a child. "I'll take care of you both."

"I don't like when you talk like that," she pouted.

His hand gripped viciously in her hair, wrenching her head backward. Sophie winced, her eyes wide with fear. "I pay a lot of money to have you here, Sophie. I'll do as I please."

Reyna gulped, but no one else batted an eye at the behavior. She hadn't thought that Beckham was being serious by saying he was kind. *Cold, distant, broody*…those were all words she would use to describe Beckham. Not *kind*. But looking at how Roland treated

Sophie, she found herself feeling fortunate.

"Yes, bring Reyna along for the ride. Beckham knows where we're going," Harrington said.

"I'm...I'm sure he's around here somewhere," Reyna said nervously.

"It'll be fine," Cassandra said. "You can ride with us."

She smiled, but Reyna wasn't sure if she could trust Cassandra, either. She wasn't as creepy as Roland. But she also had vicious eyes and a charisma that said not to fuck with her.

Reyna glanced around once more anxiously and then nodded. "Okay."

Their group took the elevator to an underground parking garage. The walls were lined with heavily tinted black town cars and limos. There were a few exotic sports cars in reds and oranges and yellows at the far end of the garage. Not a single plain car in sight. She wondered if this was the level for upper management and regular employees parked elsewhere or if these all belonged to the company for business use.

Three cars backed out and rolled up in front of them. Harrington got into the first one alone. Roland and Sophie got into the next one. He looked over his shoulder once at Reyna, but Cassandra put her hand on Reyna's shoulder and he disappeared inside the vehicle. The next car was for Cassandra, Felix, and Reyna. She walked around to the other side and sat down next to Felix.

Cassandra brushed her red locks off her shoulders and glanced over at them. "So, Reyna, what did you do before becoming an escort?"

Reyna coughed unexpectedly. Vampires called them escorts, too? "Um...nothing really."

Cassie raised an eyebrow. "Nothing at all? You had no life?"

"I, well, no, not really. I went through school, didn't have the money for college, and couldn't get a job." It wasn't like jobs were readily available. She'd spent two years looking. No one would hire her. At least not for anything her brothers approved of.

"I see." Her hand ran down Felix's arm. "So, you've no experience with being an escort, then, either?"

She shook her head.

"Hmm. And what do you think of the way Beckham tastes you?"

Reyna stayed very still. She almost snapped off that he hadn't, but for some reason that felt like the wrong answer. She didn't want anyone to think something was wrong and move her to someone else or fire her entirely.

"It's fine," she whispered.

"Fine." Cassie laughed. "Felix, do you think that when I taste you it's just fine?"

"It's like Heaven itself."

Cassandra was stroking his neck temptingly. Reyna couldn't help but be drawn to the movement. There were tiny little scars on his neck but not healing wounds. Just tiny little imperfections Reyna wouldn't have even noticed if she hadn't been looking at them.

"Yes, yes it is," she purred.

And then suddenly Felix's neck was snapped to the side. Cassandra bared her fangs and plunged them down into his neck. Reyna shrieked and plastered herself against the car door. Her mouth was open wide as she stared in horror while Cassandra pierced his artery and drank the thick red blood. A rivulet escaped her mouth and ran down to the collar of his shirt. The light-blue material darkened as it soaked up the excess.

Reyna couldn't pull her eyes away. The way Felix's eyes rolled back in his head. A look of supreme pleasure on his face. The sound of Cassandra drinking deeply. The way she held him like an animal... like food.

Then it was over. Cassandra licked from his collarbone to the wound in his neck until it was clean. The wound was already clotting from the healing properties in vampire venom. All that remained were two small marks in his neck and a pool of blood on his collar.

"Oh, look, I've made a mess." Cassandra licked her lips and glanced up at Reyna's horrified face. "Don't worry, sweetheart. We can get him a new shirt."

Then she giggled maniacally and sat back in her chair.

Reyna didn't move from her seat the rest of the drive. Even when Felix stripped out of his shirt to reveal his amazing six-pack and put on a fresh shirt. She didn't even want to think about how often that must happen for Cassandra to keep a stash of shirts for him available.

Maybe she wasn't ready for Beckham to bite her...not ready at all.

A few minutes later, they pulled up in front of a restaurant. She followed Cassandra inside the dark room. It was a chic-looking room with polished upper-class clientele. One of the suits in this room cost more than the entire Warehouse District.

They were ushered to a table in the back, and Reyna took an open seat next to Felix. He acted fine, but something about his movements made him seem a little dazed. She wondered if it was the blood loss or if Cassandra kept him drugged.

Harrington sat at the head of the table and peered over at Reyna's pale face. His keen eyes took in everything at once. "Cassandra," he admonished.

"Hmm?" she asked, applying a new coat of bloodred lipstick.

"You couldn't wait?"

She looked up at him devilishly. "Was I supposed to? I wanted a snack. It's not appropriate in public."

Harrington snapped his fingers at a passing waitress. "Get this girl a glass of water."

She nodded and scurried away. The water appeared almost instantaneously, and Reyna gulped down as much as she could at once.

"When do you think the Blood Census will go into effect, William?" Roland asked. He threw his arm onto the back of Sophie's chair, and she leaned toward him. Her neck was bare, and she exposed it to him as if inviting him to feed at any time. Reyna pulled her dark hair forward over her neck protectively.

"As soon as we can get the executive branch to push it through.

They're sluggish, but I'm funneling the money into it, so it's not taking the unreliable tax dollars to get it going. Ideally within the next month. The president keeps saying six months at the earliest, but we all know that he doesn't know what he's talking about."

"Little puppet. I wonder what puppets taste like," Cassandra singsonged.

"He's B positive, Cassie. No tasting for you."

She raised her eyebrows. "If you'd get that damn antidote already, I could try anyone I want."

"Antidote?" Reyna asked. Whatever that was, it didn't sound like a good thing for humans.

Harrington looked at her. "All in testing. Attempting to replicate the universal donor. So we wouldn't have to be as specific with subjects."

"It'd be like the good old days, then," Roland said. "Une fête."

Harrington laughed. "You have a feast already, Roland. Enjoy your little Sophie."

"Oh, I do," he said.

"Why…why would you need that?" she couldn't help asking.

"Full of questions, aren't we?" Harrington asked. He fixed his steely gaze on her, and she quickly looked down into her water. "I'm surprised Beckham allows you to be so inquisitive. He hates that kind of thing. Perhaps he just hasn't broken you yet."

She shuddered at the word choice. Broken. Was that what he had planned for her?

"If you must know, I have a very rare blood type. Do you know what the rarest blood type is?"

Reyna cleared her throat. "No."

"Rh null negative. It means that the individual is missing the entire Rh antigen group from the blood. No A, B, or O to worry about. A true universal donor. So few that only three others have been known to have the blood since I've been searching."

"Only three?"

"Indeed. Two are dead and one is dying. A universal donor would solve part of my problem," he said, gesturing to his decrepit body. "We're looking for a Permanent match for me but investigating all options, of course."

"Well," she said awkwardly. "I hope you find someone."

He smiled that toothy grin again. "Me too, dear. I'm changing the world with this company. Employing more humans than ever before. Once the Blood Census is in effect, I'll find the other Rh null subjects, if there are any others." His eyes grew distant for a moment, and then they snapped back to their normal iciness. "I'll find them."

That was the moment Beckham appeared in the doorway like a storm cloud.

Reyna straightened in her seat at the expression on his face. He walked across the room like a tightly coiled spring ready to explode.

"Ah, Beckham, there you are," Harrington said.

"Excuse me, William. I need to speak with Reyna. Alone."

She hastened out of her seat and followed him around the corner. He tugged her straight through the kitchens, out the back door, down an alley, and into a dead end. Then her back was slammed against the brick wall. His fist connected with the wall behind her, and she felt it shudder. Debris floated onto her shoulders.

"You left," he growled.

"I—"

"No." He pressed his finger to her lips roughly. She stopped breathing and stared up into his eyes as dark as night. Her body trembled under the feral stare. "You *left* without me."

The silence was weighted. All she could do was sit with their bodies nearly touching. His finger on her mouth. Her mind wandering to hellacious places.

"You are my subject. Can you imagine what it was like when I found you missing? When you turned up with three of my kind?" She shook her head minutely. He bared his teeth to her, and she shrank back. "These are meant to drink your blood. To drink you dry until there is nothing left of your body but a dry corpse. We are killers. We don't hesitate. Just because we're wearing suits and seem more like you does not mean we are like you. We are *not* like you. *They* especially are not like you. The only way you get to the top of Visage is to be fucking ruthless, Reyna. Do you understand?"

"You're scaring me," she whispered.

"Good."

He pulled away and ran his hands back through his hair, trying to pull himself together.

"What happened while I was gone? Tell me everything."

She explained what happened in the car with Cassandra and then the conversation about the Blood Census and rare blood types with Harrington.

He growled low in his throat and looked ready to punch something all over again. "I told you not to say *anything*."

"I know," she whispered. "But a Blood Census and a blood antidote—those sound really serious. Does anyone else know about that?"

"No. And no one else needs to know."

"I don't have anyone to tell," she murmured. "Becks?"

"Another question? You wear on my nerves."

She bit her lip. "If you didn't agree with the Permanent program, why did you get a Permanent subject?"

"Does it matter?"

"You won't drink from me. You don't trust your colleagues. You disagree with the work Visage is doing, yet you're at the top of the totem pole. I'm trying to understand you."

His eyes found hers again for a quick moment, a reckless abandon in his irises as he beheld her. "It would be better if you didn't."

CHAPTER ELEVEN

The rest of the afternoon went better than expected. While Beckham and his associates each had a cocktail and discussed the company, Reyna ate a completely normal lunch. But after that, Beckham kept Reyna on a tight leash. Whatever had him spooked after she left Visage without him carried over to their everyday life. She didn't leave the penthouse without him, which meant she never left. Her world had become one big routine, and it was nothing like how she thought it would be.

What stood out most was that after nearly six days with Beckham, he hadn't drank from her once. She honestly had no clue how he was still functioning. A week was max time in between meals without feeling sick and irritable. And while Beckham honestly couldn't get any more irritable than he already was, he certainly wasn't sick.

She didn't know what that meant, but after Cassandra's display at Visage, she wasn't keen on asking him about it.

Ever since talking to Harrington, she had taken an interest in the Blood Census development and research on antidotes. Rumors floated around out there that Visage had bought the Blood Census from the government for some secret mission. Reyna wished she could tell people how true that statement really was. But of course she couldn't. She couldn't do anything to risk the money for her family.

As another day rolled around, filled with utter boredom, she remembered that she had Everett's business card in her purse. She dragged it out of the bag and dialed the number.

After two rings, Everett answered, "Hello?"

"Everett, it's me, Reyna," she said enthusiastically. She hadn't left the house, and the idea of seeing another human being bolstered her.

"Ah, Miss Carpenter," he said. "Have you decided to join us?"

"Am I still welcome?"

"Of course. Where should I pick you up?"

"Oh...um, I'm still at Beck...Mr. Anderson's," she explained. She had never felt more awkward.

The line was silent for a moment.

"Right. Okay. I'll get you at the valet desk at nine on Saturday."

"Sounds good. I can't wait," she said.

"See you then."

"Wait, what should I wear?" She had never thought about that before Beckham, but now she worried that she would be over or underdressed everywhere she went.

Everett laughed. "Whatever you want. We're just going to a club."

"Club. Right." As if she had ever been to one.

That was how she ended up rummaging through her closet for something acceptable to wear at eight at night on a Saturday. She still hadn't told Beckham she was going out, but it might be better to warn him on her way out than to try to convince him to let her go. He had said on her first day that she wasn't a prisoner. If that was the case, then he should have no problem letting her go out with some friends. It would be fine.

At least she kept telling herself that.

After investigating clubbing attire online, she finally decided on a shiny black dress with a silver undertone, tiny little straps, and a square-cut bodice that hugged her figure like a glove. She paired it with some intense strappy black heels and then piled all of her dark hair on the top of her head with a few wispy strands loose around her face. It was so different than her normal ponytail. She hoped that she would blend in.

At a quarter to nine, she eased out of her room in search of Beckham. She wasn't looking forward to this.

The living room was empty as usual, and she ended up having to text him to get him to come out of the back room, since she wasn't allowed in it. When he appeared before her, he stopped short in the open doorway. His eyes widened as he drank her in from head to toe. The air crackled between them.

"What are you wearing?" he asked.

She gestured down at her outfit. "A dress? You left it in my closet."

"Yes. But not for nine o'clock at night when we're staying in."

She swallowed and worked up the courage to tell him. "Well, I'm going out with some friends."

Of all the responses she expected from Beckham, laughter was the last one.

"Your friends? The ones in the Warehouse District?" he asked incredulously.

"No," she cried. She couldn't hold back the anger in her voice. He didn't have to be an asshole about it. "The ones I've made since I've been here. I'm going out to a club nearby, and that's that."

Beckham straightened immediately. He clearly didn't like her tone or her meeting people he didn't know. "Who are these friends of yours?"

"I'm going out with Everett from downstairs."

"The valet?" Beckham asked. He pursed his lips.

"Yeah." She straightened her dress and ignored his pointed stares. She was not backing down. "I'm meeting some of his friends."

"No," he said. "That doesn't sound safe."

"What do you mean it's not safe?" she demanded. "You don't even know them."

"That's why it's not safe."

"No, you don't get to decide that. You said I wasn't a prisoner, and you've been treating me like one all week, especially after I left Visage without you. What was I supposed to do? They said I was going and you would catch up, so I went. You can't force me to stay here."

"You're not a prisoner." His eyes were steely. She was more than he had bargained for, but at this point, she didn't care. "You don't understand the city, and you have no idea what could be out there."

"*Nothing* is going to happen. I'm in a new place. I don't know anyone. The first person who isn't paid to be nice to me invited me to hang out with his friends, and I'm going to go. Can't you understand what it's like for me?"

Beckham stared at her blankly. She ground her teeth and crossed her arms in defiance. She had plans, and he couldn't dictate her life for her. If this was going to work as a permanent situation, then he needed to trust her.

"So, no? You don't get it at all," she said. "Let me explain. I'm here all alone, all the time. I don't have any friends. My brothers live an hour away and are now no longer part of my life. The only person in my life is *you*." Beckham arched an eyebrow as he watched her stoically. "And with you, I feel…I feel…useless."

"Useless?" he asked.

"Do you *ever* get hungry?"

Beckham smirked at her question, which was all the more infuriating. How was he so calm about all this? Not that she was aching for him to bite her. The idea still terrified her, but did he ever eat?

"How did I end up with the only vampire who doesn't eat?" she asked in frustration.

He eyed her curiously as if trying to decipher what was hidden beneath. "Is that what you want?"

She swallowed. This was dangerous territory. She didn't want to have this conversation again. She didn't want to think about the kisses he had trailed down her neck. How despite how afraid she should feel, when he looked at her like that, her insides ignited. It was a strange paradigm.

"I'm trying to figure you out."

"I thought I made it clear that you shouldn't," he said. His gaze was intent and deadly.

"I'm bad with instructions," she muttered.

"I've noticed."

"Well, did you just get me to please your boss?" She asked the question that had been rattling around in her brain since she had found out that Beckham hadn't even wanted a Permanent subject.

"Would you be upset if I said yes?"

Reyna stumbled at the response. "Wait, really?"

Beckham didn't seem like the type who would agree to something like this for work or who could be bullied into anything. He was formidable to say the least.

Beckham took a few slow steps toward her. Prowling like he was stalking his prey. She took an unsteady step backward and reminded herself that he wasn't going to bite her. If he hadn't already, then she didn't think he would right now. That first time had been an accident. He didn't even want her. And she shouldn't hope that he would want her.

"Do I look like I'm eager to have someone in my space? Someone I have to constantly watch?" he asked, standing so close to her she had to tilt her head back to look at him.

Her stomach twisted as his nearness encased her, trapping them in a bubble. He had such a powerful presence that she never ever forgot that he was a vampire when they were this close together. Sometimes when he got this close to her, it became overpowering. But for the first time, she saw beyond the deadly facade to the man beneath. He might be terrifying, but he was also terrifyingly beautiful—body chiseled from stone, razor-edged cheekbones, pools of onyx, effortless masculinity that oozed from every pore.

"No," she finally whispered, tearing her thoughts from the man before her and focusing on the discussion at hand. It was obvious Beckham wasn't the type to want anyone here in his penthouse. She shouldn't be upset that he didn't want her, but feeling useless was infuriating. Being useless in her job was something else entirely.

"So, what?" she asked. "You're not going to drink from me because I'm in your space?"

"I can do what I want with you, Little One."

The way his eyes landed on her body wrapped in a tiny swath of clothing made her feel completely dirty.

She glared back at him, finding only the monster in his gaze. "Fine. Drink from me. Don't drink from me. Die of starvation for all I care. I'm going out tonight, and if I don't leave now, I'm going to be late."

She sent him a scathing look and then walked to the elevator. She pressed the button and tapped her foot impatiently.

After she had stepped inside and the doors were closing, he finally said, "Be safe tonight, Little One."

Chapter Twelve

Reyna arrived downstairs late and beyond irritated. Beckham worked her up like no one else she had ever met. His very presence set her on edge. Most of the time, she wanted to slap him, and then she got lost staring into his handsome face. And she didn't even *like* him. But the tension was so thick she never knew which way the pendulum was going to swing.

"Wow," Everett said when she walked outside. His jaw dropped open. She smiled at his reaction and assessed him. He was dressed casually in a pair of dark jeans and a blue striped button-up rolled to his elbows. Maybe she was overdressed.

"Good wow?" she asked.

"Great wow. You look amazing."

"Thanks." She beamed.

"You look way too good to be going out with me and my friends."

"Oh, should I go change?" she asked uncertainly.

"Absolutely not. If Mr. Anderson let you out in that tonight, then

I'm not letting you walk back inside."

Reyna laughed. "Beckham. Call him Beckham. *Mr. Anderson* sounds like a parent or something."

"Sure. Whatever you say." Everett offered her his arm. "My car is parked in the back. Habit."

She placed her arm on his sleeve and followed him to where an old Mustang was parked.

"This car is amazing," she breathed.

"Thanks. Original body. I fixed it up with my dad. He was a mechanic before the economy tanked. Hard to afford fuel for her, but to and from work isn't that bad."

Everett opened the side door for her, and she sank into the seat. Since leaving the Warehouse District, this was the first time that she was in a car without a hired driver. She felt more normal here. Less like she had to be a doll for the show. She wasn't anyone's pet. She was just Reyna tonight.

The club Everett took her to was only about five or six blocks away. On any normal day at home, she would have walked to and from without a problem. But it wasn't safe in the city, and she didn't have her sneakers anymore, just these impossible heels.

They valeted the car and then walked through the front doors into a pulsing nightclub already half filled with bodies. Everett grabbed her hand and then pulled her through the crowd to a secluded booth. A group of people was already seated with drinks and a pitcher of beer in front of them. As soon as Reyna and Everett approached, a blond woman threw herself at him.

"Everett, you're here."

He hugged her back and then released her. He tugged Reyna closer, bringing her into view. "Mara, this is my friend Reyna. She's new at my building."

Reyna glanced at him curiously as he ushered her into the booth and slid in next to her. Mara took the seat across from Everett.

"Valet?" she asked disbelievingly.

Everett shook his head. "Receptionist."

"Killer. I was a waiter there for one week before I wanted to open my wrists on the tile floor to see all the nasty bloodsuckers have a field day."

"Oh," Reyna said awkwardly. Why had Everett lied about her? He knew who she worked for. But clearly this woman didn't like vampires, so maybe it was better to play along.

"Mara," Everett said with a head shake. "Let's leave the politics for one night."

"Fine. Fine," Mara said, raising her hands. "Let me introduce you. Reyna, this is Brianna, Tucker, and Coop."

She pointed around the table to a tall Black woman, Brianna, in a red-patterned dress with short brown hair; a guy, Tucker, in a beat-up leather jacket with thick curly black hair and tawny brown skin; and another white guy, Coop, with longish brown hair who looked like a skinny rocker with tattoos.

"So, Reyna," Brianna said, leaning over the table. "Where did you get that outfit? Did you rob a bank?"

Reyna stared down at it and realized how ridiculous it must look to them. She was wrapped in silk, wearing designer labels and shoes that cost a fortune.

"Oh, these. Well, don't tell anyone. They're knockoffs." Suddenly she realized that she wasn't really any freer with these people than with Beckham. At least with Becks she didn't have to lie about who she was.

"Best knockoffs I've ever seen," Mara said. She clearly didn't buy it.

"Want a drink?" Everett asked.

"Dying for one," Reyna said. She hopped out of the booth and followed him to the bar. "What the hell was that?"

"Sorry," he said sheepishly. "Visage isn't well-liked around here."

"How do you even know I work for Visage?"

Everett gave her a meaningful look. "A beautiful woman with an unlimited credit card hanging around Beckham Anderson? Kind of an easy guess."

"Oh." Reyna felt her cheeks heat. "You think I'm beautiful?"

Everett laughed. "Yes, but don't let Beckham know. He's a scary motherfucker."

"True." She could hardly disagree, but one thing stuck out to her. "Wait, is Beckham normally with other pretty women?" She leaned against the bar as Everett ordered drinks.

"I wouldn't say normally, but the women I've seen him with have been attractive." Everett gave her a weird look. "Why?"

"Just curious."

The thought of Beckham having other women filter through his life was unsettling. She didn't know what that meant. She had only been here a short while. But it made sense with the way the system was typically laid out that he'd have a new blood donor every month. And they all happened to be beautiful women for the wealthy elite.

She couldn't figure out why it unsettled her so much to think about him eating from anyone else. She ignored that pang in her belly. This was a job. And it had been a job for those women, too. There was absolutely nothing wrong with what any of them were doing. And really, it was none of her business. None of her business at all.

Everett handed her a dark-red drink, and she raised an eyebrow. "What's this?"

"Enjoy the irony. It's called a bloodsucker."

Reyna brought it to her mouth. The thick red liquid touched her lips, and a burst of cherry flavor assaulted her taste buds. It was sugary sweet and delicious. Everett reached forward and wiped a stray bit of the drink from her lip. She stiffened and looked away from his face. She wasn't sure what Everett thought it meant to bring her here, but she was looking for friends.

Her mind strayed to what Beckham's reaction would have been to seeing blood on her lips. It was wrong on so many levels.

Reyna followed Everett back to his friends and slid into the booth. Brianna and Coop were making out while Tucker was chugging a beer. She had never met such free-spirited people. Everyone back home worked constantly. The hours were rough, and people were too exhausted to have much time for fun like this. Even her time with Steven had been in between his shifts at the factories.

Mara leaned over Reyna and tapped Everett on the arm. "You

got her a bloodsucker?" She gave him a drunk pouty face.

"It's cool, Mara. Don't worry about it."

She pulled her hand back and rolled her eyes. "Whatever."

Brianna came up for air. "Oh, a bloodsucker. So delicious. You can't even taste the blood in them."

Reyna paled. "What?"

Mara laughed. "Nice one, Brianna."

"She was kidding," Everett said. "No blood. Just alcohol."

"Oh."

"Speaking of bloodsuckers," Brianna said, nodding her head out to the dance floor.

Everyone turned to look. Reyna didn't see any vampires. Granted, the only ones she knew were rather wealthy and probably wouldn't frequent a club like this.

"She's hot," Tucker said.

"Tucker!" Mara said with a shake of her head.

"What's the fun in that?"

"Who?" Reyna asked.

"Her," Mara said, turning Reyna's head until she found the woman in the center of the room. She was blond, with her hair pulled over to one shoulder. Her clothes were skintight and revealing, her lips bloodred, and she was so thin, her collarbones protruded.

"What about her?"

"Can't you tell?" Mara asked. "She works for Visage."

Reyna swallowed and reassessed the woman. "How do you know that?"

"Look at the bite marks on her neck," Brianna said.

"It's really sad," Mara said. "Girls like her have no options. No choices."

"I mean, they chose Visage," Reyna argued.

"Sure, but no one is choosing to be a blood escort if they can find other work," Coop argued.

"And if they can't find other work?" Reyna asked, wishing her own neck was covered, even though Becks hadn't fed on her. She still felt like her neck was on display tonight, like everyone knew.

Everett reached down and squeezed her hand as if he could feel her spike of anxiety. "I said no politics tonight. Come on."

"Look, the Visage employees need help," Brianna said. "Their blood shouldn't be up for grabs. It's sick."

"They need more than help. We need to end Visage," Mara argued.

"Mara," Everett said on another sigh. "Can we not tonight?"

"No one is going to stop working for them when it gets you high," Coop said.

"What?" Reyna asked, her head snapping to him.

"It does not," Brianna cried, smacking him on the back of the head.

Mara rolled her eyes. "Technically, it kicks your adrenaline into overdrive. Like a flight-or-fight response. So endorphins flood your system to try to counteract it. Kind of like sex."

"Enough anti-Visage, anti-vampire, anti–blood escort talk tonight. Some of us make our living working for them, and that's how it is," Everett said, gesturing to himself. But Reyna's cheeks still flamed. Everett took her hand and pulled her out of the booth. "Let's dance."

"That was enlightening," Reyna said as he pulled her onto the dance floor.

"You should ignore them. They're always spouting about social justice."

"Well, they're not wrong. A lot of people would choose something else if they could." Reyna shrugged as she wrapped her arms around Everett's neck and leaned into his chest to quiet her racing heartbeat. "God knows, I tried."

"They're not right, either. The world is fucking terrible. We make money where we can. You chose your job just like I did. Nothing wrong with that." He sighed. "Mara likes to get under people's skin."

"But she doesn't even know."

He sighed. "I'm sure she suspects."

"Why?" She didn't even have bite marks.

"Come on, Reyna. There's no one who works at my building who looks like you."

The music shifted to a slow, hypnotic beat, and their movements adjusted with the rhythm. His hands gripped her hips, pulling her closer against him.

She narrowed her eyes. "What does that mean?"

"Gorgeous."

She laughed. "That's such a weird thing to hear. Where I grew up, I'm pretty sure I was considered adequate at best. No job. Just another mouth to feed. My nicest dress was... Oh wait, I didn't wear dresses because it wasn't practical."

Everett reached up and brushed a stray lock of hair out of her eyes. "Whoever that woman was before she came here, no one sees her anymore."

Something in the way he was looking at her made her feel like all the air had been sucked out of the room. She had come here to have friends. She hadn't anticipated him looking at her like this. For a split second, his eyes were replaced with ones as dark as onyx and instead of his boy-next-door features were ones cut out of marble. Her mind conjured up Beckham out of nowhere. A vision she should not be thinking about. She pulled away abruptly.

"I need to get some air."

And then she dashed away from him as fast as she could. She couldn't breathe. No. This was all wrong. Shouldn't she want to be looked at like that by a nice, cute boy? But she didn't. And what was that vision of Beckham? Sure, he was handsome and she liked the way he looked at her, but she shouldn't be thinking about him like that or wondering how he would react to blood on her lips.

Reyna found the back emergency exit and pushed through the door, praying the alarm didn't go off. When nothing happened, she walked outside and took in a few deep, calming breaths. She needed to get it together.

A minute later, Everett busted out the back door. She whirled around and pressed her hand to her chest.

"God, you scared me."

"Why did you leave?" he asked.

Reyna looked away from him. How could she explain? "I needed some air. I felt so claustrophobic."

"I didn't mean to push," he apologized, stepping toward her.

"No. You're fine. Just so many changes in my life all at once."

"Sorry. I wasn't trying to scare you off." He looked sheepish.

"I'm not scared. I don't know. Not ready," she ended lamely.

"Let's go back inside. I promise to be on my best behavior."

"And I promise to be on my worst," a voice said from the shadows.

"Reyna," Everett said anxiously, pushing her behind him. "Let's get out of here."

And then the person moved closer toward them, and she realized he wasn't human at all. He was a vampire, but something was wrong with him. His skin was pallid and waxy. So pale, it was almost translucent. He looked as if his body might crumble into ash at the lightest of touches. His jeans and T-shirt were torn and frayed. They hung on his emaciated figure like a mother's wedding dress on a child. He had none of the formidability that Beckham or the vampires she had met at Visage had. But she recognized the same desire and need trapped in his eyes, like a living, breathing dragon desperate to escape.

"We were just leaving. We didn't mean to bother you," Everett said, slowly backing away from the vampire. He nudged Reyna and whispered, "Run, Reyna. Run."

Reyna's heart was a drumbeat in her ear as she dashed toward the door. She could feel Everett close on her heels, but she wasn't fast enough. Neither of them could possibly be. This was a nightmare. One the entire world had lived with before the cure.

She tripped over her high heels, cursing herself for wearing the damn things. But it didn't matter. They were never going to make it anyway. She glanced over her shoulder and watched as the vampire lunged for them at an inhuman speed, teeth bared. Reyna screamed and darted away, but the vampire grabbed Everett. And she stood frozen as he held Everett as if he were a rag doll.

"No," she gasped out right before he sank his fangs down into Everett's tender neck. Blood spurted from the wound into his mouth, and the vampire drank deeply.

As Reyna watched the life begin to drain from Everett's face, she let loose an earsplitting scream.

Chapter Thirteen

This couldn't be happening. A vampire wasn't going to kill Everett. She couldn't run away and leave him here to die.

Despite her better judgment, she ran over to them and pounded on the vampire's back. "Stop," she screamed. "You're killing him."

When he made no reaction, she stomped on his foot with the heel of her shoe. She heard a sickening crack as it tore through his foot and her heel snapped off. The vampire wrenched away from Everett, who dropped like a bag of rocks. He rounded on Reyna, and she stumbled back a few steps in terror.

"Shit!"

The vampire stalked forward in a way she was deeply familiar with. Her body shook as what she had done dawned on her. She could have gotten away. No matter how much of a coward that made her. She could have at least gone for help. Now she was stuck here with this monster, and she could see in his lifeless eyes that he was going to kill her, too.

Once he reached her, he swatted her across the face like an annoying fly. The force of the hit sent her careening headfirst into the metal dumpster. She rebounded, falling in a heap into a pile of discarded trash bags. Her vision blurred, and when she touched the source of the pain, a hot, sticky wetness coated her hair.

The vampire stooped to pick Everett back up and finish what he'd started. But once she pulled back her hand to find it covered in bright-red blood, the vampire's head whipped around. His stare promised death. She struggled to stand back up but collapsed back to the ground. She was disoriented and couldn't get her limbs under control. The vampire coming toward her had only one thing in mind, and still she could do nothing.

"What do we have here? Your blood produces the sweetest aroma." As he stalked toward her, Everett's blood dribbled down his chin. "Tasting you will be like drinking the nectar of the gods, if I believed they existed."

"Wha-what?" she stammered.

"I've heard of blood like this." He leaned down and breathed in deeply, savoring the scent of her like a rose in bloom. "It seems my fortunes have turned."

"I'm nothing," she pleaded, tears running down her face. "You've had your fill. Just let us go."

"I don't think so."

The vampire leaned toward her, enjoying the terror in her expression. Everett's blood had given him life, but she could see in his crazed eyes that he was going to take her for pleasure. She shuddered as he ran his hand down her cheek and tilted her head to expose her neck. And there was nothing she could do about it. She couldn't even scream. She closed her eyes and said a prayer to whomever would listen.

But the bite never came.

Then the pressure on her neck disappeared. Reyna's eyes flew open. And she couldn't believe what she saw. Her eyes widened in disbelief as Beckham held the vampire by the arm. The other vampire snarled and twisted, breaking out of Beckham's tight hold. He lunged for Beckham, who moved so quickly that the pair of them was a blur. The vampire must have been starving, because with fresh blood in his system he had more power and speed than he'd shown only moments before. The two moved together. Beckham seemed to have the upper hand. His broke down the other vampire's defensives and left his spurt of energy to be wasted. Still they fought—blows landed and deflected, feet kicking, and bodies twisting and moving to try to break the other.

In a movement that Reyna could hardly even see, Beckham whirled the other vampire around so his back was to Beckham's chest. Beckham placed a hand on either side of the vampire's head. For a split second, the guy stopped moving entirely. He realized he was defeated.

And for the first time, Beckham's face was illuminated in the streetlight. As she stared into Beckham's endless dark eyes, Reyna's gasp was audible.

His fangs were bared, and he looked furious. Beyond furious.

Dangerous.

Ruthless.

Deadly.

"Becks," she whispered in horror.

But he didn't seem to hear her. The only sound that followed was the sickening crunch as Beckham turned the vampire's head to an unnatural angle. He fell to the ground. Dead.

Reyna's mouth hung open. Holy shit! He had just killed for her. She couldn't comprehend it. She was wavering in and out of consciousness. She grasped at it, desperate not to succumb to the darkness.

"Little One," he said softly as he approached her. She watched him suck in a deep breath and then hold it as he bent down toward her. He scooped her up in his arms as if she weighed nothing.

"Everett," she mumbled.

Beckham sighed and then nodded. He would take care of it. He didn't even have to say a word.

"Thank you," she whispered before darkness carried her under.

...

Reyna awoke to find herself laid out on soft cushions. Her body ached everywhere, and she had a splitting headache. As she sat up, she groaned. A hand rested on her shoulder to lay her back down.

"Take it easy," Beckham said.

She peeled her eyes open. Beckham was sitting next to her on the couch in the living room of his penthouse.

"Becks," she said, her voice raspy.

She had never been this happy to see him. She couldn't believe that she was here right now, that he had followed her, that he had saved her. All she wanted to do was reach up and run her hand down his beautiful face and apologize for ever doubting him. Her gratitude was beyond measure. In his eyes, she no longer saw the monster who had snapped the vampire's neck in half, but a man searching her for signs of distress. A man who may have chosen to take a Permanent subject against his will but would nevertheless take care of her.

Beckham avoided her searching gaze and reached over to the table for a glass of water. "Drink something."

She took it without complaint and managed a few sips. "You saved my life," she said, swallowing back the emotions threatening to take over.

"You were supposed to stay safe."

Reyna didn't know what possessed her to do it, but this time when the need to touch him took over, she didn't suppress it. She reached her hand out to his face and placed it gently against his cheek. His skin was cool to the touch. Yet she felt like she was burning up.

Whether from the life-threatening experience or the growing shift in what his nearness did to her, she didn't know.

"Becks," she repeated softly.

He turned his head away from her hand, refusing to look at her. "I lost control," he said gruffly. "You shouldn't have had to see that."

"You saved my *life*."

She wasn't sure what part of that wasn't clear to him. She could have died out there. She'd been so close to dying, and he had come in and saved her. Everything that had been foggy before was now clear. She didn't need to fear Beckham. He wasn't going to hurt her, and she needed to start to trust him. He wouldn't have gone to such lengths to protect her if he was going to hurt her himself.

"You shouldn't have even been in that position," Beckham said. "You were in the club, and then suddenly you were gone."

"You followed me?"

He met her gaze again. "You were lucky I did. Otherwise, I never would have found you when I did."

"Yes. I was very lucky," she whispered.

It was easy to remember the horrible way the vampire had approached her. The way he had fed on Everett. The way he had come after her.

"What happened to Everett?" She sat up quickly at the realization, and her vision blurred. She put her hand to her head and moaned, relaxing back into the cushions.

"You need to rest, Reyna. Everett has been taken to the hospital. He lost a lot of blood and needs a transfusion. I had my medical team look at you and him, and then after we bandaged you up, they took him."

She touched the back of her head where she had been pushed into the dumpster. There was a large square bandage in place.

"How long have I been out?"

"About a half hour. We had to stop the bleeding." He reached back and touched her head tenderly.

The bleeding. Her blood. What had the other vampire said about her blood? Of all the strange things that had happened tonight, whatever that thing had said about her blood made the least amount of sense.

"Beckham. That vampire—he said something weird." He arched an eyebrow at her in question. "He said that my blood smelled good like the nectar of the gods and that he'd heard of blood like mine."

"You were probably delirious and are remembering wrong," Beckham said.

"No," she insisted. She remembered that. She swore she did. "I wasn't delirious. He said my blood smelled different."

"He was starving. A pathetic vagabond who refuses to get into the new system. I'm sure your blood smelled like life itself to him."

Reyna bit her lip and stared up at Beckham under thick dark lashes. "It didn't smell any different to you?"

Beckham paused for a moment before speaking. "No."

She remembered how he had inhaled deeply when he had gotten close to her and then didn't say anything, as if he was holding his breath. It had to mean something. But why would he lie to her? What could he gain from that?

"Okay," she finally muttered. "When can I see Everett? I need to make sure he's okay. He was only out there because of me in the first place."

"Tomorrow," he said decidedly. "The transfusion takes a couple of hours, and he'll need to rest. Like you, Little One."

Reyna slumped back against the pillows. "This is all my fault," she murmured. "If I hadn't gone into that alley, this never would have happened."

"Why did you go in the first place?"

He looked none too pleased, but Reyna realized this was the first conversation they'd had where they hadn't argued. This almost felt normal.

But his question brought up a whole new wave of emotions. She remembered all too well what had drawn her out of the club and led her to that alley. She had been so desperate to get away from Everett and the intimate look on his face. She had been so confused by why her mind kept drifting back to Beckham instead of the cute boy in front of her that she had just run.

"Little One?" he prodded.

She looked at him tentatively. "I was thinking of you."

Beckham stiffened under her gaze. She wasn't hiding her emotions. Her heart was fluttering in her chest and against her throat. In that moment, her eyes were a window to her soul, and he could translate what she was thinking.

"How?" he finally asked.

Reyna's blush deepened.

He reached forward and touched her dark hair, which had fallen out of its updo. His fingers threaded through the strands, careful not to touch the knot on the back of her head. Beckham was normally rough and demanding, but here he was so gentle. His thumb ran along the inside of her neck.

"That blush is dangerous," he growled, clearly trying to restrain himself.

Reyna held his gaze, her breathing making her chest rise and fall heavily.

"Touching me like this is dangerous."

He tilted his head to consider her. His eyes flicked from her eyes to her lips to her neck and then back up. "Because I could break you."

She paused at his words. He meant physically, but her heart was speaking volumes to the truth of that statement emotionally. There was a reason that she kept being drawn back to him. It was all laid out before her. It had all started with that first touch of his lips. Oh, yes, he could break her.

"Yes," she breathed.

"I'll take my chances."

Beckham leaned forward, and everything narrowed down to this one moment. His eyes bored into hers. Not asking for permission. Not asking for anything. Just looking into her soul and letting her know that he was taking her.

And she let him.

God, did she let him.

His mouth landed on hers, and it was like every kiss before this vanished into thin air. This was her first kiss. Because nothing else could hold a candle to the way his lips felt against hers. If she smelled like ambrosia, then Beckham truly tasted like it.

Sweet. Tempting. Addicting.

He was the real deal. The perfect package.

His lips as soft as feathers molded to hers with a tenderness she would never have expected from Beckham, let alone a vampire. Her hands moved up to grab his suit and pull him in closer. She needed more. She needed this taste, this sweetness on her tongue, touching her, holding her.

Reyna opened her mouth and ran her tongue along his bottom lip. He groaned into her mouth, and all of his tentative movements evaporated. His tongue darted out and caressed her. They volleyed as if there were a winner to their match.

Their kisses turned heated and desperate. Reyna hadn't actually thought he would ever want this from her. Did Beckham feel the same way she did when he kissed her? Or was this another part of ownership?

Something in the way he held her and the intensity of his kisses told her that he valued more than just her blood…or her body. He was not paying anything for this. He was kissing her like a man kissed his woman. And she wanted this.

His hands moved from her hair down over her shoulders to trace the curves of her waist and her hips. She moaned at the feel of his hands on her. She wouldn't stop him if he went further. She should. This wasn't appropriate for a professional relationship, and if she went further, there was no going back. But his hands on her body and his lips on her mouth were telling her to ignore all logic. There was here and now. There was only Beckham.

He dropped soft kisses on her cheek, to her ear, and then down her neck. She braced herself, anticipating what was to come. Her heart fluttered. This would finally be it. She wasn't anxious now that she was in his arms. She was excited. Ready.

Was what Mara had said before true? Would she get an endorphin rush from the bite? Was it anything like sex?

Her body was jittery as the kisses moved to her collarbone and then back to her neck. He hovered over her furiously beating pulse. His fangs trailed against the skin. She shivered all over, her body reacting to the erotic intimacy. She could feel her core heating, aching for him.

"Bite me," she pleaded.

He kissed the spot one more time and then leaned his forehead against her neck. His own breathing matched hers. He seemed desperate to do it, and yet he held back.

"You should rest," he said, forcing a barrier between them all over again.

She reached for him. "No," she whispered.

"Good night, Little One." He kissed the top of her head, stood, and walked away.

"Beckham, please. What did I do?"

He stilled in the middle of the room. "I am not the person you think I am. It would be best if you forget that ever happened."

"And if I can't?" He shook his head. "I think you want me to believe you're not good. Because if I *don't* think that, then I can get close to you, and you're terrified to let someone in," she said, gaining her voice.

Beckham didn't say anything for a moment. "You can believe what you wish. But that won't happen again," he said and then left.

Reyna slumped back and pressed her hand to her lips. That couldn't be the last time. The taste of him still lingered on her lips, and she knew even as she watched his retreating back that that was a promise he couldn't keep.

CHAPTER FOURTEEN

Reyna walked through the hospital. It was strange to be on this side of the Visage building. She and her brothers had never had enough money to go to the hospital in the warehouses. When she got sick, she had to sweat it out in their cramped apartment with acetaminophen and hope. Now the sterile environment, packed with sick people who had lost hope and turned to the vampire hospital to keep them alive, surrounded her.

As soon as they made it inside, Beckham had vanished with barely enough instructions for her to figure out how to find Everett. The receptionist directed her down the hall to a nurse. The next nurse pointed her down another hallway. After a few more twists and turns, she finally found Everett tucked up in a hospital bed with an IV attached to his arm.

The IV made her shudder, but at least he was alive.

He didn't look pale and sickly like when she had last seen him. A white bandage was stark against his neck, and she imagined the horrifying puncture wounds underneath. They were both so lucky Beckham had found them.

She knocked on the open door lightly.

"Hey," she whispered.

"Reyna." His face split into a smile. "It's so good to see you alive."

"I could say the same for you. Can I come in?"

"Of course you can." He patted the bed.

She walked across the small room and plopped down into a chair next to the bed. She felt sick to her stomach that they even had to be here. Of course they were tremendously lucky to be alive, but that didn't assuage the ache in the pit of her stomach. Life shouldn't be like this. The dark shouldn't hold these fears. Even back home, where it was supposedly more dangerous, she had never feared something like this happening.

After an awkward moment, Reyna broke the silence. "I'm so sorry. I shouldn't have ever put us in that position."

"No one knew the vampire was going to be there," Everett reminded her.

"That's true, but I didn't want anything to happen to you."

"Luckily, I'm safe now. All thanks to you."

"Well, thanks to Beckham," she told him. "He saved us both."

"Wow," Everett said. Surprise was written on his face. "A vampire saving humans. I'd never have guessed. What was he even doing there, anyway?"

"He was following me, I guess. I have a tendency to find danger, or danger has a tendency to find me."

"Maybe you should have warned me about that ahead of time," Everett said, but he was smiling.

She breathed out a sigh of relief that their friendship didn't seem irrevocably broken after the traumatic experience from last night. Even though Everett had seemed interested in her and she didn't feel the same, that didn't mean she wanted him to die. Nor did she want to lose her only friend thus far.

Just as she was about to say as much, all of his friends bustled into the room. Mara was at the head of the pack. She rushed over to Everett, looking stricken. Her face was puffy and her eyes red as if she had been crying much of the night. Maybe she had been.

Reyna felt a pang of guilt. She had been locked away in Beckham's apartment, sharing a kiss with him, while her friend was at the hospital getting a blood transfusion. His real friends had waited around for him to wake up. She tried to rid herself of the guilt, but it was difficult.

"Hey, guys," Everett said with a smile.

"Oh, Everett," Mara cried. She wrapped her arms around his waist and gave him a big hug. He laughed at her and patted her twice on the shoulder.

"I'm okay, Mara."

"What the hell happened to you? We thought you guys split." She gave Reyna an accusatory look.

Reyna had a feeling this was more about the fact that she'd thought Everett and Reyna left together than to find out the details. It was pretty obvious that she liked him. It was strange that Mara was threatened by her. She had never been that woman before, and honestly she shouldn't be now. She liked Everett as a friend, but that was it. Her heart was careening in a completely opposite direction. A direction she shouldn't even be considering.

"Yeah. Are you all right?" Brianna asked, nudging Coop forward into the room.

It was starting to get very crowded. Reyna felt conscious of the fact that she was seated close to Everett.

"We're both okay. We were attacked by a rogue vampire," Everett explained.

Mara gasped. Her hands flew to her mouth. Everyone else looked stricken at the prospect.

"He fed from me. Drew enough blood that I passed out, and if I hadn't been immediately transported to a hospital, I would have died."

Reyna nodded solemnly. "He came after me next. Threw me

against the dumpster, and I suffered a head injury, but uh…another vampire came and saved us."

"What?" Brianna asked, confused.

"Another vamp?" Tucker asked. "A bloodsucker fending off his own kind?"

"Yeah," she said softly.

Mara narrowed her eyes. "What the hell, Everett? Why would a vamp interfere?"

Reyna blushed and kept her eyes firmly fixed on the sheet. Everett remained silent. It would be hard to lie about this one. Lying about where she worked had been easy, but this was something else entirely. Vampires didn't act like this without motive.

"Oh my God," Mara cried. "You work for them, for Visage!"

Reyna cringed at the accusation in Mara's voice. She wanted to speak up and tell her all the things that she and Everett had been speaking about only yesterday. How stigmatizing the work only hurt the people who were in it and how she had made her choice knowing full well what was going on, and feeling *bad* for people who did this job didn't help anything. But instead she just sat there.

Everett shook his head. "Mara, that's enough."

"Visage shouldn't even exist," Mara said. "I'm sorry, Reyna, but you shouldn't be working within the system. You should be trying to take it down."

Brianna sighed. "We want to help these people, not turn them away, Mara."

Tucker and Coop were looking anywhere but at Reyna, caught in the crossfire.

"She's the one who lied to our faces."

"That was me, actually," Everett said. "And you can't blame her even if she did."

Reyna squared her shoulders. She couldn't sit back and let them voice this vitriol to her. "I'm still human. You could act like you have an ounce of humanity."

"You're giving up your humanity to them every time you let them drink from you," Mara accused.

"Guys, stop it," Everett yelled, silencing them all. "Leave Reyna alone."

"How can you defend her?" Mara demanded. "She lets a vampire suck her blood for money. The only thing worse is a fucking vampire."

"That vampire saved my life," Everett reminded them. "Maybe not all of them are bad."

"One exception isn't enough to undo generations of atrocities," Mara cried fiercely.

"But it seems enough to condemn them," Beckham said as he walked into the room.

The silence was deafening. Everyone turned and stared at his immense bulk in the doorway. The power radiating off of him was full of intensity. Tucker, Coop, and Brianna scurried to the far side of the room and huddled together. Mara stared back at Beckham defiantly, but she wasn't immune to his power. When he turned his eyes directly on her, Reyna could tell that it was the last place she wanted to be.

"What exactly is going on here?" he asked, his voice booming.

No one said a word.

"That's what I thought."

His eyes finally found Reyna's across the room, and she breathed a sigh of relief that he was here. She never would have thought that she would be so happy that he was near her. But she had felt not only degraded by Everett's friends but also cornered like a mouse in a trap. These were the kind of people who started lynch mobs, and she didn't want to get caught by the pitchfork.

"Let's go, Reyna."

She ducked her chin to her chest and hastened out of the room. She didn't care what they said after she left. She didn't want to stay there another minute. Not even Everett said anything at her departure.

They exited the hospital in silence. His driver was waiting for them at the guest entrance, and she slid easily into the darkened interior. Her tight skirt rode up her legs when she sat down. She was pulling the material down to attempt to cover herself up as Beckham got into the car. He took one look at her, the fact that ninety percent of her legs were clearly visible, and extracted his phone from his suit pocket.

As soon as the door shut behind them, the car headed back into the city. She could feel irritation radiating off of him. She didn't know if it was because of the conversation he'd walked in on or something else.

"Where did you go?" she asked. Her eyes were locked on him tapping endlessly at that damn phone. Her own phone was tucked away in her purse, unused as usual.

Beckham didn't say a word.

She sighed. Was he back to silence?

"I can't believe what Everett's friends were saying," she whispered. She slumped back in her seat, wondering if she could get a reaction from him. The only thing he had noticed was her exposed legs, but she wasn't about to stoop to taking her clothes off for him to pay attention. "Does everyone think like they do?"

Not one word. He didn't even raise his head to acknowledge that she was talking. She thought about throwing her hand in between him and the damn phone, but she was worried about the consequences of her actions.

"Are you going to keep ignoring me?"

He closed his eyes for a second before responding. "Prejudices run deep between our people. No one thinks kindly of anyone, because no one is kind to anyone else. One act will change no one's opinion. You should ignore what people think of you. You are the only one who knows whether or not it is true."

Reyna stared at him for a long time after that. It was very insightful, coming from a vampire who had saved a human's life. It proved over and over again that Beckham was not the bad person he wanted everyone, including her, to believe.

"You know it's been a week and a half, Becks."

"Have you been here irritating me for only that long? You make it seem like a lifetime, Little One."

"I obviously can't hang out with those people who hate me anymore. I can't stay locked in your apartment. I need to do something. Anything," she breathed.

Beckham huffed. "Then use the credit card and go shopping. Buy a mountain of clothes to fill your closet. Make friends with other employees, who'll understand what you are doing and won't judge you for it. Just do something that befits your new station in life."

"My new station?" she asked incredulously.

"Yes, Reyna. I'm not sure what part of this you're missing. You have more money than your wildest dreams could ever have imagined. Use some of it."

Thinking of herself as wealthy, because she happened to work for Beckham and live in his penthouse, made her feel ludicrous. The only benefit of living with him was that the compensation she did receive for the job she wasn't performing was funneled right back to her brothers. At least them receiving the money made it all worth it.

"And you want me to go shopping on the black credit card? The unlimited credit card?"

"It's unlimited for a reason," he said dryly.

"You know I have more clothes than I could ever want in my closet and absolutely nothing comfortable to wear."

"What do you want from me, Reyna?"

Well, that was a loaded question if she had ever heard one. The list of things she wanted from him that she couldn't possibly utter grew daily. Her gaze unconsciously dropped down to his lips and then slipped back up into those endlessly dark eyes. He clenched his jaw.

Yeah. Out of the question.

"I need to do something. Maybe get a job?"

"You *have* a job already."

Reyna laughed in his face. "Right now I'm getting paid to sit around in your penthouse and deal with your attitude and preoccupation with your phone. That's not a job. I can't live cooped up with nothing to do. I'm restless."

"Everyone else would die for this opportunity. Why must you be so difficult?"

"I'm obviously not everyone else."

"Obviously."

She sighed and felt the space between them heavily. "I didn't bargain for never leaving or doing anything or seeing my brothers."

Beckham shook his head incredulously. "Do you not understand the danger? Did last night reveal nothing to you?"

She lifted her chin. He was talking about the attack, but all she could think was the feel of his lips on hers. As she fell asleep last night, she had replayed that moment over and over again in her mind. She had been even more restless afterward. One taste was not enough. Could never be enough.

"Last night simply showed me what I already knew. Some people are good, and some are bad. Some vampires are bad, and some…" Reyna reached out and touched his hand across the car. "Some are good."

Beckham pulled his hand back as if he'd been burned. "That's where you're wrong. Everyone is bad. You just don't know it yet."

"I don't believe you."

"The good isn't out there, Reyna. Everyone is corrupt. Everyone is broken."

"I'm not," she whispered.

"Oh, Little One, this world will kill the goodness left within your beating heart."

"But it will not break me."

"No," he agreed. He leaned his head into her hair and drew a deep breath. "I will do that."

CHAPTER FIFTEEN

Reyna was ripped out of her dreams by a nightmare of a vampire chasing her in the streets and tearing out her throat. She screamed and bolted upright in bed. Her hair stuck to her back. Her body was clammy. And she couldn't seem to rid herself of the terrible sense of unease.

She was fine.

She was in Beckham's penthouse.

It had been days since she had been attacked by a vampire. Nothing had happened. Nothing at all since then. But she couldn't seem to shake the nightmares.

She hoped Beckham didn't hear her. She didn't want to bring it up to him. Not after the distance he had put between them. She had felt so safe and secure in his arms, but as soon as he had let her go, it was as if he had constructed a wall of impenetrable ice to keep her out.

So much effort went into it on his part that she had given up on trying to get through to him. He wanted her to be grateful for her position, and she was. But she still hoped for him, and hope was dangerous.

Rolling out of bed, she hopped into the shower to wash off the sweat. She draped a towel around her body and towel-dried her hair in the mirror. She wound her hair up in a knot on the top of her head and then went in search of something to wear. As soon as she entered her closet, she noticed a bloodred dress hanging by itself. She stopped in her tracks and glanced around. She hated when things just appeared in her room. It didn't usually mean anything good.

She moved over to the dress and skimmed the silky material between her fingers. It was gorgeous and soft and still so not her. A note was attached to the hanger, and she snatched it up in her hand.

Today.

That was all it said. No further instruction. She sighed, knowing what the word meant, and pulled it on. The dress had a strapless sweetheart neckline with a tight satin bow around the waist of the silky top. The skirt was tulle to her knees and made her feel like a ballerina, though she was hardly graceful and hadn't actually seen a ballerina since before her life had turned to shit.

After securing the dress at the back, she turned to exit her room but found something that hadn't been there the night before. On her nightstand was a large blue box. She hurried over to it and procured the card.

Perspective.

She undid the ribbon and took the lid off of the box. Inside was a sleek black camera with a large lens and a thick strap. She removed the camera reverently. Her parents had had one when she was a kid, but she didn't know exactly how this one worked. It took a couple of minutes of fiddling around with the buttons before it turned on. The screen lit up but didn't show her what she was looking at. Pressing her eyes to the small square at the top, she pointed it in the direction of her closet and pressed down hard on the button at the top. The camera clicked and whirred, and when she looked down, an image of her closet appeared in perfect clarity.

Her mouth hung open. It was amazing.

"Perspective, huh?" she mused.

She pressed it against her chest and rushed into the next room.

"A camera," she said excitedly when she saw Beckham seated at a barstool in the kitchen, staring down at his blasted phone.

He glanced at her once, scrutinizing her appearance. She stilled under that molten gaze. "And here I thought you'd complain about the dress."

"Oh. Well, this isn't the worst thing you've dressed me up in," she retorted. Her cheeks were pink from his assessment, but she was too giddy to think about the hot and cold. "But a camera, Becks."

He shrugged as if it meant nothing to him. "You said you wanted a hobby."

"It's amazing," she breathed.

Before she could think twice, she threw her arms around his neck. He stiffened beneath her, and she quickly released him. But she didn't apologize. She was too excited to care.

"Can I go shooting now? What will I take pictures of?" she asked.

"I presume whatever you want."

"Well, I should get going."

"Wait," he snapped, reaching out and grasping her hand to keep her from darting away. "We should set ground rules."

"Does everything come with rules?" she groaned.

"Yes."

"Fine. What are they? Let's get this over with."

He gave her a stern look, but she just smiled. "It's very simple. If you leave here to take pictures, you may go wherever you please as long as you take my car and have a security guard with you."

Reyna's mouth dropped open. "You think I need a bodyguard?"

He ignored her question entirely. "If the security guard believes you to be in danger in *any* way, he has express permission to remove you from the situation."

"Anything *else*?" She understood that she needed to be safe, but he could have at least made it seem less like she was going to have all her moves watched at all times.

"What do you plan to do with the photos?" he asked carefully.

"I don't know. I just got the damn thing." She shrugged. "Look at them? Is there a way I can put them on the computer?"

"Yes," he said hesitantly.

"Then probably that."

"This is important, Reyna. I don't want your photographs to show up anywhere with your name on it. I can set you up an anonymous secured website and show you how to add to it, but no one needs to know it's you or that I'm letting you do this."

"Why does it even matter?" she asked, her curiosity piqued.

"Haven't you ever heard that a picture is worth a thousand words? I don't want any of those words connected to you."

"Or you," she reasoned.

"Do you agree?"

"Yes," she said automatically. If she didn't, then he'd never let her leave again. Plus, who would care about her images? "You'll show me how to use the website?"

"I'll set it up by end of day," he promised.

She swallowed and met his gaze with earnest sincerity. "Thank you."

"You're welcome," he said. His shoulders relaxed as he seemed to have gotten through the difficult part of the conversation. "Also, you have a shopping date with Sophie."

Reyna's face fell. He gave her freedom and a ball and chain at the exact same time.

"Do I have to?" she asked, feeling like a child.

"Yes," he said, already turning back to his phone. "Visage is throwing a celebratory ball for the passage of the Blood Census. I have to be in attendance, which means *you* have to be in attendance."

"A ball?" Her ears perked up at that prospect. A ball with Beckham. Now, that could be interesting.

"Find something suitable to wear and put it on the credit card. I don't care about the cost. Whatever you want," he muttered into his phone.

"All right." She hugged her camera to her chest. "When am I meeting her?"

"Noon." He looked back up at her. His eyes remained fixed on her face. God, if she only had a penny for his thoughts. "Be careful around her, Reyna. She is a wolf in sheep's clothing."

"Then why do I have to meet her?" she asked, exasperated. The politics behind this was all so confusing. She didn't want to spend time with people she had to guard herself against.

"You said you wanted friends." He arched his eyebrow, just waiting for her to question him.

"Yeah…friends. People I meet who I have common interests with. Not a woman who also happens to be a permanent Visage employee."

"What? Like the people from the hospital? Your life has completely changed, and the sooner you realize that, the easier this will all be for you."

Her eyes drifted to his mouth again unconsciously. "What about you?"

"What about me, Reyna?"

"Your life has changed. The sooner you realize that, the easier it will be for both of us," she whispered boldly.

Her eyes travel slowly back up to his, and she knew he must feel something underneath all that bravado, but he didn't budge an inch. "The driver will be here within the hour."

CHAPTER SIXTEEN

When she left her room again, Beckham was gone. She could have skipped out on this entire escapade and taken her camera into the city all on her own. But then her nightmares hit her fresh. She couldn't do that. Not to herself and not to Beckham. He had been genuinely worried about her, and the last thing she wanted was for something to happen. Maybe it wouldn't be so bad with Sophie.

She traipsed down to the lobby and was relieved to see that Everett was back to work.

"Miss Carpenter," he said formally, not meeting her eyes.

She opened her mouth to say something, but what could she say? He might have defended Beckham for saving his life, but he knew what she was, and all of his friends now knew, too. Maybe Beckham was right. Maybe it was all bad and there was no way to break through it. Everett was the nicest, most genuinely kind and optimistic person she had met. If he couldn't get past the fact that she worked for Visage, then she didn't know if anyone really could.

"Hello," she said softly.

"Mr. Anderson's car today?" Everett responded.

"Yes. Thank you."

He signaled Beckham's driver. The minute they stood together in silence was painful. She wanted to say so much. Share how glad she was that he was back at work, reiterate how sorry she was about the attack, try to refute the things his friends had said about her.

Instead, she didn't say anything.

She let Everett opened the door for her.

"Thank you," she whispered.

Their eyes met in that brief moment after she sat down and before he closed the door. It felt as if the distance was insurmountable. Things would never be the same. Maybe *he* would never be the same.

The drive to the boutique where she was meeting Sophie was short. Reyna hoisted the large hobo bag over her shoulder. The weight of her camera in the bottom of the bag gave her confidence, and she strutted forward in her high heels. She was finally getting the hang of the things. Still, she hoped that she would have enough time after this trip to get some clothes that were more comfortable and would help her blend in to take pictures.

When Reyna entered the storefront, she teetered in her heels uncertainly. She had expected a small shop with a few dresses. When she thought designer clothing, that was what she envisioned. But this place was massive. Two or three stories high and stretching at least a city block.

A woman as tall, lean, and beautiful as any vampire she had ever met clicked her tiny pointy-toe heels toward her. She was in a black dress that hugged her thin figure and had her hair pulled up into a perfect bun at the nape of her neck. As she drew closer, Reyna startled when she realized that she was human. How could any human be this beautiful?

"You must be Reyna," she said with a smile. "I'm Blythe."

"Hello."

"Your friend has already arrived. Allow me to escort you."

"Sure," she said, trying to will confidence into her steps.

Her eyes roamed the walls filled with so many beautiful, expensive clothes that she didn't even know where to begin. How could anyone afford this? Better yet, how could they do this when there were so many starving, and working for nothing, and needy? It turned her stomach that she was even part of it.

"We're so glad that you've chosen our store for your shopping pleasure. Mr. Anderson informed us that this was your first shopping expedition and to treat you with the utmost courtesy. Are you excited?"

"Um…a little overwhelmed already."

She smiled kindly. "That's perfectly normal. We've had others come through for their first time. It's most important to outfit Visage employees. We're known for it, in fact. Some of the designers have an entire Subject–Sponsor line."

"Oh." She didn't know what to say. What kind of clothes would come in a Subject–Sponsor line? Did she even want to know?

"You're looking for a ball gown, correct?"

"Yes. Something extravagant, I'm sure." She rolled her eyes.

Blythe's eyes sparkled. "We can do extravagant."

"I'd prefer to blend into the background, but I have a feeling that isn't what I'm supposed to do."

"A beauty like you?" she asked. "Absolutely not. We'll make you and your friend Sophie sparkle beyond measure. When in a room of vampires, you have to go out of your way."

They entered a section of the store filled with ball gowns. Every shape, size, and color was available. She had no idea where to begin. All she could do was stand there speechless and stare at the extreme luxury.

"Reyna, there you are," Sophie called, walking out of a dressing room in the most revealing yellow gown. The neckline dropped almost to her navel. The sides were cut out, making her waist look teeny tiny. When she turned to stand on a box and stare at her reflection in the glass, Reyna saw that the back crisscrossed and then dipped unbelievably low before ruffling down to her feet.

"Wow," she murmured.

"Isn't it divine?"

"It's something."

Sophie pinched the sides. "I think I can go a size down, Blythe. This one is a bit baggy. Don't you think?"

Baggy where? She looked stunning. Her blond hair cascaded over one shoulder as she looked at the salesclerk seemingly innocently.

"We could have it taken in. Better to have a little bit of room so it's easier to get on and off than to go a size lower."

Clever answer.

"No," Sophie said, looking at herself in the mirror. "It's all wrong. I want to be irresistible to every man in the room."

Without another thought for modesty, she wrenched the zipper down on the bottom of the dress and let the material slide off of her body and pool in a heap on the floor. She wore nothing but a white strapless bra, matching thong, and high heels. She kicked the dress away from her and sighed.

"Find me something else. Something that would eclipse the sun." Then she turned and stalked dramatically back into the dressing room. "Come on, Reyna. Find something you like. Are you even a sample size?"

Reyna ignored her snide remark. It didn't matter what size she was.

Blythe looked Reyna up and down, taking her measurements with her eyes. "I have just the thing."

Reyna bit her lip. "Sorry about her."

"Miss Sophie is a great customer. We like to keep her happy. Why don't we get you a few choices and I'll bring them to you in the dressing room?"

"Thank you."

Reyna clutched her bag awkwardly as she walked back toward Sophie. There was another woman who offered her a glass of champagne, which she promptly refused.

"Don't be a prude," Sophie said, striding back out in another tiny yellow dress.

"I'm not thirsty. Thank you."

"Whatever. Are you excited about the ball? I've never been to a Visage ball. It's going to be so amazing. All the right people. I've only been to small parties. So, I know all the major players, but this… Gah, I'm dying," she said. She ran her hands down the silky material. "I mean, not really dying." Then she giggled.

"That one is nice."

"Nice? Ugh. You're bad at this."

She stripped out of that dress, too, and then stood there with her hands on her hips. Her body was unbelievable. Reyna felt bad for even looking at her, but she clearly wanted to flaunt it.

"Here you are, Reyna," Blythe said. She carried a handful of dresses with her into the dressing room. "Do you have your card?"

"Oh, yeah. Sorry." She fished out her credit card and passed it over to Blythe. Before it got to her, Sophie snatched it out of her hand.

"Holy shit!"

"What?" Reyna asked.

"You have a fucking black card?"

"Um…yeah?"

"How the fuck did you get ahold of this? Beckham gave it to you?"

"Yeah…"

"Fuck. I need one of these. I'm going to make Roland give me one of these. I'm on a cap. Ugh, it's frustrating as hell. I should have unlimited access to everything I want. Not that he denies me anything, but still. A black card. This is a must!"

"Miss Sophie," Blythe said, putting her hand out.

"Oh, right. So jealous." She handed over the card, giving Reyna a pouty face as if she had any control over Sophie getting a credit card, let alone getting one herself.

When Blythe walked away, Reyna closed the door to the dressing room. She had no special lingerie to try this stuff on like Sophie.

Her closet was stocked with little silk panties and bras that fit her perfectly, but she still felt uncomfortable stripping in the middle of the store.

The first dress was a baby blue mermaid design that she found impossible to walk in. She started to take it off, but she heard Sophie on the other side.

"God, you're taking forever. When do I get to see?"

"You want to see?"

"Haven't you done this before?"

"No," she admitted.

"Well, come out, silly."

Reyna stepped out in the dress, and Sophie wrinkled her nose. "No. Gross. Go change."

Reyna rolled her eyes. Why would she want to see the obvious duds?

They tried on a few more dresses before Sophie finally landed on one that she fell in love with. It was all white like a wedding gown with real crystals embedded in the dress. It sparkled like a diamond whenever she moved.

"So," Sophie said, in a better mood now that she had found a dress. "How many times did you and Beckham bang before he gave you that card?"

Reyna stumbled in the fitted dress she was wearing. "What?" she gasped.

"Oh my God, stop being such a prude."

"I...I don't know what you're talking about."

She was terrified to look at her reflection. She felt flushed from head to toe.

"Oh, please, I'm not naive enough for that." Sophie rolled her eyes. "That dress sucks."

Reyna hurried back to the dressing room for what felt like the hundredth dress. She took her sweet time, not wanting to continue that conversation with Sophie. Why did she think Reyna was sleeping with Beckham? Was that part of the job description that she had missed? Not that she hadn't thought about it or that she didn't *want* to, by any means...

"So, is he good?" Sophie asked.

"Is who good?"

"Beckham, obviously. Get with it, Reyna. Is Beckham good in bed?" she asked, but she didn't wait for Reyna's response before continuing. "I mean, Roland is rough with me and all, but you know what they say about him?"

"What do they say?" she murmured.

"Oh, you know," she said distractedly. She fluttered her fingers dismissively. "Anyway, I know Roland is nice and all, but Beckham. I couldn't imagine. Roland tells me he has such a dark past. He must be an animal in bed."

Reyna swallowed hard. How had they gotten to this conversation?

"So, is he?"

"I don't know," she said softly.

"You don't know if he's an animal? I mean, how is he compared to your other lovers?"

Reyna closed her eyes to try to stave off her embarrassment. "Honestly, Sophie, I wouldn't know. I haven't slept with Beckham."

Sophie laughed, but when she looked up at Reyna she stopped. "Wait, you're serious?"

"Couldn't be more serious."

"Oh my God, how is that possible? Roland had his hands all over me on day one. Couldn't get enough of me, until I was literally delirious from the bites and exhausted beyond measure."

"I did *not* need to know that," Reyna said, raising her hand.

"But how did you get the black card, then?"

Reyna shrugged helplessly. "He just gave it to me."

"He just gave it to you." She sounded incredulous.

"Yes."

"There you are, ma chérie," Roland crowed.

He strode into the fitting room area with purpose, bypassing Blythe without so much as a glance. His eyes were fixed on Sophie standing in her stunning white gown. Then they drifted to Reyna and widened with approval. Once the surprise wore off of his face, his smile was devious and desirous. She felt completely exposed in the black floor-length gown she was wearing with its high slit to her upper thigh and the plunging neckline.

Sophie threw herself into his arms, breaking their eye contact. For that, Reyna was grateful. "Don't you love my gown for the ball?"

She twirled in place for him, and he smiled admiringly.

"Yes. It's perfection. Go get out of it so the sales associate can box it up for us." He motioned for Blythe to follow Sophie into the room, leaving him completely alone with Reyna.

Reyna stayed stock-still, up for display on the box before a row of mirrors and Roland's prowling eyes.

"My, Reyna. You are stunning." He savored the word on his tongue.

"Thank you."

"If you show up to the ball in that, you will outshine every woman in attendance."

"I don't think…"

"Beckham is a very lucky man," Roland said, suddenly directly in front of her.

"Oh, yeah. I guess." She swallowed and looked anywhere but at him.

"Does he satisfy you? That self-restrained brooding stoic? Is he a good lover?"

She made the mistake of looking into his eyes, and he was staring at her like he would very much like to find out if he would satisfy her. Or more precisely like he wanted to find out and then snap her neck and would enjoy doing both.

"I could show you what you are missing," he growled, running his fingers up her bare arm.

His hands on her felt wrong on so many levels. Her throat tightened, and she remained perfectly still. Maybe if she didn't move, she wouldn't draw his further attention. Maybe he would walk right past her, back to Sophie, and not molest her with his eyes. All she wanted to do was run away from him, but it was not as if she could escape a vampire. Nor was he an enemy she wanted at her back.

"I appreciate the offer," she said, "but Beckham is very territorial. I don't think that he would want to share."

In truth, she didn't want anyone else. Whether Beckham wanted to share or not mattered little to her in that moment.

Roland narrowed his eyes and grabbed her by the hair. "I'd like to see Beckham get territorial."

Reyna cried out at the sudden assault. She closed her eyes and shook from head to toe. "Please…please…"

"Just think, I could taste you right here. And maybe if you're lucky, I'd let you taste my blood, too. Mingled together, and you would be remade." His hand caressed her cheek. "You'd make the prettiest little vampire."

"Please, please stop," she said, squeezing her eyes together and trying to release the tension on her hair.

"What is going on?" Sophie asked, appearing out of the dressing room.

Roland released her roughly. "Nothing. The car is waiting for you. Have the dress delivered."

And then he turned and strode out of the room. Reyna couldn't rein in her fear even after Sophie left with a mixture of pity, jealousy, and anger rolling off of her.

"Miss Reyna?" Blythe said. "Have you decided on a dress?"

"Yes. I'd like you to charge this one to the card," she said, "and then burn it."

CHAPTER SEVENTEEN

With Beckham occupied with work, Reyna hadn't found time to tell him about Roland. Maybe she was avoiding it. She didn't really want to recount what had happened. Beckham was overly protective, and she would rather stay under the radar about it all.

But as the days grew closer and closer to the ball, her anxiety peaked. She didn't want to see Roland and have his disgusting eyes on her. She had scrubbed herself clean all afternoon to get over the feel of his hands touching her. To rid herself of the desire clear on his face.

She spent more time with her camera after that, to avoid revealing to Beckham what had happened. The driver had agreed to stop at another clothing store, where she picked up a few plain T-shirts, two pairs of jeans, a baseball cap, and her coveted Converse. She had stashed all of those clothes in a hiding spot where hopefully no one else would find them and throw them away. On the rare occasion that Beckham was home when she was planning to head out, she would stash her street clothes in an oversize bag and change in the car.

It was hard enough getting pictures the way she wanted without standing out like a sore thumb. She never again wanted to encounter what had happened when she went back to the warehouses dressed in silk and heels. She might have a bodyguard, but people were not forgiving of the wealthy in this environment. And she could hardly blame them. She didn't want their anger to come down on her.

And the pictures she wanted to take weren't nice, normal pictures of the city. She preferred the ones that showcased the true heart of the city, sort of like the black-and-white ones hanging in Beckham's living room. She wanted to capture what was really happening. She wanted to find her perspective.

Most of her time was spent trying to take pictures of the poor, the homeless, the beggars, starving vampires, human–vampire interaction on every level. She wanted to remember what it felt like to see these people. She never wanted to become the establishment or forget where she came from.

Every afternoon after she finished with her shots, she downloaded them to her computer and uploaded them to a secure site Beckham had made for her to organize her photos. He had done it all for her so she wouldn't fuck up and reveal who she was—not that it even mattered. It was just pictures of the reality of city life.

But no matter what she did to occupy her time, the night of the ball approached. She had officially been in Beckham's penthouse nineteen days. He hadn't tasted one drop of her blood, and they had barely seen each other the last five days. She was both excited and anxious to spend the entire evening with him.

Beckham had hired a team of artists to do her hair and makeup for the event. When they finished and she looked in the mirror, she barely recognized herself. Her hair was piled high on her head in an intricate creation exposing her neck and collarbones, she noted anxiously. Her eyes were smoky and sultry and her face a perfect mask of porcelain. She hoped he approved.

Swallowing back her anticipation, she left her room to find

Beckham leaning against the kitchen bar in a tuxedo, completely engrossed in his phone.

"Well?" she asked, turning slowly in her ball gown. She had finally decided on a floor-length, strapless, black-and-rose-gold lace dress that shimmered with her movement. It hugged her curves and transformed her figure in the most flattering of manners. It had a tasteful slit up the right side, which revealed the strappy black heels beneath.

She could feel Beckham's eyes on her, but he remained silent. And when she finally stopped her circuit, she stared into his eyes and saw hunger, desperate hunger, reflected back.

"Is it okay?"

"You look exquisite," he said.

She beamed at his approval. It was the most he had said to her in days.

He offered her his arm, and she rested her hand lightly on his sleeve, letting him draw her out of the apartment. They didn't speak in the car. She was too nervous about what was about to happen. She had never been to a ball before and wasn't sure what it was going to be like or how to behave. Couple that with her fears about Roland, and she was completely on edge.

When they pulled up to the giant building, Beckham helped her out of the car. A red carpet was rolled out for them, and as they passed the sea of reporters, cameras flashed, capturing their every movement. Beckham kept a tight grip on her hand. She felt safe in his grasp and wished he were like this all the time. But it was futile to wish for something that would never be.

Inside, the ballroom was enormous. The biggest room she had ever seen. The lighting was dim, and crystal chandeliers dripped from the ceiling, casting soft light on the crowd. Beautiful men in black tuxedos and women in tiny black skirts and white button-ups carried platters full of hors d'oeuvres and champagne. Glitz and glamour were everywhere, from gold-crusted champagne flutes to glittering diamonds on all the women. No expense had been spared for an event that had been planned in just a few short weeks.

The room was already filled with Visage employees, celebrities, and important political figures. It was both incredible and overwhelming.

"Wow," she murmured.

"A bit pretentious, don't you think?"

She startled and looked up at Beckham. Had he just made fun of the party for his boss?

She laughed softly, loosening up. "A bit."

"Let's go make nice," he muttered under his breath.

Beckham meandered them lazily through the crowd. Everyone knew Beckham and wanted a few minutes of his time. At every turn, he stopped to say hello to a different person, and she was introduced to more people than she would ever remember. They were a blur of faces and tuxedos and ball gowns. All vampires. The only humans in the whole place were the servers, entertainment, and herself.

They finally made it to the front of the room and to his boss, Mr. Harrington.

"Beckham," he cried. They shook hands like old friends. "I see you've brought the lovely Reyna. Roland and Cassandra have just shown up with their Permanents. We've had a few others roll into the program as well, and they should be in attendance tonight. Jesse, I believe, was bringing his subject."

"That's great to hear, sir," Beckham responded cordially. "Everything working out with all the new positions?"

"As good as we could hope. One had to be taken back," Harrington said flippantly. It didn't seem to occur to him that he was talking about a human being. Or if it did, he didn't care. "They didn't seem to work out. No worries, though. Everyone else seems fine. Once the Blood Census goes into effect, we can start rolling this out company-wide."

Beckham nodded. "Sounds like another success."

"Indeed. Well, I need to go prepare for my big speech." He nodded at Reyna once more and then disappeared.

"Reyna," Sophie called, running up to her and kissing her on both cheeks. "I didn't see this gown. I'm so jealous. That cow didn't want me to have it, obviously."

"You look beautiful, Sophie. Eclipsing, of course," Reyna said.

"Of course," she said, beaming.

And then Roland snaked his nasty arm around Sophie's waist and drew her close to him. "I have to agree. Innocent virginal white suits you, ma chérie," he purred against her skin.

Reyna instinctively moved closer to Beckham. Her body tensed and felt coiled like a snake ready to strike. Everything about Roland set her on edge, and it was worse because Beckham only vaguely knew how much of a threat he was. She was mentally chastising herself for not clueing him in. Especially as Roland's eyes crawled over her outfit. She shuddered. She hated the way he looked at her.

"And you—" Roland smirked. "You chose a different dress."

"The other one made me feel uncomfortable," she said pointedly.

"Either way. It's a good choice. Beckham, your girl looks like a dream, don't you think?"

Beckham had been staring off and away at that moment, but suddenly he snapped back to attention. His eyes landed on Reyna, and everything narrowed down to him. Only him.

"A dream. A daydream," he agreed. "And a nightmare."

"Her or you, Anderson?" Roland asked. He laughed as if what Beckham had said was a joke. Reyna knew it was not.

"Me, of course," Beckham said. "I'm the one with the fangs."

"Right you are. At least nightmares get the blood pumping," Roland said devilishly.

"Excuse me." Beckham placed his hand on her arm, and she jolted from the sparks that flew between them. She met his heated gaze. "I'm going to get a drink. Would you like anything?"

"Yes, please."

"Champagne?"

She nodded. "All right."

She watched him leave, her heart beating furiously in her chest. How did one touch ignite her so? How could his words and actions be so contradictory?

Her eyes followed his progress across the room.

"And you say you're not fucking," Sophie said crudely.

"Sophie!" she snapped.

"What? Just look at the way he looks at you. That's a man ready to eat you right up."

Reyna looked over at Roland anxiously and then back to Sophie. "You are ridiculous. It's not like that at all."

Such a lie.

"Tell yourself whatever you want, but in that dress, every guy in the room is watching you," Sophie said with a hint of jealousy. "Beckham included."

"I doubt it," she said.

"Oh, but he will," Roland said, walking past Sophie. When he moved into position right next to Reyna, he leaned forward and breathed into her ear, "As am I."

Reyna shivered in disgust and yanked away from him hard. Sophie glanced between them, but either she was a twit and didn't understand Roland's objective or she didn't care so long as he continued to buy her expensive clothing.

"I will find you later, love," he murmured. "Be sure of it."

Roland wandered off, but Reyna couldn't eradicate the sinking feeling of despair at his words. She needed to find Beckham and fast. The last thing she ever wanted was to be alone with Roland. She cast her eyes around the room, looking for Beckham. His height and bulk made him easy to pick out, even in a room full of vampires. He was standing at the bar with a glass of some kind of whiskey in his hand. She watched him tip back the entire glass, grimace slightly, and then pass it back to the bartender, who refilled it quickly.

The bartender began filling a glass flute with champagne when a woman approached Beckham. He spoke with her comfortably, relaxing in a way he never did around Reyna. The woman placed her hand on his sleeve, and he didn't move it. What the hell?

Even from behind, Reyna could tell she was pretty. Her dress was solid royal blue with a tight bodice and empire waist, with ruched taffeta to the floor. Her hair was up in some fancy design that held it off her neck but still let some of the loose dark curls fall down her back.

Then she turned around, and Reyna's mouth fell open slightly. She was not pretty. This woman was dazzling. Slender like a ballerina with a perfect heart-shaped face, button nose, and full pink lips.

She searched someone out but finally shrugged and said something to Beckham. To Reyna's surprise, he tilted his head back and laughed.

Beckham laughed.

She couldn't reconcile that with the Beckham she knew. He never laughed. He was stern and solemn. There was no humor in him at all. In fact, he didn't even like people talking to him, let alone trying to make him laugh.

Without her even realizing it, ice filled her veins. All the heat that Beckham swept through her system was replaced by this ache, this inexplicable ache. Who was this woman?

"Sophie," she murmured, trying to keep herself calm. "Who is that vampire woman?"

"Which one?"

"The one talking with Beckham at the bar."

"Oh," Sophie said softly. She looked at Reyna with stark sympathy on her face.

"What?"

"That's Penelope Sky."

"Penelope Sky." Why did that name sound familiar?

"Yeah. She's the mayor's daughter. And human, not vampire," Sophie corrected.

"Human," Reyna said hollowly. Beckham was that comfortable with another *human*, and he couldn't even get near her. What the hell? How did it even make sense?

"Yeah," Sophie said. She patted Reyna's arm twice.

"Well, he seems awfully comfortable."

"Not surprising, since they've been dating on and off for at least a year," she said as if it were the most normal thing.

"What?" Reyna cried.

Shock hit her like a tidal wave. Beckham was *dating* someone?

After the kiss that they had shared, she was sure she was breaking ground with him. Now, she was second-guessing everything. He didn't feel comfortable with her. He didn't even want to be around her. He avoided her, kept her at a distance, and he had made it perfectly clear that he didn't want anything to do with her besides a professional relationship. All because he was dating Penelope Sky. The mayor's daughter. Fuck, it hurt. Way worse than she thought it would.

"Honestly, do you not pay attention to tabloids?" Sophie asked.

"No."

"They were the talk of the town this summer. A human and a vamp. As you can imagine, it was everywhere. I guess you don't get that information outside of the city."

"I guess not," she said softly. Her stomach was in knots. Beckham had never mentioned that he was dating anyone. He had never mentioned anything, though. Why was she even surprised?

"Well, it fizzled out for a while, but it looks like they're back on. Maybe that's why he's not fucking you," she said crassly.

Reyna paled. "We're not like that, Sophie. Whether he's with her or not."

Sophie patted her hand again sympathetically. "Whatever you say. But I'm glad I'm not competing with that."

That was the understatement of the century. Competing with Penelope Sky was like competing with the sun.

Reyna tried to pull her attention from them, but she couldn't help but watch him. He leaned down to whisper in her ear, and she saw the easy way that his breath hit her skin, the way she smiled up at him like a lover with the effortlessness that came with intimate familiarity.

She had about had her fill when Beckham noticed her stare. Their eyes met across the room, and her cheeks heated. Then he smiled—a dangerous, wicked smile—and walked Penelope across the room, straight toward her.

CHAPTER EIGHTEEN

"Reyna," Beckham said, "I'd like you to meet a friend of mine. This is Penelope."

Reyna swallowed back all of the anger and frustration that lanced her body in that moment. Beckham did not belong to her. Not in any way. One kiss didn't mean anything. She was his employee. And they may have a slightly unprofessional relationship, but he had made it clear that this couldn't go on.

"Hello," she said softly.

"Penny, this is Reyna."

Each woman assessed the other. Reyna didn't know what Penny saw when she looked at her. The woman's face was a mask of serenity. Which was even more infuriating. It didn't help that she was prettier up close. Her eyes were as clear blue as the ocean, and she had the slightest dimple in each of her cheeks.

When Penelope realized that Reyna wasn't going to say anything, she spoke up. "I've heard so much about you, Reyna."

"Really?" Reyna asked. She turned her attention to Beckham and arched one eyebrow.

"Yes, I was so glad when you first got here. So good for Beckham to have someone always around for him. And good for you, too, from what I've heard."

Reyna refused to be embarrassed that this woman clearly knew her history. She couldn't believe that Beckham would tell her, but there was nothing she could do about it at the moment. Her insides were on fire, and some part of her wanted to scream.

"Yep. So good for Beckham. Just what he wanted," Reyna said.

Penelope either didn't hear her sarcasm or refused to register it. "He was telling me last night about your interest in my city."

Last night. He had been out with her last night? While she had been in her room wondering what he was doing and why he was avoiding her, he had been with this woman.

"Really? Your city?"

"Oh, my father is the mayor," Penelope said proudly.

"Uh-huh. Forgive me. It's funny how this is the first time I've heard about you at all."

Beckham made an exasperated face at her. Sophie covered her laugh by coughing into her hand.

"Well," Penelope said, "I've been busy at university. We're on break now, so I'll be around a *lot* more."

The way she said it made it sound like a threat. But why should someone like Penelope even have to threaten her? The woman was drop-dead gorgeous and seemed to be a perfect match for Beckham. For anyone, honestly.

While Reyna stood before her in clothes she hadn't paid for, with her hair and makeup done by people she hadn't hired, working at a job that Penelope could hardly understand. There was no need for Penelope to feel threatened.

"University?" Reyna asked, latching on to the one thing she could comment on. "That must be nice. To be able to afford to go to college."

"I feel very fortunate."

Reyna had to restrain herself from laughing. Of course she did. Reyna would have felt very fortunate to be able to go to college, too, but instead she was here, working for Visage.

"So, how exactly did you two meet?" Reyna prodded.

Penelope looked up at Beckham with a big smile on her face. "Oh...well..." And then she flushed lightly. "It was at a political event. Beckham was there on behalf of Visage."

He gave her an amused look. Reyna could see that something about the story was off.

"You remember, don't you?" she asked, nudging Beckham in the side.

"Yes, Penny. I remember."

"You spent the entire night avoiding me like the plague. I thought I smelled funny or something. I mean, how did you ever resist this face?" she asked with a giggle. Penelope leaned her head against Beckham, but Reyna had had enough of watching that.

Reyna turned to look at Sophie. She wore a pitying expression but didn't say anything. Reyna shouldn't have asked about them. She didn't really care. Nothing was going on between her and Beckham. But still, he had brought her here tonight. If he had preferred to show up with Penelope, then he shouldn't have brought Reyna along. Sitting at home with her pictures was better than feeling left out of the inside joke between him and his whatever girlfriend.

"It must have had something to do with your politics," Beckham said dryly.

"Oh, boo on you. My politics are perfection, and you know it."

Reyna sighed. She needed to change the conversation away from the two of them so she could get through the rest of the night. "So, is that what you study?"

"Oh, yes. Politics. My father thinks it's important for me to follow in his footsteps."

"I see. So, do you have any ambition of your own?" she quipped.

"Reyna," Beckham said.

She smiled at him and enjoyed watching Penelope squirm. At

least Reyna wouldn't be the only one.

"I've always loved politics, and I believe in what my father is doing," Penelope said. "He is enacting meaningful change in the city. Something to be proud of. He has programs in place for the hungry and poor. He's working to get citizens back on their feet. He's partnered with Visage to decrease the unemployment rate."

Reyna didn't know who Penelope was trying to convince with that speech, but Reyna had lived on the streets. She had seen the city streets. Beckham had educated her, as well as the rogue vampire who had almost killed her. If Penelope thought she was doing her job, her father was doing his job, then they needed to get out more.

"That's a nice speech but unrealistic," Reyna said.

"What do you mean? I've lived through the administration. I've seen the improvements."

"You call this an improvement?" Reyna asked, shocking even herself in her enthusiasm. "Have you actually seen the streets? Like walked around on them? Seen the people starving and dirty and poor? Seen the streets littered with filth and felt the utter despair? It's palpable. Has your father—or have you, for that matter—actually *done* anything to change what's happening out there, or are you hiding behind your words? Because I'm not sure if you're aware, but words don't feed the hungry or help get the poor a job or make the streets livable."

Penelope gave her a stunned look. Everyone else around them had gone silent at Reyna's passionate outburst.

"Of...of course we're working to fix things. Everything doesn't happen overnight. We've set up some very successful initiatives."

"How exactly are you measuring success? More or fewer deaths than the day before in your wealthy districts? You probably can't even count the number of dead in the dregs of the city."

"I don't know where you think you're getting this information from," Penelope said indignantly, "but the city cares about the poor just as much as the wealthy."

Reyna laughed. Actually laughed. "The rich always say they

care about the poor as they clean up the bodies. Whatever you think you're doing, Penelope, it isn't working."

"Reyna, that's enough," Beckham growled.

"It always is when you say it is."

He full-on glared at her, but she didn't shrink away.

"Will you excuse us?" he spat.

Without waiting to hear what anyone else had to say, he grabbed Reyna roughly by the arm and hauled her across the ballroom. The room quieted down as Harrington got on the small stage and spoke into a microphone. But she couldn't hear a word he was saying over the deafening silence between her and Beckham as he dragged her out a side panel of double doors and into a small deserted lounge.

"What the hell was that?" Beckham asked.

"You forgot my champagne."

"Forget the damn champagne. What you said was incredibly out of line."

"What I said was the damn truth, and *you* know it. I'm not going to let someone tell me what it's like out there when they've never lived through it."

"You know absolutely nothing about Penelope."

Reyna scoffed. "The mayor's daughter? I know enough. I honestly can't believe you're seeing her."

"She isn't the person you think she is."

"I highly doubt that. And if she's so virtuous, then how come you *never* mentioned her?"

"I thought you already knew."

Reyna threw up her hands. "How could I possibly know?" She turned away in disgust. "Does she even know we kissed?"

"No. That's none of her business."

"It's none of her business?" she asked in disbelief. "I doubt she would agree. Why didn't you tell me you were dating someone?"

"What I do in my spare time is my own business."

"Obviously," she spat. "You made that perfectly clear. I don't even know why you brought me here."

"All of the Permanent subjects were supposed to be here tonight, to show off how well the program is working to the rest of the company."

"What a load of shit," she cried. "You brought me here for work? Did you really want to be here with Penelope? I mean, you've made it so fucking obvious to me. I should have seen it all along. I wish you would've fucking told me. Then I wouldn't be over here feeling…"

She stared up into his drawn face, wanting so much for him to understand. But he didn't. He had said that he wanted this to stop. She was attracted to him, of course. It was pure physical lust for a man who didn't even want to touch her. Yet she couldn't shake the memory of his hands and lips and body.

"Feeling what?" he prompted, stepping closer to her.

The temperature in the room spiked with him so near. She needed to step away from him, but they were like two magnets.

She reached out, took his hand in her own, and then placed it over her heart. "Feeling this." Her heart thrummed under his fingertips.

"And how is that?" he asked, his voice strained. His free arm wrapped around her waist, drawing her closer. Her breathing stopped as he held her with his hand still pressed against her heart, which was now beating furiously. She swallowed hard and wet her lips.

"Torn. I want to kiss you," she confided, "but I don't want to end up in some ridiculous love triangle."

"I cannot give you what you want, Reyna."

"Which part?"

Then his lips were on hers again and the rest of the world slipped away. Her mind grew fuzzy. Their previous arguments disappeared. Even the thought of Penelope dissolved at the feel of Beckham's lips.

It was as if she were sinking into the ocean and never had to come up for breath. She was drowning in him. Lost in the eternity sea.

They stumbled backward until her knees connected with a chaise. Beckham's body immediately covered hers. His hand rode up the slit of her dress and bunched the material around her hips. She groaned into his mouth, only urging him on further.

There was a fever to their movements. She had thought about this moment ever since he had first kissed her. Wanted a repeat of that night. Wanted to feel his rough hands on her skin. Now that she was, she kissed him back with a ferocity she hardly knew existed within her.

"Beckham!"

They both heard his name called, and a wall of ice soaked through their skin. Beckham jumped back from Reyna. A look of horror crossed his features for a second and then was immediately replaced with his cool outward appearance. By looking at him, she would have never guessed he had been furiously making out with her.

She wasn't sure she could say the same about her. She was human, after all. Slower to stand and attempt to adjust her dress. Her lips were swollen, her skin flushed, and her hair slightly tangled.

"Yes," Beckham called back. "Just a moment."

Penelope walked in through the double doors a second later. She took in Reyna's disheveled appearance and Beckham's apparent nonchalance.

"Harrington wishes to speak with you. I wanted to make sure everything was all right."

"Fine, Penny."

"Right," she murmured and then retreated.

Reyna's hand flew to her mouth. She couldn't believe what had just happened, that she had instigated it. She didn't know what was going on between Beckham and Penelope, but surely it wasn't right for Reyna and him to do this. She wished she had some answers from Beckham rather than this hot and cold.

"I have to go speak with my boss," Beckham said curtly.

"So that's it? You said you'd never kiss me again, and now you have."

"A mistake," he said callously. "Your emotions run high, and they send my baser instincts into overdrive."

"It couldn't be that you're a man desiring a woman?"

"No. It is an animal enjoying the hunt. The monster within

struggling to get out. Nothing more."

Reyna headed for the door. She didn't have to stay and listen to this. When she reached it, she looked at him one last time.

"How boring your life must be, to have no one fill you with passion and make *your* emotions run high. I'll take my chances with the monster over complacency."

CHAPTER NINETEEN

"What are you doing out there?" she mused aloud to herself. Reyna tapped her foot impatiently.

She had been waiting in her bedroom all afternoon for Beckham to leave the apartment. He should have already gone to work or done something. It wasn't like him to adjust his perfect schedule, but he hadn't left. She could still hear him moving around, and she hadn't heard the elevator.

After she had walked out of the lounge last night, Beckham had caught up with her and ordered her back to the car. She had waited thirty *long* minutes for him to finally show up. The drive home was tense and uncomfortable. She hadn't wanted to talk to him any further about what happened, and he clearly felt the same way. As soon as they had made it back, she had stormed into her room and hadn't left since.

The last thing she wanted to do was run into him in the living room and make some meaningless small talk. She wasn't going to be the first to break, that was for sure.

Footsteps in the hallway made her still and stare at her door. She could hear Beckham stop on the other side. What the hell was he doing out there?

He didn't knock. He didn't say anything. He just stood there. They both just stood there. Neither of them willing to make the first move. She didn't care if that made her stubborn. He had kissed her, treated her poorly, and on top of all that was dating someone else. She had no reason to talk to him.

After a few minutes, she heard him walk away from her room, the telltale ding of the elevator, and then she was alone.

"Finally," she breathed.

Reyna yanked the tight pink dress over her head and tossed it into a discarded pile on the floor. She walked into her closet, found her stash of normal clothes, and grabbed stuff for her to wear. Once she was clothed in a loose cotton T-shirt, a pair of jeans, and her Converse sneakers, she brushed her hair out and threw the baseball cap on her head, low over her eyes. Her camera went into a plain black bag that she hoisted over her shoulder before leaving the apartment.

She texted Beckham's driver to let him know she would need a ride. Her bodyguard, Philippé, was always waiting for her in the car whenever he was needed. Beckham must pay a lot of money for these two men to do nothing but wait for one of them to leave the building.

When she got to the front, the car had pulled up for her to get into, but she stopped when she saw Everett. His eyes widened at her clothing.

"Reyna?" he asked.

He hadn't been on duty the past couple of times she had snuck out in regular clothing. She had been glad he didn't know about her double life. He was clearly so traumatized by what had happened that he could barely look at her. She didn't want to involve him in anything else that could get him hurt.

"Oh, hey," she said. "I have to get going."

She headed toward the car, but he followed her. "Hey, are you avoiding me now or what?"

"I... What? No. Of course not." She looked up at him tentatively. "I thought you were avoiding me."

"I've barely seen you. How could I avoid you?"

"Well, you were all serious that first day back. You called me Miss Carpenter. I thought maybe you blamed me still. Or agreed with your friends."

"Sorry about that. My manager was on duty. He's been around a lot more since my attack. I think he thinks I'm fragile and going to fall apart or something. But I just got off work if you want to hang. I'd love to find out what you're doing in those clothes. Are those Beckham approved?"

Reyna made a face. "He'd probably have my head if he knew I was wearing this."

"I hope not literally."

She laughed, and it felt good. "No. Not literally."

"So, what are you up to?"

"Just occupying my time." She dug into her bag and pulled out the camera. "Trying to see the city from a different perspective."

"Cool. Can I come with?"

She looked down at his valet outfit—white button-up, black vest, slacks, and dress shoes. "No offense, but you'll kind of stand out where I'm going."

"Well, now I'm definitely intrigued. I have a change of clothes in my car around back."

Reyna considered it for a second. Beckham didn't want anyone to know that her pictures were connected to her, but she didn't think it hurt anything to take Everett along. Who was he going to tell? He was a valet for her apartment building.

"Sure. Why not?"

Reyna tapped on the glass of the front passenger window. It rolled down slowly. "Yes?"

"I'm going to go around the back with my friend. Will you meet me there in a couple of minutes to pick us up?"

"You aren't going to leave without us, are you?"

Reyna rolled her eyes. "I agreed not to. We'll be in the completely lit back parking lot."

"Five minutes," he said and then rolled the window back up.

"Charming," she muttered, following Everett around to the back.

"So, what got you interested in photography?" Everett asked.

"The attack, actually," she said softly. She stared hard at the ground. "I already had a bad image of the streets, but that magnified it. Beckham gave me the camera as a hobby, I think to keep me from getting bored, and I decided that I wanted to see the streets through the eyes of the suffering. People like me."

"People like you were…"

"Just because I live up there right now doesn't mean I'm any less like you or your friends or anyone else. I don't *belong* there, and I want my pictures to show that. Show what no one at Visage or in politics or in the upper class really *see* with their eyes."

"That's really great," he admitted.

They reached Everett's Mustang, and he found his spare clothes. She watched as he took off his vest and button-up, revealing a rather nice bare chest. Her cheeks heated, and she quickly turned around.

"Oh, sorry."

Everett laughed. "It's fine. Don't worry about it. I want to hear more about this photography. You know, it reminds me a bit of this blog everyone has been talking about lately."

"What blog?" She turned back around to face him. He had on a plain gray T-shirt and a pair of jeans perfect for what they were doing.

"I'll have to find it on my phone."

Beckham's car drove toward them as Everett fiddled with his phone, looking for the blog. They hopped into the back seat, and Reyna told the driver where to go. She had been taking pictures at a homeless shelter a lot lately. The pictures made her eyes blur with tears when she looked through them, and that was how she knew they held truth.

"Aha. Here," Everett said. He passed the phone to her. "*Perspective*."

Reyna nearly dropped the phone. There were her beautiful pictures. Beckham had named the website *Perspective*. She hadn't even realized that other people could see them. She had been uploading and organizing her images for herself.

"You said people are looking at these?"

"Yeah," he said, eyeing her questioningly. "They're anonymous, though. Everyone has been trying to figure out who the photographer is. They think the person must be an Elle sympathizer."

"A what?" she asked. People were associating her pictures with a person she had never even heard of?

"You really know nothing about politics, do you?"

"No," she admitted. "Who is Elle?"

He glanced up uneasily at the driver and her bodyguard. "Someone and something a lot of people disagree with." Then he leaned over and adjusted the baseball cap on her head. "I'll tell you when we stop."

She took the hint and changed subjects until they made it to the homeless shelter. Once they were safely inside, she slung her camera strap around her neck and walked the halls with Everett.

"So, tell me."

He peeked behind them, but her bodyguard was a respectable distance away, pretending to be invisible.

"*Elle* is the code name for the rebellion against the vampires and Visage. Back when Visage was forming, there was a series of protests against vampire-owned businesses and the mission statement that was coming out of some of these corporations, of which Visage is now the most prominent. They called this Elle's Rebellion for the woman who was the leader and was subsequently killed in the otherwise peaceful demonstration. Everyone thought that would be the end of it, but since then, there have been whispers that the Elle sympathizers have gotten together under the Elle Rebellion name and formed a more formal underground rebellion. Hence Elle, or sometimes the graffiti on the streets is a cursive *L* in a circle."

"I've seen that logo before."

"Yeah. It's everywhere. Elle rebels believe that Visage wants to be more than the biggest company in the world. They want to *rule*. A lot of them claim that Visage was responsible for the economic collapse so that they could force humans to work for them. Make everyone desperate for change so they place too much power in the hands of one company."

Reyna's mind spun. There were people out there fighting Visage?

"And they think that the person taking those pictures is an Elle sympathizer? Why?"

He pulled his phone back out and showed her the latest entry. *Her* latest entry. Everett had walked them over to the exact spot the picture had been taken in this very homeless shelter.

"Because no one photographs humanity like you," he said softly.

"I didn't…" she started, but she could see he had already figured it out. Her shoulders slumped. So much for being anonymous.

"So, are you?"

Reyna bit her lip. "Well, I didn't know about Elle or the underground rebels until you just told me, but people are dying out here, and no one cares. Visage has all the money and power, and they're doing nothing to help anyone. They're lining their own pockets and feeding their own. I believe in balance, but I'm not part of any movement." She sighed and looked around at the room, which was full of examples of the very problem she had detailed. "I want to help my family survive this. That's all I care about."

He nodded in understanding. "Don't we all."

"Maybe we should try somewhere else," she suggested, suddenly not wanting to be in the same place she had been before in case someone was trying to figure out who the supposed Elle sympathizer was. The way Everett talked about it, she was sure that it wasn't going to look good to Visage or Beckham if they thought she was one.

"I have an idea if you're interested," he said with a mischievous smile.

"I like ideas."

He laughed. "Your bodyguard might not like this one."

"He'll deal with it. Let's go," she said excitedly.

Once they were back in the car, Everett gave them an address almost clear across town. Much farther out than she had ever been. She waited for her bodyguard to recognize that it might be dangerous and refuse them, but he said nothing. She kept waiting for the other shoe to fall. But they drove all the way across the city without one word.

They hopped out of the car with her camera safe in her bag again, and Everett directed the driver where he could park. Philippé followed behind them as they walked three blocks away from their drop site.

"Why didn't you drop us off in front of the place?" she asked when they came upon a large warehouse. It reminded her of home.

"Driving up to this place in a town car is a good way to get knifed," he whispered.

Reyna shivered against that assessment and followed close to Everett. They reached the front of the building and walked through a slate-gray door.

An enormous man with bulging muscles stopped them before they could walk through a second door. "No guns. No fangs. No trouble. Five Points rules."

The guy quickly checked them over, rifled through her bag, and then let them inside.

"Wait, buddy," he said, stopping her bodyguard. "Didn't you hear me? No fangs."

Her bodyguard gave him a terrifying look and then produced a card out of his wallet. The bouncer read it over once and then nodded.

"Fine, but if you make any trouble, we have authority to stop you at any cost," he said menacingly.

"Noted."

When they walked inside, Reyna had to keep her mouth from dropping open. Everett had said this place was going to be a little different than what she had been shooting, but this was beyond anything she could have imagined. Much of the warehouse was open space, but at its center, there was a giant fighting ring. Two people faced off in the ring, wearing nothing but tight-fit shorts. All the while, an enormous crowd cheered for their champion. A makeshift scoreboard hung from one wall, and there was a box for betting on the matches.

"What is this?" she asked. She was already itching to take her camera out.

"Five Points. It's owned by the Irish mob," he said.

"Stick nearby," her guard growled. "I don't want things to get out of hand with no exit strategy."

"Okay," she agreed, rolling her eyes. As if it wasn't bad enough having a bodyguard in this kind of place, he wanted her to stay as close as possible. He could keep up with her.

"Come on," Everett said. He grabbed her arm and drew her through the thick crowd.

The people they passed were a mixed bag. Some looked like the destitute she had been photographing on the streets. Others were dressed up in suits—not quite as nice as Beckham's but not horrible, either—and they were cheering on the people in the pen as hard as the others. There was another group of people who reminded her so much of her brothers. Not hopeless but not prospering. She could see in their eyes that this was the way to escape the captivity of their daily lives. She had seen it countless times in her brothers' eyes, but with her waiting for them at home, they had never participated in anything like this. She hoped they stayed on the straight and narrow with her gone.

An ache crept into her heart, and she had to force it down. It was good to think of them. She never wanted to forget them, but it was difficult. The money had to be helping, but she was terrified that their faces were fading from her mind.

She couldn't think about that right now. It wasn't any help.

Everett reached a spot in the middle of a group of people, and a man approached him, asking for a bet.

Everett handed over a five. "Put my money on Gabe."

The man chuckled. "Guy's losing, but I'll take your money." He nodded at Reyna. "For the lady?"

She shook her head. "No, thank you."

When he was gone, she leaned over to Everett. "Why did you bet on the guy that's losing?"

"Gabe O'Connor is a legend in these parts. He might not look like much, but watch."

So, she did. She knew nothing about fighting, but the movements of the two men were like a choreographed dance. The bigger of the two had the upper hand in height, weight, and strength. He was all bulk and threw it around with a prowess that clearly had been established over many matches. The smaller guy—Gabe—was quick on his feet, though. He dodged and blocked, striking out at the bigger guy when he least expected it. Despite this, it was pretty clear that the bigger guy was going to win.

Reyna slowly extracted her camera from her bag and stared at the pair through the zoomed-in lens of her camera. She snapped picture after continuous picture of the fight, trying to see what Everett saw.

Then it happened in a flash.

Gabe smirked. That was all Reyna needed. She took that picture and knew it was going to be a brilliant one for her collection. Gabe was toying with his opponent. He wanted to make it look like he was going to lose, keep the odds against him, so when he was victorious it was even more exceptional.

"He's playing cat and mouse," she whispered.

"Yes," Everett agreed. "You can tell in his footwork."

"No. In his eyes and in his smile."

She zoomed back out and took pictures of the crowd, the venue, the sense of desperation in the room. She was focused in on one woman's angry cries when everyone roared their disapproval. Her eyes flew to the stage, where the bigger guy was laid out flat on his stomach, blood pouring from his face. Gabe hadn't stopped. He kept pummeling until they hauled him off.

The crowd surged forward, and Reyna almost lost grip of her camera. She stuffed it back into her bag as Everett clamped his hand down on her elbow.

"What's going on?" she cried.

"People lost a lot of money. We have to get you out of here."

Her eyes searched for her bodyguard, but he was too far away. She made up her mind to get to safety with Everett and let him drag her through the mob. She lost sight of the guard, lost sight of everything, just held on to Everett for dear life. Fights broke out all around them. People were angry that they had lost more of their precious little income to a gambling debt. The noise grew unbearable, and suddenly guards rushed down with batons, Tasers, and guns to keep the crowd in line.

She and Everett burst through an unguarded door that she had assumed went outside, but it led to a flight of stairs. Everett didn't hesitate as he took the stairs two at a time. She had no choice but to follow him. She was breathing hard when they finally got to a landing with a long hallway.

"Where are we?"

"I think this is office space," Everett said. "Let's find a room to wait this out."

"My guard is going to be freaking out," she said.

Everett shrugged. "Isn't it a little freeing?" He smiled back at her, and she couldn't stop from laughing. She had been afraid running through the crowd, and now she released all her nerves.

"Yeah. It kind of is." She pushed open the first door. "How about this one?"

She stepped in the first room and fumbled for the light. Her mouth dropped open.

"What the hell?"

CHAPTER TWENTY

"Whoa," Everett said, following her into the room.

"What is all of this?" Reyna mused aloud.

The room was stark white and as clean as the Visage hospital she had first been tested in. One wall was full of gray containers stacked waist-high, filled with packets of blood. The other wall had blood hooked up to some kind of strange system. A blood packet dripped into another packet and then into a third packet from the ceiling to the floor. The room hummed softly with the machinery directing the operations.

"I heard rumors of this, but I didn't think it was true," he whispered.

"Thought what was true?"

He turned to look at Reyna with a drawn expression on his face. "Black-market blood banks."

Her mouth dropped open. "That's a thing?"

She lifted her camera back out of the bag. She would surely never remember what this room looked like exactly if she didn't take a picture. She wouldn't post them. Not knowing that people were watching her images now. She would keep these for herself.

"A rumor. I didn't think it was possible that they would be doing this."

"They who?" she asked, suddenly scared. She pulled her camera down to look at him.

"Anyone. Visage has a monopoly on blood for vampires. These people must be against them to have all this blood. This could be an Elle operation."

Reyna paled. "Then we should leave. I don't want to be part of anything, even if by accident. Someone could be watching."

Her eyes searched the room for some kind of recording device, but it was difficult to see anything through the rows of blood drips. She didn't like being here, anyway. It gave her the creeps. Blood meant needles.

"I don't want to be here anymore," she said.

"All right. Let's find our way back out."

Reyna stashed her camera again, and they backtracked into the hallway. A man in a white coat and two women in scrubs came out of an adjoining room.

"Hey," the man yelled. "You two aren't supposed to be here."

"Sorry, we got turned around," Everett said, trying to be placating.

"Security!"

"Let's go." Everett grabbed her arm again and dashed down the stairs.

A man followed after them, down the first flight of stairs, and then a second. She was panting by the time they reached street level and Everett shouldered open the door. She was disoriented when the door deposited them out on the streets. Where were they? They were supposed to be back in the warehouse.

But she didn't have time to think. She just followed Everett. The guy behind them did not look happy that they had accidentally broken into the blood bank. She didn't know if Everett knew where he was running to or if he was winding them through the backstreets aimlessly until they lost the guy. But eventually, he yanked her hard into a tiny alcove and covered her mouth with his hand.

The guard rounded the corner and ran right past them. After a few minutes, when they were sure that he was gone, Everett released her.

"This way," he said. He opened a side door, and they went up two flights of stairs.

"Where are we? I'm so lost," she admitted, still panting from exertion.

He opened the first door on the right. "Home sweet home."

They walked into a small apartment, and he quickly closed the door.

"This is where you live?"

He nodded, color touching his cheeks. "It's not much, but it's mine."

It really wasn't much. With his impeccable appearance at work and the nice car he drove, she thought he would have lived in a slightly nicer area of town. Reyna didn't know how far they had run, but it couldn't have been *that* far away.

"Do you live here by yourself?"

"Yeah. Just me and Hopper," he said as a dog promptly hopped out of the bedroom and ran right into Everett. He smiled and picked up the tiny puffball of a dog and let it lick his face.

"Oh my goodness, how cute," she cooed.

"Here. He loves everyone."

Everett handed her the dog, and she plopped down onto his couch. Hopper nuzzled her and forced her to pet him the whole time. After the previous incident, it was actually really relaxing. She couldn't believe that they had gone to an underground fighting ring, found a black-market blood bank, and were chased by some scary-looking security guard.

"When you said we were going somewhere exciting, I didn't expect all this."

He sighed and sank down next to her. "Me either. I never would have taken you there if I had thought all of that was going to happen."

"What do you think they're doing with that blood?" she asked.

"Selling it?" he guessed. "I think the more important question is—where are they getting it from?"

Reyna shuddered. "Ew. I don't want to think about that."

"And you shouldn't. You should forget everything that just happened. You don't need to be mixed up with anything like that. You have your own life."

"What about you?"

He cracked a smile. "I'm too smart to get mixed up with anything. I don't share my friends' belief that all vampires are bad by the sheer virtue of them being vampires."

"Right. Just like not all humans are good because they're humans."

"Right."

They sat like that on the couch until Reyna's breathing evened out. She felt like she could pass out right then and there from exhaustion. It all hit her at once.

"I like your place," she murmured drowsily.

He laughed. "I'm sure it's nothing compared to where you are."

"This feels more like home," she told him. "I grew up in the Warehouse District."

Everett cringed. "Really? I heard it's awful out there."

"It's awful everywhere. But at least at home I had my brothers. They made it all worthwhile."

"Where are they now?"

"They're still there." Tears sprang to her eyes unbidden, and she quickly swiped them off her face. "I miss them a lot. It feels like an eternity since I left."

"But you'll get to go home to them soon, right? Isn't that how the program works? One month and then you switch?"

Reyna closed her eyes and swallowed hard. "That's how it normally works, but they rolled out a new program. Better pay, better benefits, and you live with the Sponsor permanently."

"What?" Everett asked. "Can they do that?"

"They're already doing it. I'll be with Beckham until…well, I don't know until when. Indefinitely."

Everett was stunned into silence, which was the only reason Reyna heard her phone vibrating in her giant purse. She fished it out of the bag and sighed when she saw that Beckham was calling.

"It's Beckham. Sorry."

"It's my fault, really. We shouldn't have ditched your guard."

"I shouldn't have to have one," she muttered irritably.

"Take the bedroom," he offered, pointing behind him.

"Thanks." She walked into the bedroom and answered the phone. "Hello?"

"Reyna," he said, sounding out of breath. "Where are you? What happened? Are you all right?"

"Yes, I'm fine."

"You lost your guard."

"I know," she said softly. "I know it's against the rules, but there weren't really a lot of options."

"God dammit. This is why I didn't want you in places where anything could happen." He actually sounded worried, not pissed like she thought he would be.

"Well, it doesn't matter. I'm fine."

"Where are you? I've been trying to get ahold of you. I just got to the warehouse. The fighting bosses were not pleased to see me," he told her.

He had driven all the way out to the warehouses for…her?

"Just tell me where the hell you are. Last time this happened, you almost died."

"I'm at Everett's place," she finally admitted. She hadn't wanted to tell him, since she was still pissed at him. He wouldn't approve. He didn't really approve of anything she did.

"You're at another guy's apartment?"

Her anger flared up all over again. "Yes," she said defiantly. "Don't you go to *Penny's* place?" She drawled out his nickname for the woman.

"That's none of your business."

"And this isn't yours."

"Your whereabouts are my business. Send me the address so I can have a car swing by and get you."

"What if I don't?"

He said some choice words under his breath. "I have ways of finding out where he lives. Don't make me use them."

"Empty threats," she muttered.

"Don't test me."

The life was draining from her again. This afternoon had been more eventful than she had anticipated, and all she wanted to do was curl into a ball on her bed and go to sleep.

"Fine. I'll get it from Everett." She hung up the phone before he could reply and returned to the room. "Did you hear that?"

He looked up at her sheepishly. "Yeah. Sorry. Everything okay?"

She shrugged. "I guess."

"You know, you can stay here if you want."

"I appreciate the offer, but no." She couldn't do that. It would be the same as when she had lived with her brothers. She couldn't get another job any more than she could have gotten one at home. Just another mouth to feed here, too. At least Beckham could take care of her and she could send the rest of her money back home.

"Oh, okay."

"It's not you. Really. I need to help my family, and this helps. So, I need the address to your place."

She handed over her phone, and he typed the address into it for her.

"Thank you for the exciting afternoon," she said. "Oh no, your car. Do you want me to take you back?"

"No," he said immediately. "I mean...I don't think Beckham is the first person I want to see right now after I endangered your life a second time. He was kind enough to save my life and pay my hospital bills. I don't want him to put me back in there. I'll take the subway or catch a ride with someone else."

"Okay. Sorry about all this."

"It was fun hanging out with you. Can't seem to do it without risking your life, but hey, where's the fun if you don't live on the edge?"

She laughed and gave him a hug. "See you later."

When she made it down the stairs to street level, Beckham's car was already waiting for her. The driver opened the back door, and she slid into the darkened interior with a sigh.

They were halfway home before Beckham said anything. He had been so fixated on his damn phone, she wasn't sure if he had even paid attention to her getting inside.

"I'm glad that you're safe," he said.

"Yeah." She kept staring out the window.

"Did you get the shots you were looking for?"

She thought about the images she had taken tonight and smiled. "I think so."

When she wasn't looking, he reached out and removed her baseball cap. She had forgotten she still had the thing on. She turned to look at him. He released her ponytail, threading his fingers through her dark hair and letting it fan out.

"You never came out of your room."

She swallowed. "I know."

"I waited for you."

"Why?" He had been pissed at her, and her even more infuriated with him. She couldn't handle these mixed signals.

"I don't know. It didn't feel right to leave things like that with you," he admitted.

Reyna's mouth dropped open. "Oh."

"Then I heard where you were and what happened." He almost looked vulnerable, but that was the absolute wrong word for the formidable man in front of her. "If I'd known you wanted to go explore like that, I would have taken you."

"Really?" she asked, flabbergasted. "You would have taken me to the fights? Would you even have been allowed inside?"

Beckham laughed, and it was the best thing she had ever heard. His laugh was electric, lighting up his entire face even in the briefest of moments. It was like a glimpse into the past. Before he had turned, before he had let the monster take over, before he had closed himself off from feeling. She would do anything to see it again.

"Nowhere is barred to me. All you had to do was ask."

"Forgive me, but asking you for anything is a bit like pulling teeth, Becks. You don't make any of this easy."

"I know. I am not an easy man to be around."

She frowned and nodded. That was true. And also false. He was so easy to be around at times. When he let his guard down. When he didn't hide his relationship with another woman. As much as she wanted to claw his eyes out for that one, and for kissing her despite it all, she knew that she didn't really have the right.

Part of her wanted to hold on to her anger and remember how it had flared up when he kept pushing her aside. She didn't want to be taken advantage of if he was with someone else, but she also didn't want to be away from him. She liked being near him. She liked his broody company. Even though she hated never knowing exactly where she stood.

But staring up into his eyes as black as night wrapped a spell around them both, and she was not going to be the one to break it.

"Will you take me?" she whispered.

Their shared gaze turned heated. Her words held more than one meaning, and until they left her mouth, she hadn't realized how much she wasn't talking about the photographs. She might have wanted to close her heart off to him, but her body certainly wasn't listening. The back seat of the car suddenly felt stifling hot, and the short distance between them crackled with desire.

Beckham broke her gaze and stared down at his silent phone. She let out a strangled breath and pulled herself together.

Jesus, Beckham…

"By the way," he said, "what the hell are you wearing?"

CHAPTER TWENTY-ONE

Beckham let Reyna keep the clothes.

She half expected her baggy T-shirts, jeans, and Converse to disappear from her closet the next day, but they remained safely tucked away. In fact, they were freshly laundered and returned to that same location.

But since Beckham had picked her up, she hadn't gone back out into the city. She *could*, but she was waiting for Beckham to take her. She was secretly thrilled about the idea. If he wanted to take her to see some more of the city that she could photograph, then it had to be good.

Plus, the excitement of uninterrupted time with Beckham away from his work and his colleagues and Penelope did sound inviting.

While she waited, she spent a lot of time studying the images she had taken while out with Everett. She posted a few of the fighting ring to her site and wondered if anyone was looking at them.

She particularly loved the close-up she had gotten of the smaller guy fighting. His face was so clear, and he had this defiant smirk. It was a perfect candid. Humanity rising above despite the circumstances. The world they were living in was horrible enough. It should be noted that there was still some hope out there.

Not that she was the shining example of that. Visage wasn't hope. Visage was a Band-Aid, covering up the real problems so many were suffering from.

The elevator ding pulled her out of her melancholy. She quickly exited out of everything on her laptop. The fighting images disappeared, and then the mysterious blood bank pictures followed. She had been sure to keep those in a separate locked file. She didn't want those to end up online.

Beckham opened the door without knocking, and she quickly closed her computer. It was late. She hadn't expected him to come see her. All she was wearing was a pair of tiny silk shorts and a tank top. She wore small, tight dresses around him all the time, but she felt so much more exposed in her sleeping clothes.

"Have you put pictures anywhere but on that website I set up for you?" he asked. No greeting. All business.

She shifted her weight on her bed. "No."

"Where are they?"

"They're in storage on my computer and then online. Why? You said that was all right."

"That's fine. Just don't ever show them to anyone. Ever."

Reyna sighed. "Um…but I went out with Everett taking pictures. He was there at the fights with me, and we went to a homeless shelter."

"Did you tell him that the website was you?" he demanded.

His tone was so sharp she jumped. He hadn't wanted her to tell anyone, but Everett had figured it out. She never would have told him otherwise.

"He guessed."

Beckham scrunched up his forehead and walked into her bedroom. His hands were balled into fists at his sides. He looked ready to punch through a wall…or a person. But she didn't understand why he was so mad. She hadn't told Everett. He had figured it out. She hadn't meant for it to happen. But it wasn't life or death.

"I'll have to look into him. I can't have this get back to you," he said, his voice determined.

"You said that before, but I don't think Everett is going to say anything. Who would he tell, anyway?"

"Can't take the chance."

"Why are you freaking out? What happened?" Reyna hopped off the bed and stopped his pacing. It was starting to scare her. Had something happened? Was this related to the rebellion things that Everett had told her about? She didn't want to cause Beckham trouble even if she was secretly glad that her images were making a splash.

"Nothing. Nothing happened. I want to make sure you're protected," he said. He pulled away from her touch. He looked shaken, and that only scared her more. "Remember when I said a picture is worth a thousand words? Some people have different words for images than you or I. Those images can then become dangerous."

She stood very still and imagined what could scare Beckham into worrying about those images. And if he was worried, why was he allowing her to keep them?

"Should I stop posting them?" she asked.

"You like them?"

She nodded. "Very much. It gives me purpose."

He wavered before shaking his head. "Then they stay."

"Can I ask you something without you getting angry?"

Beckham narrowed his eyes. "Okay?"

She took a deep breath and then ventured forward with her question. "Is this about the rebellion?"

Beckham stiffened, and his eyes narrowed. He was perfectly still and silent like a statue. He searched her face for something, but she wasn't sure what it was. "What rebellion?"

"Elle," she said. His eyebrows rose. "I heard that there was a rebellion or a resistance to Visage."

"Where did you hear that?"

"Does it matter?"

"Yes. Was it at the fight? Did you talk to someone or see anything suspicious?"

She looked away from him. She wasn't ready to tell him about the blood banks. If Elle was a real thing, it was very clear that Beckham was on Visage's side. He was such a high-ranking official, it would be ludicrous to think otherwise.

It didn't matter that he was different than the other vampires she had met in the upper echelon. He wouldn't want to give up his power. Power made people hungry and greedy. Two things at which vampires were already experts.

"You mean besides the fight, everyone's reaction to the fight, and getting chased out of the place? No. Nothing out of the ordinary."

Beckham scowled at her. "Then where did you hear about it?"

Reyna bit her lip before answering. "Everett. He was telling me about the fact that my images could be used to support the Elle rebels or something. That they showcased the crux of humanity's difficulties. But I'm not part of the rebellion. I'm clearly with the system, here, working for you and Visage. I wouldn't go against what you wanted with the company. I mean, I think people need help, but I don't think we should take down Visage, either. Some of the things they're doing are really helpful. I think we need an alternative way to also help the people who don't work for them. Okay, I'll stop now." When she realized she was babbling, she quickly shut her mouth.

Beckham didn't immediately respond. He ran a hand back through his hair in frustration and seemed to want to say so many things. She could feel the indecision rolling off of him.

God, she hadn't meant for any of this to happen. When Beckham had given her this camera, she hadn't thought that her pictures would ever be seen by anyone.

"Get dressed," he said suddenly. "We'll talk about it on the way."

"The way where?"

"You'll see. Just bring your camera." And then he stormed out of her room in a hurry.

That damn man was always in a hurry.

Reyna slipped out of her sleeping clothes and threw on a soft black backless dress and red-backed heels. She longed for her jeans and Converse, but when Beckham said "dressed" that wasn't what he meant. He let her keep the clothes, but that didn't mean he wanted her to wear them.

At least she was getting used to the shoes.

They left the penthouse shortly afterward and got into Beckham's car. The driver drove them through the darkened city, which seemed all closed up for the night.

Reyna was anxious to find out where they were going and what he would tell her about the rebellion. She hadn't thought he would actually say anything. Or at the very least she had thought he would get angry with her for bringing it up. Since neither of those things had happened, she waited rather impatiently for him to explain.

"You don't talk a lot, you know?"

Beckham was gazing straight ahead, but she was staring at him and didn't miss the upturn of his lips. "You only lasted through three minutes of silence."

"Well, if I kept waiting for you to say something, I'd be waiting forever."

"Silence gives me time to think and not act impulsively."

She gave him an innocent look.

After another quiet minute, Beckham continued. "For a long time, I didn't think before I acted, and I've now cultivated this new skill to protect everyone around me."

"How does silence protect people? It seems to keep them at a distance."

"Where they belong," he said firmly. "Everyone should be kept at a distance."

"Everyone?" she asked. She couldn't help leaning toward him. How could he think that? What had happened to him to make him want to push everyone in his life away?

"Yes. I do not relish the thought of acting on my every whim."

"Do you act on *any* whims?"

"Some," he admitted.

His eyes looked at her body and then up to her lips. She tensed as the memory of his kisses flooded her mind. She couldn't get them out of her head. Even when she was mad at him, the touch of his lips still brought chills to her skin. She wanted more. She craved him like an addict craved the next hit. She didn't know what he did to her, but when they got like this, she didn't care. It didn't matter how infuriating he was—she was caught up in the whirlwind of their desire.

"Be glad that I do not act on more. If I did, far fewer people would have their throats intact."

Reyna's mouth dropped open. What the hell was she supposed to say to that? She turned back to face the front. "Oh."

The car finally stopped outside of an outrageously tall building on the outskirts of the city. It wasn't a bad area by any means, but Reyna had never been out this far. She didn't even know that nice areas existed outside of downtown proper. Everything was pitch black; even the building didn't have any lights on. It looked closed, but Beckham had said nothing was barred to him.

Beckham helped her out of the car, and then she followed him up to the front door. Reyna peered inside, but the interior wasn't visible. The glass must have been tinted, or it was just that dark. Beckham slipped a card out of his wallet and scanned it against a magnetic strip she hadn't noticed, and the door clicked open soundlessly.

He ushered her inside and then took her hand to guide her through the darkened interior. She relished the feel of his hand engulfing hers.

"What is this place?" she asked, looking around at the dark blank walls.

"Office space."

"For Visage?"

"No."

"Then what company?"

"For once, be silent and enjoy the ride," he told her, pushing them through the elevator doors.

She laughed. "Fine. You win."

"I usually do."

He pressed the button for the top floor, and the doors shut behind him. A dim light illuminated Beckham's face and cast eerie shadows throughout the elevator. But her eyes were locked on Beckham, who hadn't taken his gaze off of her since they entered the elevator. The room crackled. She wanted to clear the distance that he always kept between them. It would be so easy to do. But the sharp sting of rejection still bit into her. It had only been a few days since he had kissed her at the ball and then turned her aside.

"Becks," she murmured.

"Don't, Reyna," he said, but it sounded more like he was pleading with her.

Her heart thumped in her chest. That was the last thing she wanted to hear, and he hardly sounded like he meant it. But she would stay still. Being in his presence was intoxicating enough. She wouldn't throw herself at him in desperation.

Slow, agonizing seconds ticked by before the elevator opened again. He exited, and she followed him down a hallway and to a stairwell.

"Where are we going?"

"Up."

"But isn't this the top floor?"

He smiled a heart-stopping smile. "The sky is the limit."

They traveled up two long flights of stairs and reached the apex. Another door stood in their way. When Beckham pushed it open, she walked out onto the roof. The wind was whistling at this dizzying height, and the temperature had dropped a considerable amount. She rubbed her hands up and down her arms to ward off the chill as she moved to the edge of the building and stood paralyzed and awestruck at the beautiful rooftop garden view.

"Wow," she breathed into the wind, with Beckham at her side.

The entire city was laid out before them. Where she had thought it was dark and silent, it was so clear now that it was bright and bustling. The buildings and streets were lit up to show the crisscrossed blueprint of the city.

"It's beautiful."

"Yes," he agreed. She felt his gaze sweep her face and wondered if they were talking about the same thing. "Yes, you are."

CHAPTER TWENTY-TWO

H is words were like a dream. She wanted to respond, but she was worried she would wake up and the dream would dissolve into reality.

She couldn't help herself. She turned her head and looked at Beckham. Their eyes locked, and everything crystallized. Whatever had been going on between them was real. He might deny it. She might try to deny it. But she saw even in that brief moment that he felt something. A thread connected them, and all she wanted to do was tug on it and bring him closer.

"This is one of my favorite places in the city," he told her.

"Why?"

She felt as if she could hardly breathe in his presence. No more than a foot was between them, but it was suddenly as if all the air had been sucked out of the sky.

"The city almost looks whole from up here."

"And not from the streets?"

He circled the dew on the railing with his finger. "You know it doesn't look whole from down there. You're the one with the camera."

At the mention of the camera, she suddenly remembered that was the whole purpose of the trip. The thread grew longer, pushing distance between them again. It was a bit of a tug-of-war, keeping up with the rawness of his shifting emotions.

To keep her face neutral, she dug into her bag and retrieved the camera. Putting a physical barrier between them should keep her steady. At least she hoped so.

She took the cap off of the lens and shifted the camera up to her face. She snapped a few pictures of the city skyline. The familiar click of the camera calmed her nerves, and she let the rhythm of the pictures take over.

"Much easier to see the big picture from a bird's eyes, but the aggregate doesn't equal the individual. From up here you would assume everyone was happy and successfully living out a fairy tale. From down there you see the reality, the lie," she told him.

Beckham was silent, and she wondered what he was thinking. Was he judging her answer? Weighing it against his Visage rose-colored glasses? Her words weren't a popular opinion among the wealthy, but she couldn't forget the things she had seen and experienced.

"Are you not living the fairy tale, then?" he asked.

She looked at him over the lens of her camera and made a face. Hardly.

Despite the stirring of emotions about Beckham, she would not consider this life a fairy tale. Maybe it was every girl's dream to live in a penthouse, have an unlimited credit card and a closet full of designer clothes, but it was a cover-up. Beckham was not a shining prince on a white horse riding in to save her. The world they lived in was not a peaceful kingdom where all worries disappeared.

"If this were a fairy tale, there would be no need for a rebellion, would there?"

"Perhaps, but you are not part of any rebellion."

"No," she agreed.

She was a silent voice among countless other silent voices against the establishment. People with no energy to fight, no means to accomplish anything, and worst of all, no hope.

"So, tell me about this covert group, Elle, and how it relates to the rebellion. You said we would talk when we were up here," she reminded him.

Beckham grumbled under his breath and turned back to look out at the city. "What do you want to know?"

"I don't know, but if people think my images are part of Elle, I want to know what they think they stand for."

"I'd rather you not know much," he said into the breeze. "It's safer that way."

"Safer for who? You or me?"

"Both," he said thoughtfully. "Everyone."

Reyna blew out a frustrated breath. They were going nowhere fast with this line of conversation. It wasn't as if she were part of the rebellion. She wanted to know what the hell was going on out there.

"Well, what *can* I know?"

Beckham sighed. He was stalling, hoping she would change her mind, but she wasn't about to do anything of the sort. She stared at him and waited.

After a moment, he seemed resigned to the task. "Don't repeat anything I'm about to tell you. You already made quite a spectacle at the ball." He waited until she nodded before continuing. "There are two factions among vampires. One is of the belief that humans are food."

Their eyes met briefly, and she blushed. She didn't know why she would find that embarrassing. She should find it horrifying. Maybe she would find it more horrifying if he had bitten her.

"We control the food." He gestured to her. "And we shouldn't have to limit ourselves. After all, we are supreme. We should be able to have whatever...*whoever* we want." His eyes drank her in. "In fact, many believe it is a limitation to only drink from a blood type match."

Reyna gasped. "But then wouldn't you be savage? You would kill people. No one would be safe."

His eyes darkened, and a scowl appeared on his face. "Yes. People would die. It would be the way it was before, but now with so much more power in the hands of the vampires. But this faction feels entitled to it. Vampires are the greater species, higher on the food chain, predators." His voice took on a dark, menacing tone. "You are no more than a fly caught in our web with no chance of escape."

She couldn't help but shudder at the bloodlust in his voice. She laughed as if what he was saying didn't affect her, but it came out strained and desperate. She hated to imagine a world like he described, where humans were crushed like ants under his boot.

"And the other faction?" she asked.

"Abide by the cure." His fingers tightened on the railing. "Most vampires did not ask to be made into this monster. We were created. Forced to drink the blood of our maker, drained dry of our blood, and then left for dead to reawaken like *this*. The virus or curse, whatever you want to call it, inhabits our body and mind, crawls under our skin, and begs to be released against our will. It makes us *want* to be the first group."

"But the blood type cure changed that, right?"

"Yes," he said.

Which made her wonder all the more why he refused to drink from her. He didn't seem like the animal he described. Shouldn't he want to drink from her?

"To an extent, the cure curbs that tendency. It makes us almost human, makes us feel human. Alive, when we've been dead inside for so many years. Some enjoy that feeling and want to live beside humans without any more death, and some think it's an abomination to want to be like a weaker species."

A weaker species. Wow. Did he really think that?

"And you? Which faction do you fall into?"

His eyes found hers once more, and she was immediately lost in the dark depths. They were deceptively blank yet entirely enticing. He took a step closer to her. She felt frozen in place.

"I've lived a shorter life than most of my kind. I can still remember the feel of being human," he said, running his hand down her arm for emphasis. Goosebumps broke out on her skin. "But I can also vividly remember the feel of taking a human life." His hand gripped her arm. "I've killed viciously, savagely, and enjoyed it. I've sought people out, tortured them, drove them mad just to kill them slowly through their insanity. I've done horrible things and enjoyed it, Reyna."

"Okay. I get it," she whispered. She grasped his hand on her arm to try to get him to loosen his grip. He was going from hurting to bruising her.

"As a universal donor, an O negative blood type means there are so few matches out there for me, unlike an AB positive, which is a universal receiver. Before there was a cure, the majority of humans I drank from were not a match. The things I did were unspeakable."

Reyna was starting to feel sick at the mention of the horrible things he had done. That was not her Beckham. She knew it with her entire being. He was not that person anymore. He couldn't have ever really wanted that.

"So, you ask me which faction I'm in, and I have no answer for you. To be human is to be weak and fragile," he said, suddenly releasing her arm. She clamped her hand over the area where she was sure her skin was already turning purple. "But to be a vampire is to be a murderer."

"Well, I don't think you want to hurt anyone."

"What makes you think that?" He peeled back her fingers and looked at the swollen skin. "I've given you no reason to believe that."

"I've seen Cassandra and Roland toy with humans and act as if they're beneath them. But you don't. If Sophie were dying, Roland wouldn't care or do anything to save her. But you risked a lot to ensure my safety, not to mention Everett's." Beckham opened his mouth, likely to object, but she held her hand up. "And I know it's not just because I'm an investment, Becks. You don't drink from me, and you could replace me with ease. It's because you care for humanity, for me."

"Believe what you wish," he said.

Which was the biggest nonanswer she had ever heard. He didn't have to admit it. His actions showed very clearly the person he was.

Beckham motioned for her to bring her camera up to her face, effectively ending the conversation. She sighed but did as he directed.

"Now find Visage."

She searched out the massive building. They were far enough away that so many of the buildings appeared as if they were on top of one another. But Visage was the tallest and stuck out like a sore thumb on the horizon.

"Okay?" she said.

He had moved to stand behind her. He was bent forward so that he was level with her camera. His chest nearly pressed against her back. His breath tingled against her ear. He reached forward, covered her hand with his own, and slowly adjusted the angle of the camera.

"There," he breathed. "What do you see?"

She focused back on the matter at hand instead of the feel of him against her. Twisting the lens until it zoomed in on the roof of Visage, she concentrated, trying to see what he was showing her. It looked like a regular roof with a large antennae-type thing on the top with a flashing red light.

"What am I supposed to be seeing?" she whispered.

"The roof," he said softly. His lips brushed her ear, and then she shivered.

"But it's just a roof."

"Exactly."

"I don't…"

"Visage may seem all-powerful, impenetrable, but everything has limitations. Their building is not infinitely tall. From a distance or the right perspective, you might see that it's really just a building after all."

Reyna clicked the picture a couple times. She didn't know exactly what he meant. Was he saying Visage was vulnerable? Was he saying *he* was vulnerable? There were clues in what he was telling her, but none of it made sense. Wasn't Beckham further proof of Visage's power?

But her train of thought vanished when she felt his lips move from her ear to her neck. She closed her eyes and tilted her head back to give him better access to the area, then ground her body against him. She stuffed her camera into her bag and then let it drop to the ground, forgotten.

His hands grasped her hips, tugging her closer. Thoughts fled her mind as his lips cast a spell on her. The tension from the past few weeks cracked wide open. All that there was in the world was Beckham.

His presence was overwhelming. Everywhere he touched, she felt superheated. All she wanted was to push him to go further. Beg for more. But she wasn't about to test his limits. The thought about how dangerous he had been before the cure flitted into her mind and then quickly out again. He wouldn't hurt her. Of that, she was certain.

Beckham turned her abruptly in his embrace and then dropped his mouth down on hers. Here at the top of this abandoned building, the world was spread out before them, and nothing could stop what was crashing down all around them. And she didn't want it to ever end.

Her hands were around his neck as she kissed him with fervor. The feel of him was incomparable. Her heart was ready to burst. Her fingers trembled with the anticipation of this moment. Being near him did nothing but ignite her desire for him. She saw no reason to turn back.

"Reyna," he murmured in between kisses.

"Don't stop," she pleaded.

He groaned into her mouth. She could tell he was fighting with his inner demons, and she felt horrible but she hoped they won out. She wanted him so desperately. She ached for him. There was no second-guessing this decision. He grabbed the backs of her legs and hoisted them up around his waist. She gasped, and a devilish smile crossed his face. She liked his forcefulness, when he so often pushed her away.

Beckham carried her through the rooftop garden. He reached a large circular lounger and carefully laid her back on the plush cushion. Her body was flushed even in the chilled air, and she couldn't tear her eyes away from the gorgeous man in front of her. She didn't even want to blink, for fear that all of this would disappear and she would wake up in her bedroom, aching for him all over again.

His hands crawled up her legs, then her stomach, across her sides, and then up to her face. He cupped her cheeks in his strong hands. He was in complete control, and she surrendered power at the touch of his hand.

"You disarm me, Little One."

She broke into a smile. "And here I thought I was the one tangled in your web."

"Oh, what a tangled web we weave," he murmured, planting soft kisses down the hollow of her throat.

She tilted her head back and closed her eyes, ignoring the deception laced in his words. He kissed back down her front and then ran his fingers up her inner thighs. She trembled under his practiced touch. She couldn't even be embarrassed that she was so ready for him.

When his mouth replaced his fingers, she had to do everything in her power to keep from bucking against him and begging for him to take her. His lips reached the hem of the black dress she was wearing. He bunched the material around her hips, leaving her exposed to him, all save for her tiny silk thong that she had already soaked through.

"You smell incredible," he groaned, running his nose the rest of the way up her leg to the edge of her panties.

She tightened as desire raged through her.

"Would you like me to taste you?"

"Yes," she said without hesitation. Fuck, did she *ever* want him to taste her.

"You know there's the most incredible artery in your inner thigh." He spread her legs wider and ran his teeth lightly along the spot. Her legs shook with anticipation. "I can almost smell the blood pumping through your body this close to the skin."

He nipped at her lightly, and she nearly lost it there. She almost prayed he would break the skin so he would get over his aversion to drinking from her. She was ready. She was well past ready.

"Becks," she moaned.

His hand grasped the soft fabric of her thong. She heard the material snap apart, and then he ran a finger down her folds. "My two favorite things all in one place."

He spread her lips wide and then pushed two fingers deep inside of her. She arched her back off of the lounger at the feel of him penetrating her. Then his tongue swirled around her clit, and she thought she might actually combust. He languidly pumped his fingers in and out, building her pleasure while his tongue flicked against her.

Reyna dug her fingers into the material of the lounger. She couldn't even think properly. All that she felt was the work Beckham was doing to her body. It was hard to believe this was happening, let alone on the rooftop under the starlight.

In a matter of minutes, her walls clenched almost painfully around his fingers.

Her breathing was ragged as she said, "Becks, I'm so close."

He thrust into her faster at her comment. "Good," he growled. "Come for me."

Her body shuddered at his command and obeyed as his fingers hit just the right spot. She came undone at the skill of his hands and lay back panting, shaking, practically intoxicated from her climax.

"Come here," she pleaded breathily, reaching out for him.

He didn't move, and she hastily sat up and unfastened his belt. Her hands deftly unbuttoned his pants and slid down the zipper. She reached her hand over the band of his boxer briefs and trailed her fingers lightly along the sensitive skin. She could feel how hard he was for her through the material. It made her want him even more, knowing how much he clearly desired her. She moved her hand down farther and brushed against the head. He jerked against her and then grabbed her wrist forcefully.

"Stop."

"What?" She looked up at him, confused.

"Reyna, just stop."

"Stop?" she asked as if she didn't understand the word.

"Yes. Stop. That's enough." He took a step away from her and fixed his pants.

"What the fuck?" she asked. "Why are you stopping?"

"None of this should have ever happened."

Reyna quickly straightened her dress and stood. "Don't lie. You want this. I know you do."

"No. I can't believe I almost went further."

"Went further? You mean you almost let me blow you or that you wanted to have sex with me? Because you clearly want both."

"Reyna," he snapped. "Enough. You somehow unravel my restraint, but *this* cannot happen again."

"Why? Why won't you let it? It keeps happening over and over again," she cried desperately. "You've already set off a chain reaction that can't be stopped."

Beckham met her eyes. "This isn't fair to Penny."

Reyna cringed at her name. It felt like he had slapped her with the word. "Oh yes, the mysterious girlfriend who only comes up at these inopportune times. Bastard."

He didn't even respond to her comment. She took a deep breath and untangled the knots in her hair.

"Whatever," she grumbled, walking back to her bag and hoisting it over her shoulder. Beckham followed her, and that only pissed her off more. She whirled on him. "No, you know what? This isn't over. You can't bring her into this like that. Either you're dating her or you want me. Whichever it is, you have to choose, because I can't do this push and pull. You're hot. You're cold. You want me. You don't. I don't want to hear about the warring monster. I want to hear from the human silencing the voices. Because right now I feel like you're actually torturing me and driving me out of my mind just like one of your victims."

"I did say I would break you," he whispered.

"I think you're too damn afraid of what the old you could have done to take any real risks. It's sad, because the new Beckham is better than this."

"There is no new and old. There's just me. And if you think this is torture, you have no idea."

"By the look in your eyes, I guess I'll find out."

"For your sake, I hope you never do."

CHAPTER TWENTY-THREE

Reyna had no patience the next morning. She had barely gotten any sleep. She had tossed and turned in her bed, replaying everything that had happened between her and Beckham until she thought she was going to scream.

Why couldn't she get him out of her head?

She was beyond pissed at him, and still she couldn't stop thinking about their evening. He had been so real. Sincere, even. He had been himself with her. He had let his guard down and they'd had one beautiful moment, then poof!

Gone.

Slide the wall back between them. Two steps forward, fifty steps back. It was maddening, and she wasn't going to put up with it anymore. Last night had solidified that in her mind. Beckham wanted Penny. If he was an asshole who cheated on his girlfriend, then she didn't want him.

Not that she had any right to him anyway.

That thought propelled her out of bed. She threw on her street clothes and pulled her hair into a slicked-back ponytail. After she grabbed her camera, she left her room, and without even a glance around the penthouse, she walked to the elevator.

Once she reached the bottom floor, she exited through the front doors. Everett smiled as she approached the valet station.

"Your car?" he asked.

"No, thanks. I'm going for a walk. If anyone comes looking for me, will you tell them I needed some air and will be back later?"

He raised his eyebrows. "Do you expect someone to come looking for you?"

"No," she said immediately. Her eyes flitted to the lobby in irritation.

"Be safe. You're kind of prone to danger," he said, only half joking.

"Yeah," she acknowledged. "True. Well, I'll stay out of the shadows."

"Good."

"Hey," she said, stepping a little closer. "Did you ever find out anything more about that place we went?"

She couldn't believe it had only been a couple of days ago that she had found an underground blood bank. She still didn't know what it meant, but she wasn't sure how to go about investigating them. Part of her wanted to post the images on her site in the hopes that someone else would look into the issue, but Beckham had been freaked out enough about her images. She wasn't sure if she was ready to go public with them.

"No. I think we should probably leave it alone. There's no way we could get back in there undetected. It was a fluke."

She nodded, but she still felt like they *should* be able to do something. "You're probably right. But maybe we could give it a try," she said with a wink.

He laughed. "You really do like danger. You didn't think it was bad enough the first time that we almost got caught?"

"But this time we know what we're looking for."

"I don't know," he said uncertainly. "Maybe."

She smiled brightly. "That sounds like a yes."

"That's a maybe."

"All right. I'll find a time to get away and contact you about it."

"I haven't agreed yet, Reyna," he said as she backed away.

"Oh, but you will."

He sighed. "You're right. Anything for you."

Reyna ignored the look he was giving her. She liked Everett, but not like that. Her already fucked-up love triangle wasn't going to suddenly become a love square. She wanted to get rid of one of the sides, not add another one.

"I'll see you around." She waved and then trotted around the corner.

There was a park across the street from their building. She had only been there once, because it wasn't exactly the kind of place she liked to shoot. Since they lived in the wealthy part of town, the park was clear, uncluttered, and all around a safe place.

At the moment, she didn't feel like any of those things at all.

But it didn't matter. She couldn't sit in Beckham's apartment all day. The feel of his lips all over her body was still too fresh in her mind. If she stayed behind, she was pretty sure she would have stormed into his side of the penthouse to demand to know what the hell his problem was. She wouldn't care that she wasn't even allowed back there or that attacking Beckham would likely accomplish nothing.

"Ugh," she grumbled. She couldn't keep thinking about him. That was why she had left in the first place.

Grabbing her camera out of her purse, she snapped images. Flowers in bloom, a couple on a park bench, the lake where small boats with wooden paddles were docked. She let out a deep breath and tried to enjoy her work. It wasn't as emotional as the other things she captured, but it calmed her nerves nonetheless.

Reyna rounded the corner and caught a smudge of black in her peripheral vision. She stopped in her tracks. Her eyes searched the area but saw no one. She was in a well-lit part of the park, but it was mostly empty this early in the morning. She turned toward the fields where nannies brought children to run around and play games. When she was almost there, she noticed footsteps falling faintly behind her.

She was being followed.

Her heart rate sped up, and she increased her pace to a slow jog. She was glad that she was in her Converse today. She wouldn't have been able to get anywhere in the ridiculous heels that lined her closet. Her feet carried her to the edge of the park, and she took one look behind her. That was when she caught a glimpse of the person following her.

She slowed to a walk and then turned to face the now-empty trail. Reyna crossed her arms, planting herself firmly in place.

"I know you're following me," she called out. "Can't I have a moment of peace, Beckham?"

He stepped out from the tree line and approached her. Anger welled up inside of her. She did not need an escort through this park. And it didn't matter that he was truly gorgeous in dark-wash jeans and a black long-sleeve button-up that he left unbuttoned at the neck. It was the most dressed-down she had ever seen him. It fit him as well as the suits he always wore. This whole thing would have been much easier if he wasn't attractive. She gritted her teeth in frustration.

"You left without security," Beckham said.

"Yes. Don't you think there was a reason for that? Can't take a hint?" she snapped.

"I'm sure you had a reason for your actions, but I don't think they preclude you from staying safe."

"Do I look like I'm in any immediate danger?" She spread her hands wide and gestured to the park around her. "The only person stalking me is you."

Beckham ignored her comment. "I wondered where you wanted to go to be all alone."

"Honestly? Anywhere away from you, and even then I can't get away, can I?" She hated that she sounded petulant, but she was hurt. After what happened last night, he deserved to get a little slap in the face. She couldn't even believe he had the nerve to follow her.

"No. You still work for me, Reyna."

She rolled her eyes. "You signed the paperwork. You pay my wages. You provide the penthouse. There is no work involved here. And if there is, perhaps I should file some sexual harassment paperwork."

"Oh, Reyna, you don't mean that."

He didn't exactly sound hurt by her words, but his response wasn't like him, either. Well, she hoped he was hurting half as much as she was.

"I need to be away from you right now," she told him.

"I can't let you go off by yourself."

"Then send someone else," she said. "I can't even look at you."

She swallowed and turned away from him. She hated so much how small she felt in front of him. Last night had been incredible, and then he had ruined everything. Now whenever she saw him, she remembered the slap to her face she had received when he had mentioned Penelope's name.

"I won't apologize for last night," he said.

Reyna walked away from him. He caught up with her easily. "Stop following me."

"Stop acting like this."

She glared at him. "You said you wouldn't apologize. For what? For going down on me or the fact that we almost had sex or the part where you stopped because you had a girlfriend," she spat.

"Any of it."

"Fantastic. Aren't you supposed to be with your precious *Penny*?" she said, drawing out the nickname. "That's where you always disappear to, isn't it?"

Beckham didn't answer, but she already knew the truth.

"Whatever. You disgust me."

"Finally you're talking sense."

"Sense?" she cried. "You want to disgust me?"

He shrugged noncommittally. "Well, you sound jealous of Penny."

Her face heated in response as the words sank in. "And you seem to enjoy it. All of it. You love the way I smell, the way I taste. You want me. You want more," she said, running her hand up the front of his shirt. "What would your Penelope think if she found out about how bad you want to fuck me?"

He grasped her wrist in his hand. "That's enough, Reyna."

"I don't think so. You like that you can have her and me, too. You like the control, the power, Beckham."

He released her forcefully and stepped away. "I've always enjoyed power. It's the only thing I allow myself to crave anymore."

She gave a stilted laugh. "Just because you stopped yourself from having sex with me doesn't mean you don't crave more. I can tell you do. It's written all over you. So, you're right. Maybe I am jealous of Penelope, but I think you're just as jealous of the fact that I can stand here without hiding my emotions like you have to do every day of your life."

Reyna continued walking through the park. Why did this damn man make her feel so out of control? All she hoped was that he got the hint this time and left her alone. She was in no real danger in this park. He clearly wanted to follow her to torment her.

But then she felt his presence behind her a few minutes later. "Oh my God, is this part of my newfound insanity?" she asked.

"You didn't eat."

"Nice change of subject, but I'm not hungry."

"I know a great place nearby."

She arched an eyebrow. "Do I look like I eat the same things you do?"

"I used to go there before I was turned."

"It must be really old, then," she muttered.

"Not *that* old," he said with a smirk.

She just glared. "Stop being nice to me."

"Reyna, you are a fact of life in my world. I neither asked for you nor wanted you here. I had to take you because of my job. You leave yourself so open. I don't even know if you can help it. If you guarded yourself better, then you would not be hurt so easily."

"My emotions are my own. Don't try to take away my humanity."

"You would surely know if I was," he said, flashing his fangs. She took a step back at the sudden movement. "Now let me ensure that you don't starve."

"What? Like you?" she asked, angling her neck suggestively. He wasn't going to do anything.

"And yet you continue to tempt me, Little One?"

She shrugged. "Doesn't seem to hurt anything."

His eyes darted to her neck and then away quickly. He did seem paler than normal. Maybe he really was hungry. He never acted this way. Normally when he was near her neck, he was completely in control. The way he stuffed his hands into his pockets and avoided looking at her too long now proved otherwise. As much as she wanted to needle him further, she decided to let it be for now. Arguing with him took so much effort, and he wasn't going to change his mind today.

"All right. Where is this place?" she asked.

As they walked across the park, Reyna kept her camera out and snapped pictures. She turned her camera on Beckham, catching a picture of him looking thoughtfully ahead.

"Huh. A reflection. And here I thought you needed a soul to have a reflection," she joked. She had photographed vampires before, but never this close and none as good-looking as Beckham.

"All of those rumors about vampires are really pretty ridiculous, you know. Reflection, sunlight, stakes."

"What? Stakes don't work?" she gasped.

"Please, you think it's that easy to kill one of us?"

"You think it's easy to get a stake through someone's heart?"

"Very."

"Oh. Well then."

They came up to a small restaurant inside the park that Beckham directed her into. The place was packed with a line of businesspeople waiting to be seated, but when Beckham entered, the staff immediately escorted them to an empty table. Had he planned this, or did they just know him?

Once they were seated, Reyna looked over the menu. She ordered a sandwich and a drink, and then sat there before Beckham, tapping her foot impatiently. It was times like this that really frustrated her. It was so easy and natural to be here with him. Yet there were so many complications regarding their relationship—professional or otherwise.

She was trying to untangle her emotions when a voice brought her out of her thoughts.

"You don't mind if we join you, do you?" Roland asked. He strode right over to their table with Cassandra, Sophie, and Felix in tow as if he had already known they would be there.

Beckham stiffened. "Of course. I didn't know you were coming here for lunch."

Cassandra ran her hand through Felix's hair as if he were a pet dog. "We love this place and thought we'd call in for an early lunch."

The staff quickly pushed the table next to them into place so they connected, and then the entire group sat down. Reyna sat very straight and still. She might be pissed at Beckham, but even she wouldn't make that knowledge known among his colleagues. She didn't trust either of them. Sophie was vapid, and Felix was clearly besotted with Cassandra.

Reyna kept quiet as Beckham discussed work with his colleagues. She was halfway through her sandwich when the conversation shifted to her suddenly.

"So, are you excited for Friday night?" Roland asked, staring straight at her.

"I... What? What happens then?"

Roland looked from her to Beckham and back. "You know. Going to the Vault for the first time."

She raised her eyebrows. "What is the Vault?"

"Beckham, were you going to surprise her with the party? Did I ruin everything?" Roland asked. He sat back in his chair, laughing softly as if it were all some kind of joke.

"No," Beckham said. He didn't elaborate further, but he refused to look at her.

"Well, then do tell us why you're keeping this juicy secret from your beautiful pet," Roland said. "Cassandra is bringing Felix. I'm bringing my Sophie. It'll be a real party."

"I'd planned to bring Penny," Beckham said.

Reyna inhaled deeply. She didn't even know what the Vault was, but she couldn't believe he had been keeping it from her. If everyone else was going, wouldn't it be weird that she wasn't there? She suddenly felt sick to her stomach over the whole situation. Plus, he was taking Penelope. This whole thing was a mistake.

Cassandra giggled as she ran her finger up and down Felix's neck. The memory of her sinking her fangs into him made Reyna shudder all over again. "Pets are more fun, Beckham."

"She's right. Penelope can miss one such occasion for you to introduce Reyna to our world. It will be her first time, after all. There won't be another one for a while. She'll want to see it. Won't you?" Roland asked, directing his attention back to her again.

She swallowed but answered truthfully. "Yes."

Beckham scowled at her. "The plans are already in place."

"Oh, break the plans. Little Reyna is so young and innocent. Don't you think it will be positively *delicious* to see her reaction?"

"Delicious," Cassandra purred against Felix's throat.

"Plus, she wants to go."

"I do," Reyna agreed. Though she had no idea what she was agreeing to.

"I see," Beckham said stiffly. "Then I'll have to change my plans for the evening." He gave her a look that said, *You have no idea what you're getting yourself into.*

She just smiled back deviously.

CHAPTER TWENTY-FOUR

"**W**hat the hell is the Vault?" Reyna asked later when they were leaving the restaurant.

"You'll see," Beckham said.

"You're not going to tell me?"

"No," he said curtly.

Reyna bit her lip. The way they talked about it at lunch made it sound both exciting and scary. What was she about to walk into? And why the hell wouldn't Beckham tell her where they were going?

Once they were finally back in the apartment and Beckham was halfway to his room, she spoke again. "Are you going to tell me anything about it? What I need to wear? Where we're going? What we're going to be doing?"

"You agreed to come. You plotted this whole thing so you would be there. You'll have to deal with the consequences. Follow my instructions when I give them and do what I say. Everything else will be decided for you."

"I can follow instructions. I can *come* on command." She said that double entendre under her breath.

Beckham arched an eyebrow but otherwise didn't respond to her. She was pretty much used to that—and all the more irritated with him. Beckham disappeared for the rest of the afternoon, leaving her to think about everything that had happened recently with him and wonder what they were going to do.

To try to clear her mind, she sent Everett a text message.

> *Want to do that thing this weekend? I have plans Friday, but maybe Saturday?*

He answered almost immediately.

I don't think it's a good idea. What if we get caught?

He had a fair point. She didn't know what would happen if she got caught sneaking into a black-market blood bank, but she didn't exactly think it would be rainbows and butterflies.

> *Then let's not get caught.*

You make it sound so easy.

> *Last time, the room was unguarded when the crowd was in an uproar. Maybe we just make something like that happen?*

How exactly do you expect to do that?

That was a great question. She had no idea, but she wanted to get back in there and find out what they were up to.

> *I don't know.*

Maybe we can meet this weekend and figure it out.

Reyna shrugged. She didn't have any plans except this Vault thing, so it sounded fine to her.

Saturday night?

See you after I get off work.

. . .

T ime felt endlessly slow on Friday. She was cooped up in her room, waiting for this Vault thing to go down. Waiting for something that she knew nothing about made her unbelievably anxious. When she looked up the Vault, her search came back with a bunch of meaningless websites. Certainly nothing that would have the need for this level of secrecy.

At around eleven at night, two women showed up in her room and got to work on her hair and makeup. When she attempted engaging them in conversation, they remained silent. She didn't know if they were under orders from Beckham not to give anything away or if they really didn't know what was going on. Either way, they transformed her face until she almost didn't recognize the sexy vixen wearing the smoky makeup. The hairstylist pulled her dark hair into a sexy updo with loose tendrils framing her face and falling out of her twist.

When she walked out of her bathroom, she found a small white bag on her bed. She peeked inside, and her eyes widened. Of all the things Beckham could have suggested, the last thing she'd expected was skimpy lingerie. She hoped that something was going over this.

She ran her hands over the soft silk and laces of the outfit and then stripped out of the dress she was wearing. A woman came in a minute later to assist her into the red-and-black corseted top. She tightened the laces until Reyna was afraid she wasn't going to be able to breathe. The corset was paired with ruffled black boy shorts, thigh-high stockings that attached to the bottom of the corset with ribbons, and a pair of black-heeled boots. She felt ridiculous but also sexy in a way she never had before.

"Where is my dress?" she asked.

The woman handed her a black silk kimono that didn't look like it would even cover her ass. "Here you are."

"Wait, but where is the dress that goes *over* this?"

"This was all we were provided."

Reyna slid the kimono over her shoulders and pulled it closed over the revealing outfit. Not that it did much to hide the fact that she was wearing very little. She pushed down her apprehension and decided to own it. She had gotten herself invited to the Vault. There was no way she was about to walk away just because she was dressed in even more scandalous clothing than normal. Beckham had seen her half naked. This wouldn't be so bad.

When she left her room, Beckham turned his gaze to her, and she let the front of the kimono drop open. His eyes swept her body. He inhaled deeply, and his lip quirked upward for a split second. He tried so hard to hold on to his cool demeanor, but she could tell that her outfit affected him. She may be pissed at him, but it was always nice to feel sexy.

"Stay close to me," he said, walking toward her. "Everyone is going to want to get their hands on you in that."

"Everyone?" she asked.

He smirked. "Oh, yes…everyone."

"Even you?"

His eyes darkened, and he looked away from her. "Just don't leave my side. You have no idea what you're about to walk into."

She wanted to ask him to tell her, but the look on his face stilled the question on her tongue. He wasn't going to answer. She knew that much. He was enjoying the anticipation.

She focused her attention instead on imprinting the way Beckham looked in that moment to her brain. Head cocked to one side, dressed in a black suit with a black shirt underneath unbuttoned at the top. All black from head to toe and utterly delectable. It might be easier to avoid wanting to jump his bones if he didn't look so damn attractive.

In the place of their normal town car was a sleek black limo. Her eyes lit up. She had never been in a limo before. Never even dreamed that she would have use for one. The driver opened the door for her, and she slipped into the back seat. Beckham followed after her.

"There's one more piece to your outfit," he told her once the car pulled away.

"Oh?" she asked, intrigued.

He removed a thick black ribbon of silk from his pocket. He looked devious in the dim lighting.

"Have you ever been blindfolded?" he asked.

She swallowed. "Is that necessary?"

"The Vault has strict security. No one is supposed to know the exact location unless they're an elite member. It's a precaution." He twirled his finger in place. "Turn around."

She slowly did as instructed. Her heart pitter-pattered in her chest with anticipation. She hated herself for getting so worked up over it—but damn, she wanted him.

He slid the fabric over her eyes, and everything went dark. He tied it in a tight knot at the back of her head. His hand slipped down her back once he finished. "How is that?" he asked.

"I can't see anything."

She tightened her legs together. Without her sense of sight, she was susceptible to everything else tenfold. The smell of his musky cologne, the light touch of his hand against her skin, the small physical distance between them—and how desperately her heightened awareness made her want to bridge it.

But after touching her back, Beckham left the space between them vacant. She felt cold and empty without him, but she wouldn't be the one to cross the line. Not after what had happened on the roof. Her nerves got the better of her, and with each passing mile and turn of the car, she grew more anxious about where they were going. About a half hour later, the car drove beneath the city.

The car finally came to a halt.

She was ready to pry off the blindfold herself and find out where she was. She had been turned around thirty minutes ago and had no hope of ever leading anyone to the underground location.

Beckham leaned toward her in the limo and tugged the blindfold from her face. She found herself staring into his dark eyes as she adjusted to the new light.

"We're here," he said.

"Where is here, exactly?"

He shook his head. "It's best if you leave all the talking to me."

"Okay," she said hesitantly.

"And I got you something."

"What? Something else?"

He removed a black box from his inside jacket pocket and handed it to her. She took it in her hands in awe. A jewelry box. Who would have thought she would ever own a piece of jewelry that would warrant a black velvet box?

She pried the top open and stared down at the most beautiful silver bangle bracelet with inlaid diamonds. The top was engraved with the words *ANDERSON, O-*. Her mouth was open, and she couldn't seem to recover herself. A *diamond* bracelet?

Beckham slipped it on her wrist, where it sat cold against her skin. "Never take this off once you're inside. It shows that you're with me. It will protect you."

"From what?"

"Everything."

That was another nonanswer, but she at least trusted him to keep her safe. Even though the bracelet had something to do with the Vault, she relished the feel of it against her wrist. She loved that it meant she was with him even if it in some way meant she *belonged* to him.

"Are you ready?"

"As I'll ever be."

Beckham opened the door and assisted her out of the car. There was a door that blended in with the surrounding concrete and opened at their approach. They entered a nearly pitch-black hallway. At the end was a small room with a giant vault door. Beckham passed a white card through a slot next to the door, and then a hand slipped them two similar cards.

"Welcome to the Vault," a woman purred from the other side.

"What's that?" Reyna asked, pointing at the cards.

"Participation cards. You won't need yours."

Reyna arched an eyebrow. "Why not?"

"Because you *won't* be participating," he growled low.

She looked up at him defiantly. "And what if I want to participate in whatever this is?"

Beckham tugged her close to him so they were nearly pressed together. "This bracelet says you're mine, Little One. No one can get near you but me, and they would be a fool to do so."

Reyna nodded despite her trepidation about what was to come. Their conversation made no sense to her—participation cards, bracelets that claimed her—so she steeled herself for whatever she was about to witness.

The large handle on the door turned in circles and then pushed inward. When the door opened all the way, she was transported into another world and gasped.

"It's a sex club," she whispered.

CHAPTER TWENTY-FIVE

"A brothel, technically," Beckham said.

Reyna stared around the room in awe. The whole place was decorated in swaths of red, purple, and black. Divans covered with pillows littered the perimeter of the large open room. Tables were set up with dozens of plush chairs around them already occupied by attendees. Everything was centered around a stage with a large white bed on it.

She tore her eyes from the empty stage and to the patrons in the establishment. Many were pulling people into shadowed alcoves where they could do things she could only imagine. Bare-chested men in nothing but tight black shorts carried around trays with cocktails and a little dropper filled with something as red as blood. She didn't even want to know what that was for. Stark-naked women lay on buffet-style tables filled with all varieties of food. The irony wasn't lost on her.

The patrons were all vampires dressed to the nines with lapdog humans on leashes and all forms of debauchery. Even though Reyna matched the general attire of most other women in the place, she felt out of her depth. In fact, most people wore less than her. But it was the feeling of power that reverberated throughout the room. Vampires had all of it, and the humans were subjugated to their desires. She shuddered at the thought.

"You said you wanted to come," Beckham reminded her.

"And now I'm here."

He leaned over and whispered into her ear, "Take off your robe."

She didn't even question him. She could tell by the vibe in the room that this was not the place for questions. She swallowed back her discomfort, looked up at him, and let the material slide to the floor. His eyes crawled over her body again, and she noticed a slight tremor in his hand.

"I need a drink," he said.

Reyna smiled at the implied meaning in his words.

She followed him across the room and tried to keep her eyes on him alone rather than the decadence and debauchery around her. They took a seat at the back of the room. She tucked her chair under the table until most of her body was obscured.

Beckham sat next to her, and a waiter approached them. She accepted a glass of water, because she wanted to keep a clear head, but Beckham ordered scotch.

"A drop, Mr. Anderson?" the waiter asked.

He waved his hand. "No."

The man nodded, handed him a drink, and then disappeared.

"What is a *drop*?" she asked.

Beckham sighed. "One day I will get you to stop asking questions."

"Unlikely."

"A drop is a drop of blood."

"What kind?"

He gave her a sobering look, and she understood.

"You mean people here are drinking blood that isn't a match," she gasped in horror.

"It's just a pick-me-up. Nothing that would cause anyone any harm or any more harm than they already wish on themselves."

Reyna was still trying to process that when Roland, Cassandra, Sophie, and Felix showed up at their table. Roland was in a suit, while Cassandra had opted for a long black lace dress that was entirely see-through and somehow managed to be more revealing than Reyna's lingerie. Felix was in nothing but black boxer briefs and a gold studded collar. He already had bite marks in his neck and as usual looked a bit dazed and out of it. Sophie was confident and cool in a white bridal lingerie set that contrasted with the dark tones of the room.

"Good to see you, Beckham," Roland said with a tip of his head. Reyna noticed the red hue of his drink and shuddered. Just what she needed — a feral Roland Batiste.

The way he looked at her made it seem like he was slowly undressing her with his eyes. She felt as naked as the women laid out on the tables in front of him, and she shifted uncomfortably.

"Glad you could make it, Reyna," Roland said.

She glanced away from him and kept her mouth shut. The memory of what he'd said at the ball came back to her, making her sick. *I will find you later, love. Be sure of it.*

The lights flickered twice, signaling for everyone to take their seats. Sophie sat next to Reyna, who breathed a sigh of relief at the fact that Roland wouldn't be within arm's reach. He creeped her out, and knowing he was drinking a drop didn't help anything.

A busty woman in a black lingerie and long sheer robe that trailed behind as she walked stepped onto the stage at the front.

"Welcome ladies, gentlemen, and all manner of deviants." She extended her arms out to the crowd and strutted across the stage. "I'm Dee, the Madame of the Vault. You're now locked in to my world of debauchery. No one comes in, and no one goes out. You know the rules." She winked as she sashayed across the floor. "Tonight, I have a special treat for you. A rare delicacy draped all in white. Some strapping young lads and a few...taste testers. Prepare to be bewitched. I give you a feast."

She gestured to the bed. Reyna leaned forward as a trembling young woman stepped out in a white dress with a hem that brushed her knees. She looked the part of a sacrificial lamb, and she had everyone's rapt attention.

Fear rolled off of her, and she was powerless to do anything to stop it.

"Our little delicacy may look like she's frightened." The woman tapped her on her perfect red mouth. "In fact, she probably *is* frightened, right, darling?"

The woman nodded, trembling.

The madame circled the woman. "But everything that will be done to her tonight—and *everything* will be done to her tonight—will be exactly what she asked for." She slapped her gently with a riding crop. "Tell them your safe word."

Reyna grasped Beckham's hand as the woman answered. She thought Beckham would throw her off, but he closed his hand around hers.

"Where have you brought me?" she whispered to him.

His gaze was hot on her body, and when she turned to face him, she found him gazing at her exposed throat. He licked his lips with an appetite that he never showed. His free arm ran along the back of her chair, and he leaned in to whisper in her ear.

"Exactly where you wanted to be."

"Is this a…a *blood* brothel?" Reyna asked.

"Precisely," Beckham said into the hollow of her throat.

Reyna was both terrified and intrigued by the prospect of a blood brothel. The woman was shaking like a leaf, but she didn't try to run or cry out. Reyna saw herself in that woman onstage. Take away the penthouse and the one-man show, and in the end, it was all the same thing.

"And they're going to perform sex acts?" Reyna's voice trembled at the question.

Beckham's lips brushed her skin. "It's a scene. Everyone agreed to be part of it. But do you agree? Do you want to watch?"

"I…"

Did she?

Two men walked out from backstage and reached for the woman. One pushed her hair off of her face, revealing that she wasn't quite as young as Reyna had originally thought. Probably early twenties. The guy on her right had short dark hair, and he pressed his lips to her mouth tentatively. But the guy on the left with shoulder-length blond hair grabbed her from the other guy and kissed her with vigor.

Reyna was enraptured. She could no more say that she didn't want to be here than the woman on the stage.

"Reyna?"

"I want to watch."

The second man shoved the woman to her knees, pulled his enormous cock from his shorts, and pushed it against her lips. Her whimper could be heard through the audience, but she opened her mouth and took the whole thing in. After a few seconds of her bobbing back and forth against him, he grabbed her head and fucked her mouth until she was left gagging and short of breath. She doubled over and coughed.

The other guy took pity on her and lifted her into his arms. He carried her to the bed and lay her tenderly down with her legs toward the audience. He pulled the white thong over her hips and then tossed it onto the stage floor for dramatic effect. He fell to his knees before her and licked her until her cries were almost violent in nature.

Reyna pressed her legs together under the table. She had never seen anything like this before, and as conflicted as she was about what was happening, the woman certainly seemed to be enjoying herself. It was quite obvious that the two men were enjoying themselves. Half of the people in the audience were already enjoying themselves. She couldn't help but get hot at the thought of doing those things with Beckham, and the exhibition aspect only heightened her desire.

"Reyna," Beckham groaned into her ear, "you are so turned on."

"I…I'm not," she whispered back.

He dropped the hand she had been holding, slid it under the table, and spread her legs open. The table hid what he was doing, but she couldn't help but flush from head to toe. He pushed his hand up to her black lace underwear and pressed against the material.

"I can *smell* you," he insisted. "Are you sure?"

"Why don't you find out?" she dared him.

He slid the material aside and rubbed against her slick, sensitive skin. She bit her lip to keep from groaning. Then he easily slipped two fingers inside of her and stroked in and out.

She leaned forward into the table and let her mouth pop open. Holy shit!

No one was paying them any attention, but Beckham was *fingering* her in a club while there were people onstage having sex.

She focused back on the stage—anything to keep her from crying out from an orgasm. The guy had positioned himself at the woman's opening and fucked her. The blond male was now seated with his cock on her face, slapping it around and then roughly shoving it into her mouth.

Reyna shook from Beckham's fingers and had to close her eyes. His teeth grazed her neck.

"Open your eyes," he told her. "You won't want to miss this."

She peeled her eyes open as a male and a female vampire slinked gracefully onto the stage. The man wore black dress slacks and nothing else. The woman was in a black spandex leotard and thigh-high leather boots. She pushed the blond man aside easily, and he took a few steps and pumped his hand on his cock.

The woman leaned over, smiled sweetly, and then sank her fangs into the other woman's throat without warning. At first she screamed, silencing everything else in the room, and then she was abruptly cut off into moans of delicious pleasure.

The first man lost it inside of her at her shrieks, and the male vampire replaced him. He lifted her legs in the air and then punctured the vein in her inner thigh that Beckham had teased Reyna about the other night.

Reyna's own blood pumped fiercely at this point, and she was close to her own climax. She could barely keep from coming undone immediately as Beckham swirled his thumb around her clit.

"Stop making this so hard," Beckham groaned.

"What?" she asked, reaching her hand and placing it purposely on his cock.

His hand stilled for a second as she grasped him, but he didn't stop her. "Staying away from you."

"You want me, Becks. I'm yours," she said hoarsely. "Just choose me."

Reyna squeezed him again as the woman onstage let loose another violent scream. The male vampire was now buried inside of her and running the blood from her wounds across her pale skin and over the white lingerie. The vampire woman licked down the other woman's chest as the second man came up behind her and fucked her.

"Reyna," Beckham groaned, and the sound did her in. She lost control as wave after wave of sweet ecstasy ravaged her body. She tilted her head back and closed her eyes. This was everything. Dear God! Her body shook with the force of her orgasm, and she had to wait until her breathing steadied again before she could open her eyes.

Once she was still again and Beckham had removed his hand, she reached her own hand between her legs and slicked her finger. She pushed the wet finger up to his lips temptingly.

"Do you see what you do to me? Taste me," she demanded. He slid the finger into his mouth and sucked her. "That's yours."

"Fuck," he said as he released her.

"Yes, exactly," she said. "That's exactly what I want."

Beckham and Reyna stared at each other as the couples onstage finished their performance. There was a charged minute before Beckham turned back to the stage. Reyna felt dejected at his lack of response. She *knew* he wanted her. He had proven it just then, and yet he still turned her aside. He still refused to choose her.

Madame Dee walked back onstage to a round of applause from

the captivated audience. "Thank you, everyone," she said, sweeping her hand to the participants. "Thank you. You are all free to use your participation cards as you see fit."

"Well, that was the best performance I've ever seen," Roland said, turning to face them. "I'd say you two enjoyed it."

Reyna averted her gaze and prayed she wasn't as red as she felt. All she wanted was to disappear with Beckham and figure this out or fuck it out. At this point, she didn't even care. She was so desperate for him she was considering pushing people off of the stage bed to take him.

"Come along, darling," Cassandra said to Felix. "I have someone I'm *dying* for you to meet."

They disappeared into the crowd, and then Reyna was left alone with Beckham, Roland, and Sophie. Sophie looked impatient, but even she realized that this was a place of vampire control.

"Ah, there you are," Roland said, standing. "I'd wondered if you were going to come after all."

Reyna dragged her eyes away from Beckham to look at the person Roland was talking to, and her mouth dropped open. What the fuck?

"Penny," Beckham said with as much surprise in his voice as Reyna felt.

And of course Penelope looked gorgeous. Her hair was draped over one shoulder, long with perfect voluminous waves. She wore a black bustier, fitted black skirt, and fishnet tights. Not as revealing as most of the other humans in the room, but then again, the mayor's daughter wasn't exactly like most of the other humans in the room.

"Sorry I missed the show," Penelope said. Her eyes landed on Beckham, and Reyna saw concern flash into her eyes. Reyna wondered what the hell that was about, but the look was quickly replaced with malice when Penelope looked between Beckham and Reyna.

"What are you doing here?" Beckham asked.

Penelope shrugged. "Roland said you wanted me to come," she

purred, walking around the table toward him.

Reyna felt sick to her stomach. How could she sit here and watch her do this? He had just been inside of her, and now he was going to hang out with Penelope in a sex club?

Beckham gave Penelope a pointed look, but she smiled and touched his shoulder playfully. "I am still invited, right?"

Her other hand ran along her exposed collarbone and to the soft contour of her neck. She was tempting him, teasing him. Reyna watched Penelope flit her eyes over his head to look at Reyna and then back. Penelope was winning. Reyna could feel it. Whatever had transpired had wiped away everything that had happened the last couple of days. It made perfect sense that he would want Penelope, but it broke Reyna's heart that it always came right back to this.

"Of course you're invited," Beckham finally said.

Reyna had had enough. She couldn't believe this utter bullshit right now. She scrambled out of her seat. "Here, take my place," she offered. "I've no use for it."

"Reyna," Beckham said softly, almost pleadingly. But she would hear none of it.

"No worries," Penelope cooed. Without warning, she plopped down directly into Beckham's lap. She looked into his eyes, draped her arm around his neck, and then giggled. "You look ravenous." She tilted her neck toward him. "Have a taste, love."

Reyna jarred at the near-exact phrasing she had used with Beckham. Her heart was beating out of her chest, and she felt like she might be sick.

"Penny," he growled.

"What?" she teased as if she were innocent.

Beckham hesitated only a split second before sinking his fangs into her throat. Reyna felt paralyzed as she watched him drink from Penelope. She looked like she was in bliss with her head tilted back and her eyes closed.

Reyna couldn't believe he would sit there and drink from Penelope. The one thing he always refused Reyna. She had thought it so erotic, watching the people onstage drink, and the thought of Beckham drinking from her was so personal. All of that gone in a blink of an eye. She felt ridiculous, but tears marred her vision, and she needed to get out of there. Get far, far away.

So, without looking back or a thought for her safety, she turned and fled.

Chapter Twenty-Six

Reyna stumbled out of the main room of the brothel. It was difficult to see where she was going through the tears in her eyes, but she pushed past people anyway. All she wanted to do was be alone. She felt a breakdown coming on and couldn't allow herself to do that in front of people.

Yet she couldn't seem to find anywhere unoccupied. The Vault was built like a maze, trapping her inside and refusing to let her out of its grip. All she did was move in the opposite direction of the traffic. After a few minutes, she found a long hallway lined with doors that was practically empty compared to the rest of the building.

She wiped her eyes softly, trying not to smudge her makeup, and then walked down the hallway in search of an empty room. She wrenched open the first door. A man had a woman bent at the waist and was drilling into her from behind. Reyna squeaked and then quickly slammed the door shut.

She raced farther down the hallway and tried another door.

This one was even more disturbing. There were at least ten people involved in whatever sex acts were going on.

"Don't you see the room is occupied?" a woman yelled at her.

"Sorry. Sorry. I didn't know," Reyna murmured.

A nude vampire man who had been watching the display grabbed her wrist. "Hey, love, not so fast. You look absolutely delicious. Why not stay and join us? Plenty of room for one more."

Reyna felt panic setting in. "No…no, thank you."

"Oh, come on. We'll be gentle. Won't we?"

His eyes clearly said that *gentle* wasn't even a word in his repertoire. Reyna yanked away from him, but he circled her waist and drew her farther into the room.

"Let me go," she shrieked. "I said no!"

"You're part of the Vault," he said, breathing in the scent of her hair. "*No* doesn't exist here, doll."

Reyna blanched. "That's rape."

"You're here. You already gave consent," he said callously. "How tasty you must be with all that blood running so fast through your veins. I can feel your heartbeat skyrocketing."

"Please, please let me go." She sounded breathy and desperate, and she didn't care. She *was* desperate. She hadn't wanted this to happen. She had wanted to be left alone to sort out what had happened with Beckham.

"Let's see what type you are. Not that it matters in here." He cackled.

Reyna froze in place. This was exactly what Beckham had said. These people were obviously part of the first faction of vampire who had no regard for humanity. They didn't care if they raped her or if drinking from her would inevitably kill her or everyone else in the room.

The man grabbed her wrist, his nails biting into her skin. He glanced down at the diamond bracelet Beckham had put on her wrist earlier that evening. When he read the inscription, he dropped her hand as if he'd been burned.

"Beckham Anderson?" he asked.

"Yes," she said, stumbling backward.

"I'll take my chances with someone else. The man is a feral murderer."

Reyna didn't need to be told twice. She bolted out of the room to the sound of laughter. She ran all the way down the hallway until she was sure no one else had come down this far, then entered an entirely empty room. She crashed back onto the bed, curled her knees up to her chest, and let the tears flow.

After a minute of near-hyperventilation, she forced herself to get it under control. She could be upset—about Beckham, about Penelope, about the man who had wanted to rape her—but she couldn't let it leave this room.

No wonder Beckham hadn't wanted to bring her here. He didn't even drink from her. He certainly didn't want to share, and yet he was out there drinking from Penelope. Doing who knows what to Penelope.

Ugh! She couldn't even think about that.

She had fallen for him. That much was certain. It wasn't just physical anymore. She saw the real Beckham in the glimpses. The way he told her about the Elle rebels, the way he constantly looked out for her and protected her, the black card he had given her while asking nothing in return, the camera he had given her when she needed an escape, the way he talked to her about photography. Everything. He wasn't the hard businessman that he showed everyone else. He was a different man entirely, and it was breaking her heart into a million little pieces to accept that he wasn't going to be hers.

As sexy as this place had seemed when she first entered, the Vault was a disease. It did nothing but perpetuate the very behavior the blood type cure had tried to curb.

She longed for her camera to reveal the *real* dark side of the vampire elite, but of course she couldn't do that. She didn't have her camera, and even if she did, she wouldn't implicate Beckham in this. As much as she hated him right now, she wouldn't hurt him the way he had hurt her.

All she wanted was to go home to her brothers. She had saved enough for a little while, and she would redouble her efforts to get another job once she got back to them. Anything would be better than this game they were playing.

She sat up on the bed and took a deep breath. Yes. That was what she would do.

Just as she came to that conclusion, the door to her room popped open. She scrambled to her feet, ready to tell the person to leave her alone. Then Roland walked in, closed and locked the door, and she knew immediately that she was royally fucked.

"Hello, pet."

Reyna attempted to mask the fear rolling off of her. Roland was not like the other vampire, who had released her at the mention of Beckham's name. Roland knew no fear. He had been toying with her for weeks, waiting for the right opportunity to strike.

"You've been playing cat and mouse with me." He ambled forward slowly. He watched her with close attention.

"No, I haven't." She put conviction in her voice, but she worried it was lost. All she had was fear at this point. How could she escape Roland in a locked room made for this very thing?

Roland tsked her like a petulant child. "No lying, pet. I've been watching you. I knew I would find you alone eventually."

He stepped even closer to her, and she hurried away from him. The deadly smirk on his face only increased with her fear. He backed her up until her knees hit the bed. She sat down heavily and scooted out of his reach.

"Beckham is probably looking for me," she told him.

"No. He's not," Roland said with conviction. "He's thoroughly occupied with Miss Sky and will be for some time, I assume. He always is."

Reyna winced at the mention of Penelope and Beckham alone together. The worst of it all was that it was true. Beckham hadn't even seen her leave when he drank from Penelope. He wouldn't be looking for her, and Roland clearly enjoyed watching the realization come over her.

"But no worry." Roland ran his hand down her arm. She felt sick to her stomach. "I plan to keep you occupied on my own."

Reyna dashed to the other side of the bed and ran to the door. But before she had even made it past the bed, Roland grabbed her arm. She cried out as he held her in a bruising grasp before throwing her back against the foot of the bed.

He laughed. "You will not leave. I've ensured it." His hand brushed her dark hair out of her face like a caress. She gritted her teeth. "Now, where were we? Oh, yes. Don't tell me that you haven't imagined this moment. I know I have."

"I've never thought about you in that way," she growled.

"You would think of *him* that way, but not me?" he asked in disgust. "He has no interest in you but as a passing fancy. I find your will entertaining. A thing worth breaking like a prized stallion. Back home in France, we used to pay a pretty penny for a broken horse. I will see it done to you, too. Starting tonight."

Reyna screamed as he lunged for her. She darted out from under his arm and dashed toward the door again. She grappled with the lock, but she wasn't fast enough. Roland's hand clamped down on her hair and wrenched her backward. She yelled as some of her hair was pulled from the root and her twist unraveled from its pins. As he dragged her by her hair across the room, she lost her footing and he dug in deeper to yank her along.

He threw her back on the bed and crawled on top of her. Tears streamed down her face from the pain in her scalp and the terror of what was to come.

"Look at the way you tremble and cry and taste," he said, bending down and licking her tears off of her cheek. "Oh, I plan to savor your taste."

His hands fell to her corset, and he ripped it open from top to bottom, revealing her breasts to him.

"Please, no," she cried. "Please, please, no. No, no, no, no, no."

"Oh, yes, you will be a delicacy." Roland bent down and kissed her on the lips. She recoiled from his touch and refused to yield. "How I love this game, but I was told not to play with my food."

Her head was jerked back, exposing her throat. His fangs bore down toward her. She felt the touch of his mouth on her neck. It was over. This would be her first vampire bite and probably her last.

Then time slowed. The door to the room burst open. Roland lifted his head to see who dared disturb his private room, and Reyna caught a glimpse of Beckham looming in the doorway. He was a murderous shadow in all black, his face a storm cloud ready to release.

"Let her go, Roland," Beckham said, his voice low and dangerous.

Roland laughed, on the edge of madness, but he made no move to release Reyna.

"She is *mine*."

"Then come take her from me," he challenged.

Beckham took one deadly step forward, and Roland moved to puncture her neck. Reyna screamed, but before Roland's fangs reached her, he was yanked off of Reyna and hurled across the room. His back hit the wall, and he landed in a crouch on the ground.

"You would fight me over her?" Roland asked.

"You leave me no choice."

Roland came to the same conclusion. Neither of them waited; they launched themselves at each other, moving so fast they were a blur. Reyna had thought Beckham's fight with the rogue vampire in the alley had been too fast to follow, but this was something well beyond that. Roland and Beckham were both excellent fighters. They were on equal footing. Both deadly and terrifying, with pasts that spoke for themselves and had earned them the highest positions at Visage. She didn't stand a chance of keeping up with the fight. Punches were thrown and blocked, bodies hurled against walls that shuddered and released plaster from the ceiling, and furniture broke into pieces at their assault. It was like a synchronized dance made lethal.

Reyna stayed out of the way of what was happening. She crouched in a corner, hugging her tattered corset to her chest. Neither of them slowed down as their attacks turned more and more brutal. Finally, everything slowed down to the one moment when Beckham landed a perfectly executed hit to Roland's temple, and he dropped like a ton of bricks. Whatever Beckham had done had left Roland completely immobilized.

He wasn't dead, Beckham wouldn't want to kill him, but in that moment, she hoped for it.

"What is going on in here?" someone called, entering the destroyed room.

Reyna hadn't even noticed that they had drawn a crowd. She held her corset tighter to her and curled deeper into her corner. She wanted to leave. She wanted to forget this night had ever happened. Beckham adjusted his suit and faced the man, who was pushing everyone else out of earshot.

"It's been settled," Beckham said.

"You know the rules, Mr. Anderson. No fighting of any kind."

"I'm well aware of the rules. Mr. Batiste was taking possession of my property without my permission. I was within my rights to stop him."

The man glowered at him. "Fine, but we must ask you to leave, as you have made quite a spectacle of yourself."

"No one in, no one out," he reminded them.

"We protect our own. We'll take you out the back way."

Beckham still looked murderous, and the man seemed ready to relent at any minute. But rules were rules, apparently, and Beckham had broken one of the cardinal ones to save her. Finally, he nodded.

Beckham turned to address her, and he realized she was mostly naked and shaking. "Oh, Reyna."

He helped her to her feet. She couldn't seem to stop herself from shaking at what she had witnessed. Beckham shrugged out of his jacket and quickly threw it around her shoulders. The jacket smelled like him, and she pulled it tight around her. He placed his hand on her lower back, but she stepped away from his touch. He might have fought for her, saved her, but that didn't make up for all the other bullshit.

She was done. She was so done. Beckham Anderson had no right to her body or her mind any longer.

"Reyna," he said, his voice straining.

She shot him an ugly glare and then teetered across the room. She made it only about halfway to the door before her legs gave out and she fell forward. Beckham was at her side in an instant, holding her up. She wrenched away, but the adrenaline was wearing off. She felt ragged and exhausted, humiliated and exposed, and angry. She felt so angry. But her body wasn't listening to her. Her legs were not working.

Shock.

She was in shock.

When she didn't move another step, Beckham scooped her up into his arms and carried her out of the room. She didn't even have the words to argue with him. To shout at him and tell him to leave her alone. To tell him how much better her life had been without him in it.

The man who had forced Beckham to leave directed them down a hallway to where another door was located. It wasn't quite as large as the Vault door but still looked sturdy.

"I'll have to lock up behind you."

"That's fine. I'll have my driver pick us up from our location," Beckham said.

Then he carried Reyna through the door and out into a long tunnel completely devoid of any- and everything. The club door slammed behind them, sealing itself shut and casting them into utter darkness.

CHAPTER TWENTY-SEVEN

O nce the door closed behind them, Beckham eased her back onto her unsteady feet. She stumbled a bit and clutched onto the wall to right herself. Even if she had been about to pass out all over again, she wouldn't have wanted to stay in Beckham's arms. The wall was cool to her touch, and she used the sturdy feel of it to bring her back to herself. Images flashed through her mind—fangs sinking into flesh, leering expressions, a ripped corset, shuddering walls. She closed her eyes and forced away her panic.

She was out of there.

No one could hurt her.

Except the man before her, who from the start had promised to break her.

Reyna peeled her eyes back open and let them adjust to the darkness. Beckham was standing before her, but his eyes were cast down the tunnel contemplatively, which was when she noticed that the tunnel wasn't as dark as anticipated. It was dimly lit from the roof at random intervals.

Beckham pulled his phone out of his pocket. That damn phone. The screen lit up his face, where fear lingered despite the fact that they were out of the club. Reyna didn't know what Beckham could fear.

"Fuck," he cursed. "No signal."

Reyna groaned. Great. Just great. "I shouldn't have come here."

"Finally, something we can both agree on," Beckham said stubbornly.

Reyna rolled her eyes and then glared at him. "How dare you even say that shit to me right now," she spat, her voice cold and hard. "If you hadn't wanted me to come, if you had *really* wanted Penelope all along, then this is your fault."

"I *told* you not to come. You insisted and boxed me into a corner."

She shook her head. "No one bullies you. I'm your employee, remember? You tell me what to do."

"Yeah, and right now I'm telling you to stop talking."

"No," she said, straightening. "I'm not finished. This entire thing was bullshit, and I'm over it. I cannot believe you drank from Penelope."

"Reyna," he said, his voice lethal.

"How could you do it?" she asked, almost desperate. "After the rooftop...and everything else. How?"

He ground his teeth and then looked away. "It's complicated."

"No, it's not. You won't drink from me, but you'll drink from her? That's not complicated. That's bullshit."

"We need to leave. We'll talk about this later."

"No, we'll talk about it now. And we'll start with this—I don't want you to ever touch me again," she growled. "You're a liar, a cheat, and a coward."

His eyes were steely as he stood taller and flashed his fangs at her. She tried not to show fear, but when he wanted to appear menacing, he was damn good at it. "I have been called many things before, Little One, but I am *no* coward."

Reyna held her ground. "A coward is a man torn between two women and leading them both on. So, I'll make the decision easy for you. I will not be in the middle anymore. I want to go home."

"Yeah, we're about to leave. We'll talk about this when we get there. We have to walk until we get a signal."

"No," Reyna spat. "I mean I want to go *home*, to my brothers, to the Warehouse District."

"What?" Beckham's head snapped over to her, and he stared long and hard.

"You heard me. I'm done. I want to go home," she told him more forcefully. "I want to get away from this world, this horrible, awful world."

He clenched his jaw, breathed out harshly, and looked away from her. "We'll talk about this when you calm down."

"I'm not going to change my mind."

"Right now, I don't give a damn, Reyna. We're locked out of the club in a dark abandoned tunnel after I ruined a *very* important business relationship for you. So forgive me if I don't want to hear about you wanting to leave and go back home right now. You've proven to be more trouble than you're worth," he said, gesturing wildly, "and I want to get out of here. We can decide about *you* later. So, let's go."

He started down the tunnel, and with no other choice, she followed. Her numbness turned into full-on sickness at Beckham's words. She had told him she wanted to leave, but she hadn't expected that reaction. Why did she even want him to fight for her to stay? It wasn't enough that he beat Roland up for touching her—that was just protecting his interests; this was him not caring one way or another whether she stayed or left. In fact, he had even said she was too much trouble. All while refusing to explain what the hell was happening between him and Penelope. And she couldn't stand it any longer.

Reyna stumbled along in her heeled boots. Her feet were sore and it was cold in the tunnel, but she didn't complain. She refused to let him see her pain.

"Do you smell that?" Beckham asked, turning his head up to the ceiling.

Reyna breathed in deeply. "I don't smell anything."

"Fuck. No. Not yet."

Beckham picked up the pace, and she had to take long awkward strides to keep up.

"Beckham, slow down. I can't keep up with you, and I don't know where I'm going."

"We have to hurry, Reyna."

She jogged after him in her boots, but he was flat-out running now. There was no chance of her catching up with him. "Beckham," she yelled breathlessly.

She lost sight of him in the dark, and her voice rose an octave in panic. "Becks!" she called again.

He reappeared a minute later, winded and almost delirious. "She's not there. She's not there."

Reyna bent over at the waist with her hands on her knees, gulping in air. "Who? Where?"

"Penny. She's still inside. Fuck! No, this wasn't supposed to happen," he said, pacing in front of her as he rambled on to himself.

"You're not making any sense. What's going on?" Reyna reached out, grabbed him, and shook him with as much force as she could muster. He looked into her eyes, but he appeared wild and lost. Not at all like the cool, confident Beckham she knew. "Snap out of it and tell me what's wrong."

"She wasn't supposed to get stuck inside."

"Why is she stuck? I don't understand what you're saying."

"I have to fix this," he said, his eyes suddenly alight.

Beckham picked Reyna up as if she were a rag doll, against her protests, and ran until they reached the front door. She had no idea what was going on. Beckham seemed frantic, and he was freaking her out. When they reached a group of people—human drivers, mostly, but also one female vampire and her escort—gathered outside of the door, Beckham planted Reyna on her feet and pushed through the throng. A group of people banged uselessly on the door. Reyna's eyes darted down to the bottom of the door and saw smoke curling out of the entrance.

Her heart stuttered to a halt as she realized what Beckham had smelled.

Smoke.

Fire.

"Oh my God," Reyna said. Her hand flew to her mouth.

Now that she smelled it, she coughed at the intrusion in her lungs. The horrid realization took over that everyone was trapped inside the building with no way to get out. No wonder Beckham had been panicking about Penelope. As much as she was envious and detested Penelope, that didn't mean Reyna wanted her to die.

She watched as Beckham took charge of the group. He still looked crazed, but less so with a solution in mind.

"You over there. Call 911. Get an ambulance and fire truck here now."

The driver wavered in place. "But they can't know about this place. We're under orders."

Beckham looked at him incredulously. "If they don't, a lot of people will die. What's more important to you? Now call! Hurry!"

The man nodded and reached for his phone. Reyna feared that the fire department wouldn't get here fast enough to save the people inside. Smoke inhalation couldn't kill the vampires, but the flames surely could.

Beckham sent the vampire woman and her escort to the entrance they had just vacated to try to breach the door. She didn't know why people weren't already getting out that way or through the front entrance. Both had locks on the inside. Beckham sent a group of drivers to the brothel sleeping quarters. He left the largest group at the entrance to try to ram through the near-impenetrable door while Beckham took off toward the last exit he was aware of.

Reyna ran after him as fast as she could. She reached him as he was banging against a side exit much like the one they had left through.

"You shouldn't be here," he said when he saw her.

"I'm not leaving you." With his wild and crazed demeanor, she said it as a reassurance, but what she meant was she had nowhere else to go.

He didn't say anything else after that, and after a few minutes of work, he managed to pry the door open at the top. Smoke poured out from the hole he had made. She could hear screams on the other side.

"Whatever happens, Reyna, stay here."

"What are you going to do?" she demanded, her eyes wide with fear and already itching from the smoke.

"I have to get to Penny."

"How?" she demanded, her mouth agape. "Go walk into the flames? They could *kill* you. Be reasonable."

"Penny is in there, and I won't leave her there to die," he said, wrenching the door open farther. She could see his hands were blistered and bleeding from the exertion. For it to do that to a vampire, the heat must be outstanding. "If that's unreasonable, then fine, but she wasn't even supposed to be here tonight. I won't let her die because of me."

With a screech, the door came off the hinges. Vampires and humans streamed out of the hole, bloodied and coughing, trying to expel the toxins from their lungs.

Beckham shouldered past the first wave of people, and Reyna followed him. She grabbed onto his hand and tugged.

"Please stop," she cried.

"Stay back, Reyna. I can't worry about both of you right now."

"Come back to me," she pleaded. No matter how furious she had been with him tonight, watching him walk into that fire was like teetering on her own brand of madness. The flames engulfed her heart as surely as they were about to consume his body.

Without warning, he crushed his lips to hers in a fierce, possessive kiss. "I will."

And then he disappeared into the burning building.

Reyna rushed back out with the evacuees and stood in a location where she could watch and wait for Beckham to return. She couldn't believe he was risking his life for Penelope. And yet, at the same time, she completely understood it. He had feelings for Penelope, but Reyna wanted to believe it went beyond that. Beckham valued human life, and he was proving it more than ever with this rescue. He could have, like Roland likely would have, abandoned the building to the fire. Even if Roland would have gotten a door open, it only would have been for his fellow vampires. But when Beckham had told the man to call 911, he had said otherwise a lot of *people* would die. People, not vampires.

So she waited anxiously for him to come out, but Beckham didn't show.

"That's it," a man called. "That's everyone we could get. The main room collapsed and killed dozens. There's no hope for the others."

"No," Reyna yelled desperately. "He couldn't have gone in there for nothing."

The distant ring of an ambulance and fire truck announced their arrival. News crews and police showed up on the scene shortly thereafter, wrangling the victims and getting statements of what happened. Reyna was oblivious to everything but the opening to the brothel. This was not the end. He had not gone in there to his death.

"Ma'am, are you all right? Can you tell us what happened?" a camerawoman asked, sticking a microphone in her face.

"No. Leave me alone," she said, shouldering her out of the way.

It had been too long. He had gone in after Penelope on a fool's mission. He was a vampire, but that didn't make him invincible.

Tears ran down her face like black rivulets, but still she refused to turn away from the doorway. Even when her eyes itched and her throat grew scratchy, she couldn't step away. Even when a medic approached her to check her health and a policeman tried to reason with her.

"Miss, you need to back up. We need to clear this area."

"No," she sobbed. "He's still in there. He swore he'd come back to me."

"Ma'am, we have firefighters inside right now trying to look at the rest of the rubble. Why don't you tell me who to look for and where they might be? We'll relay the information to the people heading inside."

"He swore he'd come back," she repeated like an anthem.

"Please, let me help you." The policeman snapped his fingers at a couple of medics, trying to get them to come help.

She repeated the same thing over and over again. "He said he'd come back to me."

"No one has come out of the door alive in fifteen minutes," he said, touching her hand softly. He probably thought she was going to faint.

"No. He'll be back. He promised."

"Miss…"

Then out of the smoke came a figure in black, carrying a small woman with her head lolling to the side.

"Holy…" the police officer cried in horror.

"Beckham!" Reyna pushed past the policeman, who grabbed for her, and rushed to Beckham. "You came back."

Beckham had a haunted look on his face, but when he saw Reyna, he breathed in new life. "We need to get her to a hospital immediately."

"Ambulances are here," she assured him.

As if on cue, two paramedics appeared with a stretcher. Beckham placed Penelope on it, and they went to work trying to revive her. Once she was out of his hands, Reyna threw her arms around his soot-stained suit.

"I thought you were gone," she breathed in horror. "Thank God you're all right."

"He doesn't answer our prayers," Beckham said, monotone and lifeless.

"He answers mine," she told him.

Beckham patted her hair as if he wasn't fully aware she was there and then moved closer to watch the medics work on Penelope.

"We need to take her to the hospital. Are you responsible for this girl?" the paramedic asked Beckham.

"Yes," he answered at once.

"Then come with us." They rushed through the crowd that parted for the stretcher and lifted Penelope into the ambulance.

Beckham put a hand on Reyna's shoulder. "The car will take you back to the penthouse. Gerard is on his way to retrieve you."

"Becks," she pleaded.

"I have to go with Penelope. Get back to my place, and we'll discuss you leaving when I return."

She swallowed, hating the way that sounded. Leaving would be the smart thing to do, but she couldn't keep her heart from reaching out for Beckham.

"Beckham, please."

"All ready to go," the paramedic called.

"Go, Reyna. I have to take care of Penelope. She needs me, and you made it perfectly clear you don't."

Beckham jumped into the ambulance just as the door slammed shut, and she stared at Beckham's dark eyes through the glass before he sped away.

CHAPTER TWENTY-EIGHT

Reyna walked into the empty penthouse, feeling utterly exhausted. She tore off her boots in the entranceway. Her feet were blistered and sore. Her mind and heart felt even worse.

She moved numbly from the living room to her bedroom and stripped out of what remained of her brothel clothing. Even though it was ridiculous, she pulled Beckham's suit jacket back over her and crawled into bed. It still smelled like him, and she wasn't quite ready to give it up yet.

So much of her wanted to say *fuck this shit*, grab her stuff, and go. But she didn't know if that was a rash decision that she would regret later. She was so tired from the evening, and even if she left, where would she go at this hour?

She didn't even realize she had drifted off until the sound of the elevator drew her out of her slumber. She glanced at the clock and realized she had slept the entire day away. Reyna tensed, waiting for Beckham to come to her, to explain, to tell her what had happened.

She heard him walking around the apartment, then the distant sound of his feet retreating away from her.

He never came to her.

He never even checked to see if she was all right.

Nothing.

She could have already left the apartment, and he wouldn't even know or care. She should be beyond caring what Beckham Anderson thought. She should have deduced that last night, but it hit her again full force.

Stretching her sore muscles, Reyna rolled out of bed. She grabbed a black bag out of her closet and threw her meager possessions into it. The bag was nicer than anything she had ever owned at home, but there were no other options except designer purses. She changed into jeans and a T-shirt. Her feet slipped into her Converse, and she pulled the baseball hat low over her eyes. By the time she was finished, she really didn't have much—three changes of clothes, a few toiletries, and her black card. She decided she would empty what was left of her bank account on her way out and then cut up the card. She left her phone on her dresser, then exited her room.

When she walked into the living room, she expected Beckham to come out, ready for a confrontation. But he never left his room.

Frustrated, she was turning to leave when she caught a glimpse of her name on a leather case on the kitchen counter. She unzipped it, and inside was a note. She flipped it open.

Freedom.

She scrunched her brows together and pulled out the other item in the bag. It was a check. Her mouth dropped open when she saw the seemingly endless zeros scrawled in Beckham's hand.

Her chest constricted, and her throat went dry. This amount of money would mean she would never have to work again in her life. It meant she could live comfortably, get out of the shithole her brothers lived in, go to college, have a life. She could do anything she wanted.

But the money wasn't freedom like he proposed. He was letting her go without even saying goodbye.

She pushed the case away from her with shaking hands. She would only take the money that was owed her. The money that she had earned. She never wanted to feel as if he were buying her out. She never *ever* wanted to feel like she owed Beckham anything. This would be a clean break.

Reyna glanced down at the check one last time, then exited the apartment with just her backpack over her shoulder.

Everett wasn't working the night shift at the valet station. She was glad he wasn't around to see her go, but she was also sad that she wouldn't get to say goodbye to him, either. But this was necessary even if it was the hardest thing she had ever done...even harder than deciding to work for Visage in the first place.

She took a cab to a bank and transferred the rest of the money to her brothers' accounts. She didn't want to have anything to do with the money anymore or the account Visage had set up for her to deposit it into.

Then she was on the road to the Warehouse District. It was surreal to think she was really going back. She had thought about it so often but had resigned herself to the fact that she would never see her brothers again.

She paid the cab with her black card, swearing it was the last time she would use any of Beckham's dirty money, and then hopped out of the car. She stared up at her brothers' place. It was dark and ominous. No one was on the streets, and all the windows were shut up tight.

Home sweet home.

Three flights of stairs later, she was standing in front of their door. It was hanging slightly off the hinges, which she didn't remember from when she had been living here. She grew suddenly anxious and knocked once on the door.

"Who is it?" Brian asked gruffly. "We don't have anything. Try another place."

"Brian?" she whispered. She hugged herself in the dark.

The door swung open. "Reyna?" Brian asked. "Oh my God, is that you?"

Drew jumped up from the dingy sofa and rushed to her. He barreled into her, scooping her into a fierce hug. "What are you doing here? We thought we'd never see you again."

It so perfectly mirrored her own thoughts earlier that she couldn't help it—she burst into tears. They were tears of both joy at seeing them and grief over what she had left behind.

"It's so good to see you guys. I've missed you so much. You have no idea," she said through her sobs.

"I'm so glad you're home," Brian said, joining in on the hug. "Stop crying. Come inside."

He urged them back into their apartment, then closed and bolted the door. Another new addition. Her eyes scanned the room. It looked bare in the feeble light. Not just in comparison to Beckham's immaculate penthouse but to her memory of their apartment. The place was bare-bones, as if someone had moved but left all the big furniture.

"Are you on vacation or leave?" Brian asked curiously.

"No," Reyna said. She drew her out of her thoughts. She hiccuped and wiped her eyes. "I left. I couldn't do it anymore."

"Were they mistreating you?" Drew asked.

"Are you hurt?" Brian chimed in.

They both went into full-on big-brother mode, and it almost made her smile.

"No." How could she explain what had happened? It was a world they would never understand, and she honestly hoped they never tried. "I was never even bitten."

Brian's face darkened. She didn't blame him for not wanting to hear about that.

"Then what were you doing this whole time?" Drew asked.

"You wouldn't believe me even if I told you."

Drew urged her to sit down. "Start from the beginning. No one has been feeding off of you?"

Reyna showed him her neck. Up close, it was clear it was perfect. No marks at all. Not even the tiniest little ones. Not that that was the only place a person could get bitten, but it was the most common.

"What was I doing?" she repeated, laughing bitterly. "Going to balls in gorgeous dresses, clubbing, shopping in designer boutiques, and learning photography. Absolutely nothing of any practical use."

Brian and Drew exchanged a hesitant look.

"That sounds like a fairy tale," Drew said.

"I know."

"So why did you leave?" Brian asked. He took the other seat next to her. They both looked honestly curious. She could tell they were glad to see her, and she hoped that meant they wanted her to stay.

"It was a fairy tale at first," she said cautiously, "but the dangers of that world are too much. I can't describe it. You'll just have to trust me."

"We can talk about it when you're ready," Drew agreed easily.

Drew was always far more trusting than Brian, who was giving her a look as if he wanted to ask more questions, but he held his tongue for now.

"Thank you for sending the money, by the way."

"Oh, guys, I'm sorry," she apologized immediately. "I'll try to get a job to cover me being back."

"We'll make do," Brian said. "We're glad you're home."

"What happened to this place, anyway?" she finally asked, gesturing around the room.

Both guys looked down and away from her. Neither wanted to tell the story. Finally, Brian blew out a breath. "After a bunch of the guys found out that you were sending us money, they ransacked it and took everything. We have nothing, Reyna."

Reyna's mouth dropped open. All this time, she thought she was helping, and she'd been making it worse for them.

"I'm so sorry."

"It's not your fault," Drew said consolingly.

"It is."

"It's not," Brian insisted. "We've been working doubles to make up for it."

Reyna threw her head into her hands. She had tried so hard to give them what they always deserved and allow them to take fewer shifts at the warehouse. She had wanted them to have their own lives. Everything had backfired.

She stood with a newfound purpose. "I put the rest of my wages into your account, but I'll start looking for a new job today."

"We don't care about the money, Rey. We care about you." Drew took her hand. When he saw that she wasn't relenting, he added, "Give it a day or two. We'll figure it out."

Reyna wavered but ultimately decided a few days wouldn't hurt anything. She needed some time to get used to being back, anyway.

"So, what have I missed?" she asked between them.

Brian immediately colored. It was impossible for him not to get embarrassed. It was probably where she had gotten it from.

"Laura and I are getting pretty serious," he admitted.

Drew laughed. "She's already hounding you for a ring."

"Hasn't she been doing that since you started dating?"

"Yeah, but, well, now that you're gone…" He cleared his throat and looked away.

"Now that you don't have someone else to take care of," she added.

"She doesn't come right out and say it, but I'm saving up for a ring."

Reyna looked down at her hands. Her brother was going to get engaged soon. Wow. She'd known that stuff would change while she was gone, but she hadn't realized how fast their lives would move in her absence.

"Well, I'm happy for you. Perhaps it's time for that ring after all."

Drew nudged him in the ribs. "That's what I've been saying."

"And you?" Reyna asked him. "Any woman in your life? Or do you insist on getting old all alone?"

He shrugged, averting his gaze as he said, "No women in my life, Rey." Then he cleared his throat and looked up at her. "Just you. And

I'm glad you're back. Everything else can wait."

She slung her arm around Drew's waist and leaned into him. It was nice to feel loved again and to have the easy, comfortable companionship of her family. But it didn't dull the ache of her missing Beckham, and she wondered if he had realized yet that she'd left the house and the check behind. What would he think when he saw it? Would he cut his losses? Would he care at all?

She tried not to think about it any further. There was nothing she could do. The past was the past, and she doubted she would have changed any of her decisions.

They stayed up talking half the night until the guys swore they had to get to bed to stay on schedule for work. The next day was their one day off that week, and they spent it messing around like old times.

In the morning, Reyna cooked breakfast and was pleased that someone else was there to enjoy it. They walked around their seedy neighborhood, and though it felt like home, it made her miss the clean park where she had taken a picture of Beckham. It made her miss her camera.

She splurged on lunch at a nearby restaurant that had been there forever, not that it was anything fancy. Then they spent the night playing board games and reading to one another from Drew's favorite fantasy novel. It was warm and comfortable being with them, but her heart was missing Beckham. Even if she hated herself for thinking so, she still went to bed that night wishing he was nearby.

The next morning, she got up extra early to walk her brothers to the warehouse for work. She couldn't count the number of times she had done so in the past. Reyna took a sorrowful look around the apartment, then followed her brothers down the stairs. It was a nice day despite the fact that she had a heavy heart.

When they reached the warehouse, her brothers each gave her a hug and promised to see her when they got off work. She watched them walk away with dueling thoughts battling in her mind. On one hand, she was so happy to be here with them, and on the other, she had never felt more alone, watching them disappear and having absolutely no options.

Before, she had always had Visage as a last resort. After she'd exhausted her last option on getting a job, she could always become a blood escort. She had hated the idea—not because she had anything against vampires, but out of fear of the unknown, her fear of needles, and the thought of becoming a food source, which wasn't exactly appealing. Now that unknown had been her reality, and she couldn't turn back to it. Not now. Not ever.

With a sigh, she left the warehouse and started toward the road for home. She only made it a few feet before she heard her name called. It was strange being in a place where people knew her again. She could have walked anywhere in the city and never had a single person recognize her. She only knew a handful of people in total, anyway.

And in the warehouses, this was the last person she wanted to see. Steven.

"Hey," she said, trying to act casual. After the last time she saw him, she wanted to punch him in the face. But he was much bigger than her, and she couldn't rely on her brothers getting her out of the situation this time.

"Little Reyna Carpenter!" he said in greeting. "Back from her blood whore days."

Reyna rolled her eyes. "What do you want?"

He smiled at her, and she wondered why she had ever found him attractive. He was nothing compared to Beckham.

"Vampires get tired of your blood? Or something else?" He eyed her up and down suggestively.

"I've had a really long weekend. I don't want to deal with you right now." None of what he said was true, but it didn't hurt the sting that Beckham had let her go.

"Let's have fun like old times, Reyna."

"No thanks. I don't want any of your fun."

She walked away, but he grabbed her arm. "You can't tell me you'd rather have vampire cock than mine."

"And if I did?" she spat.

He was staring at her menacingly, but then his eyes widened and he didn't respond.

"What?" she asked, turning to see what he was staring at.

"Your chariot awaits."

Her mind couldn't keep up with the sight of the familiar black town car slowing to a stop in front of the warehouse. The car was still rolling when the back door popped open. Beckham stepped out and headed toward Reyna.

She was pretty sure she was hallucinating. She blinked twice and even contemplated pinching herself. This had to be a dream. Except Steven hadn't let go of her arm, and her dreams never really got right how utterly gorgeous Beckham was.

CHAPTER TWENTY-NINE

"Beckham?" she asked.

"He's come to reclaim his whore," Steven spat. He didn't exactly drop her arm; it was more like he threw it toward Beckham as if he were offering a prize.

Beckham's eyes left hers and looked to Steven standing behind her. Steven stepped backward as he took in Beckham's immense size.

"Is this your ex-boyfriend?" Beckham asked.

"Yeah," Reyna said softly.

Beckham grabbed Steven by the collar of his shirt. He hoisted Steven off of his feet until he was eye level with Beckham. "If you harass her or anyone she knows ever again, I will personally kill you. That's not a threat. It's a promise."

Without waiting to hear if he would say anything back, Beckham threw him as if he weighed nothing at all. Steven landed hard on his back a few feet away. He scrambled to his feet. Fear was written all over his face.

Beckham could have done worse. She'd seen his speed and agility in a fight. Steven should just walk away. This wasn't a fight he could win.

"Bloodsucking disease on our world," Steven called. "You're all the same. One day, we'll rid the world of your plague."

"But not today."

Steven glared and then stormed away. Reyna breathed out a sigh of relief. As much as she despised Steven at this point, she didn't want him to get himself killed for his insolent mouth.

Once he was gone, Beckham refocused his attention on Reyna.

"What are you *doing* here?" she repeated.

"You left the money," he said. It was more of a statement than a question, and she didn't know what he wanted her to say.

"Yeah." She shrugged.

"Why? It was enough to support you, to keep you safe and secure, to have your own life."

"Because I don't need your charity."

"It's not charity," he insisted.

"It is. You wanted to buy me out, but I can't be bought. I'll work and get a decent wage like the rest of the country. I won't be indebted to you for the rest of my life."

Beckham eyed her curiously. "I wasn't buying you out. You said you wanted to leave. That was what you wanted."

"And then you *never* came back for me. You saved Penny. I get it. She was injured. I understand her being important to you. But you never checked on me again. Honestly, I assumed you wanted me gone."

"I thought you wanted space," he said.

Reyna cast her gaze away from him. "I was angry. After everything that happened that night, I was angry and scared. I didn't know what I wanted. Answers, mostly. I guess I figured out your answer when you chose her."

"Reyna, I had to take care of her."

"I know. She was hurt, but you didn't have to hammer the nail into the coffin. You said I made it clear that I don't need you, but you've saved me more times than I can count now. I clearly need you in that life, but I don't *need* that life. I have another one, equally terrifying in its own way, where I fight my own battles. But in your world, I can't fight for you anymore. You won't let me and it's breaking my heart, Beckham."

He reached out for her hand and took it smoothly into his. She locked eyes with him and saw something swirling around in his she had never seen before. A vulnerability that he had never shown her.

"Come back."

"What?" she asked.

"Come back to the city with me. Stay with me."

"Why? So you can keep stringing me along?"

"No, because with me is where you belong."

Reyna swallowed and searched his face for some form of malice. She couldn't dare to hope without an answer to her next question.

"And Penelope?"

He sighed heavily. "They're calling me the Saint, and her the Martyr, because in the video footage from the fire, she looks dead." Reyna cringed at the painful memory. "Her face is burned beyond recognition on one side. The rest of her body isn't in much better shape. She took the brunt of the fires. She might be glad that she is alive, but I can't tell her how I feel in her unstable state."

"And how do you feel?" Reyna asked. She swallowed hard, unable to believe that the words she had craved for so long were so near.

"That I need you to come back. I *need* you, Little One."

"I don't know what that means, Beckham. What does that mean?" She needed him to lay it out for her.

"I thought you wanted to leave, and I wanted to give you what you wanted. I thought I could keep you separate from my life, but I realized I can't. I can't live without you. I don't want Penelope. I've never wanted Penelope. I want you, and I want to share all my secrets with you." His hand cupped her cheek. "I want to be the man you saw on the roof."

"Really?" The words were melodic, like hearing a siren's song. But doubt crept through even the best words. "Why the change of heart? All of this just because I left the money, because I left you?"

"Because I can't live without you. I thought I could, but I was wrong. Come back with me."

Beckham's lips were soft on hers for the briefest of moments. When they broke apart, she looked around at her home.

Could she ever be happy here again? Or would it always be missing the one thing she had standing right in front of her? Maybe her home wasn't even her home anymore. Her home was with Beckham, and he was *finally* choosing her.

"Okay," she whispered.

Her heart fluttered in her chest. There were actual butterflies. When she walked out of Beckham's apartment, she had never thought in a million years that he would be standing here asking her to come back. She had wished he had stopped her, but wishing for him was like wishing for rain in the desert.

The sound of feet pounding on the pavement behind them tore her out of her dreamy daze. Beckham stood in a defensive pose, but Reyna placed her hand on his arm when she realized it was only her brothers.

"It's okay," she told him.

"What the hell are you doing with our sister?" Brian asked. He stared Beckham down like he had any chance of beating the shit out of him.

"Yeah, back off," Drew chimed in.

"Guys, it's all right." She put herself between Beckham and her brothers. She didn't want *any* fighting. There had been enough of that lately. It was one thing for him to rough up Steven, but it was a different story with Brian and Drew.

"What are you doing out here?" Reyna asked.

"We came to check on you. Steven said that there was a guy out here harassing you," Brian said.

Reyna shook her head. What an asshole. "Yeah. He was the one harassing me. Beckham, however, is not."

The guys sized each other up, and it was completely ridiculous. She wished she could correct male behavior, but instead she let them have their moment.

"Beckham, these are my brothers, Brian and Drew," she said. "Guys, this is Beckham. He's the person I was staying with in the city."

For some reason, she stumbled over the word *vampire*. It wasn't as if they didn't already know Beckham was a vampire if he was who she'd been living with, but it felt weird to call him a vampire. Maybe because he was just Becks to her.

Beckham extended his hand. "It's nice to meet you. I know Reyna has missed you both very much."

Brian gave him a wary look but then took his hand. "I'm Brian, and this is Drew."

Drew took Beckham's hand next. He was more welcoming and had a smile on his face. He had always been less reserved than Brian.

"We're glad to have Reyna back home," Drew said.

"Yeah. She had quite a traumatizing experience in the city," Brian said accusingly.

"Brian," she whispered.

Beckham glanced at her but gave no indication of what he was thinking. "Yes, she has. I hope to change that."

She smiled and turned from his gaze. Her brothers were going to see what was going on, and she couldn't even stop herself. He had chosen *her*! How could she not be giddy?

"And how do you plan on doing that with her here in the Warehouse District?" Brian asked, crossing his arms over his chest. "What exactly are you doing here, anyway?"

Reyna spit the truth out. "I'm going back with him, guys."

"What?" Drew asked. His eyes were wide with hurt. Brian looked pissed.

"No, you're not. You've cried yourself to sleep the last two nights. Going back with him is a recipe for disaster. This is your home," Brian said.

"You don't get to make that choice for me," Reyna said. "As much as I want to be here with you, I need to be with Beckham."

"So, there was a part of the story you left out," Drew accused.

She blushed. "Yes."

Beckham cleared his throat uncomfortably. "I'm going to give you a few minutes. I'll be by the car."

She nodded with a sigh. "Sorry."

Beckham walked away, leaving her alone with her brothers. She whirled on them. "That was rude."

"Rude?" Brian asked. "You're in love with a vampire. We don't have anything against their kind, but are you out of your mind?"

"I'm not in *love* with him," she said, hoping he couldn't hear this conversation. She hadn't figured out how she felt about him yet. She hadn't wanted to dive too far into it when her heart was at risk.

Brian scowled further. "Have you thought this through at all, or are you rushing back into it because he's here to collect you?"

"I know that this whole thing freaks you out, but it's exactly how you would have reacted if I'd told you I was going to Visage in the first place. The same reason I *never* told you. I'm not a kid anymore. You can't keep treating me like one. I am capable of making good decisions, and Beckham is one."

"So, long term, what does this look like?" Brian asked. "He feeds off of you, fucks you, then what? Do you want to become immortal? Are you going to become a vampire and leave your family behind? What is it, Reyna?"

Reyna paled and avoided his gaze. "I don't know. Okay? I don't know. Does it have to be one or the other?"

"In case you aren't aware, vampires live forever. You turn fifty, they stay the same age. You turn eighty, they stay the same age. You die. They live. There's no getting around it."

"Okay. Okay. I get it. I know, Brian," she snapped. "I don't see why I have to decide that today. You've been dating Laura for five years and still haven't even proposed. I've known Beckham less than a month. Maybe I can wait a couple of years like other *normal* people and see if it still works out."

Drew sighed and reached for her hand. She saw he was really upset with the whole thing, and she hated hurting him most of all. "You left us once already, Rey. Don't do it again," he pleaded.

"I know," she said. "I don't want to leave you. I'll come visit. I think I can make it work this time. It will definitely not be forever. But if I don't go with him, I'll always, *always* wonder what if. You might be willing to do that, but I can't."

"Reyna," Beckham called.

"Just a minute," she said, holding up her hand. She looked at her brothers imploringly. "Tell me you love me and want me to be happy. You don't have to approve of him, but respect my choice."

Drew sighed and pulled her into a hug. "We're going to miss you so much."

"I'm going to miss you, too."

"Come on, Brian," Drew said. Brian joined in on the hug.

When they pulled away, she could tell Brian was still upset, but he managed a smile for her. "You always have a home here if it doesn't work out. Promise to come back."

"I will. As often as I can."

They followed her over to Beckham's town car. They each shook his hand. "Take care of our sister," Brian said.

"I fully intend to," Beckham said.

They nodded in some unspoken agreement. Then she and Beckham got into the car and were driving away. She swiveled in her seat and watched her brothers as she left the Warehouse District behind all over again.

CHAPTER THIRTY

When her brothers were finally out of her line of vision, she plopped back down in her seat and tugged her baseball cap off of her head. "How much of that did you hear?" she asked.

He gave her a pointed look, and she nodded.

"Right. All of it."

"They love you," Beckham said.

"Yes, they do. Very much so."

"You could have stayed."

She shook her head. "You and I both know that isn't true."

"They wanted you to."

"And a part of me still wants to be with them," she admitted. "But I want to see where this goes, Becks. It's not an easy road, but it's one that I'm willing to travel with you."

He reached for her hand, and they laced their fingers together. It was nice and made her sigh. Everything wasn't right with the world, but the here and now was too wonderful not to relish in.

Beckham was staring at her, not saying anything. He wasn't even looking at his phone. She had become so accustomed to the thing glued to his face that she wasn't sure what to make of it.

"Nothing urgent or pressing?" she asked.

"No."

"No text messages you need to send? Emails you need to reply to? Charts you need to look at?"

He smirked. "No."

"I thought it would be a busy day after what happened."

"It might be," he acknowledged.

"I'm not complaining, but normally you're kind of attached to your phone." It was almost a little bit disconcerting to have the full weight of his gaze on her.

"Did you never ascertain that *you* were the reason I was always plugged in?"

Reyna cleared her throat and looked anywhere but at his penetrating gaze. "I mean, I didn't think that was the sole reason," she volunteered. "I figured you were busy?"

He laughed, and it had a lightness she had never heard before. "Sure. I'm busy. All the time. But when you're in the car with me, I can't concentrate. I get nothing done. All I could think about was this," he said, grasping the back of her head and pulling her in for a fierce kiss.

She practically climbed into his lap she was so ready to have his lips on her. She didn't care that she was in ratty jeans and a T-shirt while he was in a two-thousand-dollar suit. All she wanted was to feel him again, feel him as *hers* for the first time. God, she couldn't wait to get him home. She was going to finally get to rip off this damn suit and find out *exactly* what was underneath it.

"Reyna," he groaned. He bit her lip lightly and dragged it between his teeth. She arched her back and pressed her pelvis down onto him.

"Mmm?" she moaned.

"I need to talk to you. I have things I need to tell you," he said, his hands doing all the talking for him.

"It can wait," she assured him.

All talking could wait. He had said that he was going to tell Penelope he wanted to be with Reyna, and that was good enough for now. He had chosen, and he had chosen her. She wasn't sure she could wait until they got home to get her hands on him.

"Reyna, please," he groaned as she fumbled with his tie.

She silenced him with a kiss and then yanked the tie off of him. Then she began undoing all of the little buttons of his shirt. He stopped protesting at that point. He couldn't win against her when all of his barriers had been shattered. His hands pushed the soft cotton of her shirt up and over her head. A thin lacy bra covered her breasts, and he cupped both of them in his hands, flicking a finger inside to caress one nipple.

She moaned and grabbed onto his chest for support against the pleasure coursing through her body. She circled her hips on top of him, desperate for the passion that had been building between them to finally come to fruition. Her hands tugged on the belt he was wearing, unfastened the buckle, and then unsnapped the button of his trousers.

"Beckham, take me here," she pleaded against his mouth. "I don't care where we are. I just want you."

He growled deep in the back of his throat and then threw her down roughly onto the seat. His tall frame had difficulty adjusting to the cramped space, but his body covered her and his hands were everywhere. She threw her head back, and he kissed down her throat in a heated desperation. Her legs came up to circle around his waist, drawing him closer.

In the silence that followed, the buzzing of his phone was as clear as day. "Ignore it," she pleaded, running her hands down his jaw.

"Let me turn it off." He reached into the inner pocket of his suit jacket and retrieved the phone. His brow furrowed when he checked the screen. "Hmm…"

"Hmm good or hmm bad?" she asked. She was anxious to get back to business.

"It's Roland."

Reyna cringed away from the name. After what had happened with Roland in the club, just the mention of him made her body shudder with revulsion.

"I have to take this." He gave her an apologetic look and sat up. He didn't want to talk to Roland any more than she did, especially not under the circumstances.

Recess was over.

She righted herself in the car and reached for her T-shirt on the floor.

"Hello?" Beckham said gruffly into the phone.

Beckham listened as Roland said something into his ear.

"Yes," he responded after a minute. "Today?"

He pulled his sleeve back to check the time.

"That's in half an hour."

Roland was clearly saying something that Beckham didn't agree with, because his face was growing darker and darker. All traces of the fun, sexy Becks who had been seducing her in the back seat of the car evaporated.

"I understand."

He hung up the phone, clearly aggravated, and tapped on the console that let him speak to the driver. "Change of plans. Head to the city hall building downtown."

"Yes, sir."

"What happened?" she asked.

He carefully rearranged his suit, buttoned his shirt up, and retied the knot at his neck before getting under control enough to answer.

"He didn't say exactly. Purposefully vague. Just that I needed to get to city hall. That I wouldn't want to miss what was about to happen."

Reyna swallowed, hating all of this. "Why do I feel like we're playing into his hands by going?"

"Because we are," he admitted reluctantly, "but I see no alternative."

She hated bringing this up, but they were going to the building where the mayor was. "Do you think this has anything to do with Penelope?"

Beckham shook his head. "I doubt it. I would have heard if her condition had changed. She was stable when I left. This sounded personal."

Reyna frowned. "Personal how?"

"He asked me to bring you."

"What does that mean?" she demanded. She did not want to see Roland. If she had to face him down eventually, she would. She wouldn't cower, but she had hoped that time would come in a distant future, not today.

"I guess we'll find out once we get there." He took her hand in his and kissed the top softly. "Don't worry. I won't let anything happen to you."

They made it to about a mile from the city hall building before their car was stopped in bumper-to-bumper traffic. People filled the streets for as far as the eye could see toward the main intersection.

"What the hell?" Reyna said, craning to see what all the traffic was from.

"This will do for now. We'll have to go on foot the rest of the way."

Beckham told their driver their plans, and then they hopped out of the town car into the middle of the gridlocked intersection. They jogged over to the sidewalk and past the people mingling around the road in confusion. Reyna was glad that she wasn't in some ridiculous high heels in that moment. If she didn't have her Converse on, she never would have been able to keep up with Beckham. As it was, she still lagged behind.

He reached back for her, and after another ten minutes, they finally made it in front of city hall. Reyna leaned over to a couple who were chatting animatedly.

"Excuse me. What's going on?" she asked.

The woman glanced worriedly at Beckham before saying, "The mayor is about to make a big announcement. We're finally going to get the change we needed. After those horrible fires and all the unnecessary death, we are so eager for what the mayor is going to be heralding in with these policies."

"What policies?" Reyna asked, astounded. She had only been gone a couple of days. How could all of this have passed so quickly? What was the media saying that was convincing these people that it was a good idea?

"Human and vampire equality, of course."

"Of course," Reyna deadpanned. She looked up at Beckham as the couple disappeared into the crowd. "I don't like this. Something seems wrong."

He nodded. "I can feel it, too."

"You didn't hear anything about this?"

"No. That's what worries me."

Reyna and Beckham pressed in closer to the city hall. A stage had been erected in front of the building, with a podium and a row of chairs on it. Even with Beckham's height and bulk, they could only get so far into the crowd before it was impossible to move forward. Reyna couldn't see a thing. Not that she really would have been able to see much at this distance anyway. But Beckham could see to the stage with his enhanced sight.

The crowd was bustling with activity. Everyone was excited to hear what the mayor was going to say and had their own opinion about what they thought that meant. All Reyna knew was that whatever the big announcement was, it couldn't be good.

A group of people walked out on the stage in a single-file line and took their seats. As a man approached the podium, the audience quieted down.

"Welcome," the man called into the microphone.

"Harrington is seated to the left of the speaker," Beckham whispered down to Reyna.

"Do you think this has something to do with Visage?"

He pressed his lips firmly together. She could tell it was killing him not to be in the know. As a senior official, he should have been informed of what was about to happen, especially if it had something to do with Visage.

"Stick close to me." He pulled her closer to his body and reached for her hand. "There are too many people out right now, and I don't want us to get separated."

"Thank you all for coming this afternoon. It is my pleasure to introduce our very own Mayor Sky."

As the mayor stepped up to the microphone, the audience broke into applause. He was well-liked and had been elected over and over and over again by the people. Reyna didn't really feel like he had ever helped. While she felt bad for Penelope's situation, she and her father were both beyond wealthy in a world where the poor were quite literally starving. Living on the inside with Beckham had really shown her the difference, and if she had the chance, she would vote him out of office in a heartbeat. Though there would never truly be a better alternative in today's environment.

The mayor waited for the immense crowd to quiet down again before speaking.

"Welcome." His voice boomed. "It is both sad and troubling, the circumstances in which I stand before you today. Our city has endured a great tragedy this weekend. I've spent my time meeting with the family of the victims of the underground fires, my daughter among them. It is with a heavy heart that your city government and I have had to come up with a drastic solution in these trying times."

He paused for effect to let his words sink in. Reyna held her breath as she waited to find out where he was going with this.

"Henceforth, all illicit activity will be severely cracked down upon for both humans and vampires. Many have let the animosity between our races drive them to violence. No matter the measures we have already put in place, more death and destruction befall the people of our city than ever before. The fires are the tipping point to a horrible plague. My own daughter was burned."

Reyna clutched Beckham's hand tighter at the mention of Penelope. His face was drawn, and she wished she could make his worries go away.

"Your brothers and sisters dead. We need to come together as one and stamp out the evil in this world. That should be our ultimate goal, and it was the goal in crafting this legislation. Today, I bring you a new plan to remedy the rising crime. The government must take responsibility for what has gone on, and today is the beginning of a new era!"

Beckham and Reyna glanced at each other. She couldn't tell what he was thinking behind his dark eyes, but hastily drawn legislation couldn't have been well thought out. Nor did she assume that meant it was truly benefiting everyone.

"Your legislators have passed a sweeping anti-crime bill that I have signed into law in response to the rapid increase in deaths within our city limits. As a result, we are immediately initiating these measures:

"First, our city has decided to commence the Blood Census starting tomorrow morning at locations all over the city, including city hall."

"What?" Reyna said. "I thought that wasn't supposed to happen for a few months."

"Looks like they're in a hurry to get it started," Beckham responded stiffly.

"Our city is thrilled to be the first in the country to herald in this new program. Each of you will be assigned a location to register in the city, and everyone must be tested for their blood type within a month. We want this to happen as quickly and seamlessly as possible, so we can report back all test results to the federal government and complete the national crisis database. Anyone who fails to complete the test will be heavily fined."

The crowd rumbled with speculation. Some were outraged that they were being forced to participate in this. Others were frustrated that a blood type database was even necessary. Many of them mirrored Reyna's own sentiment about the existence of a Blood Census. It could mean only one thing: Visage was in the government.

"Additionally, all Census sites will be equipped with these." The mayor held up a small band in his hand. "They are bracelets issued by the city, programmed with your identification information. All officers will be issued band scanners to verify your identity."

The rumble turned into a roar. It was enough that everyone had an ID card, but it definitely wasn't mandatory. And now they were taking it a step forward with these mandatory ID bands. What else would the government force on them?

"These must be worn at all times as proof that you are registered with the state and have passed your blood test. Anyone caught after the deadline for the Census without an ID band will be arrested and fined. We hope these new identifiers will help check crime in the city. After all, our mission is to make your city and the city where your family and friends live a safer place."

Reyna realized she was shaking. How dare they do this? Who the hell did they think they were that they could pass sweeping legislation like this without hearing what the citizens thought? She wasn't a prisoner to the system. She believed in change, but she didn't believe that they were going about it the right way at all.

The mayor continued despite the growing unease. "Finally, we are enforcing a mandatory curfew within the city limits."

"What?" she cried along with everyone else. "Curfew."

"Reyna," Beckham growled, pulling her closer. "We need to get out of here. This doesn't look good."

"We can't leave. We have to voice our opinion. We have to tell them that this is wrong. They can't do this."

"They can and they are. We don't need to get caught in the middle of it."

"Maybe if more people were willing to get caught in the middle, something would have been done *long* before they enacted these rules."

"I agree," he said. "But right now, my thought is for getting you out of here before everyone gets crushed under a stampede."

"Fine." She couldn't change his mind, and even less so the

government's mind. But she wanted to. She desperately wanted to.

The mayor droned on as Beckham clutched her hand and veered through the crowd pressing in on all sides.

"Only night workers will be able to go out after curfew, and they must have a permit that allows it. I hate the thought of shutting down our city after midnight, but we feel at this time it's necessary for peace."

"Freedom. Freedom. Freedom!"

The chant started up in the crowd. The people heaved forward toward the podium, and Reyna's hand was wrenched from Beckham's.

"Beckham!" she screamed over the crowd.

CHAPTER THIRTY-ONE

Reyna searched for Beckham in the crowd, but she was carried away by the mob. He was gone. He was lost. She couldn't believe this. She should have listened to him. They should have gotten out earlier.

"This is further proof that these measures are necessary," the mayor called.

Gunshots rang out in the crowd, and everything happened at once. People were yelling and running and crushing together. Some were trying to storm the stage, but the police were holding everyone back. All were quickly ushered offstage at the sound of the gunshots.

In the middle of the madness, the only thing she could think about was Beckham. She searched frantically for him. He was so tall that he should have been visible. But she couldn't find him. She looked over her shoulder as she was pushed in the opposite direction.

Her feet couldn't keep up with her, and she tripped, landing heavily on her hands and knees. Several people stepped on her as they rushed forward to fill her vacated spot. Someone kicked her face, and she saw stars. She cried out and tried to stand but kept being shoved back down to the ground. Finally, she lay there in a ball, trying to stay as small as possible as chaos erupted all around her.

Tears leaked out of her eyes as she lay on the dirty ground, her head throbbing. She couldn't believe this was happening. She had no means of contacting Beckham without her phone, and she didn't even know if she would ever get out of this crowd. It was an endless barrage of people running into her. She couldn't seem to escape.

An arm reached down out of the abyss and hauled her up by her shoulder. Reyna grunted as her shoulder popped with strain. She stared up into the eyes of a female vampire.

"You smell amazing," she growled. She reached out with her finger and touched it to Reyna's forehead. Reyna cringed away from the pain as she realized she was bleeding.

"Let go of me," Reyna cried, trying to pull free.

The woman ignored her plea and placed her finger in her mouth. She sucked on it, and her eyes grew ravenous. The vampire flashed her fangs at Reyna.

"This won't hurt a bit."

"You're out of your mind." Reyna clawed at her, but she might as well have been trying to move a mountain, for all the good it did.

"Stay still," she snapped.

"Get away from her," Reyna heard behind her. She sighed with relief. Beckham. "She's *mine*."

The woman glanced over Reyna's shoulder and then released her. It was clear that even in the midst of all the madness going on around them, fighting with a senior official of Visage would draw attention. Not to mention, there was no way she would win.

"Fine. She's yours. But she does taste amazing."

Beckham glared at her. "You tasted her?"

"Just a drop," she said with a wink.

"Get out of here before I remove your head from your shoulders."

Her eyes widened at the threat, and then she scampered off into the crowd.

"Reyna, I'm so glad you're all right." Beckham pulled her close to him. Her heart was beating fiercely, and in that moment, she was happy that he was there and had stopped the woman before anything terrible had happened.

He inspected the cut on her forehead. "It's minor. Hold this to it." He offered her a handkerchief, because of course he had one, and she held it to her head.

"You found me," she breathed.

"I'll always find you." He kissed the top of her head and then reached down for her hand. "Let's get out of here. I don't want another close encounter."

Beckham tightened his grip on her hand, then shouldered his way through the crowd. It took forever before they finally reached a city block that had thinned out. By then she had a headache. Her clothes were rumpled, and one of her sleeves was torn. Nothing she could do about that right now.

"This way," Beckham said, directing them back toward the center of the city.

"How did you find me?"

"I could smell you," he told her. "Your blood."

"Oh."

She removed the handkerchief and stared down at her own dried blood. The cut had stopped bleeding already. It had been small to begin with, but still that vampire had been able to smell her. Beckham had been able to smell her.

"Here." She offered the handkerchief back to Beckham.

He frowned, taking it from her. "We should burn that."

"Burn it?" she asked. "Beckham, what is going on? That woman had the same reaction to my blood the vampire had outside of the club, but you claimed it didn't smell any different. *Does* it?"

Beckham was silent for a few more blocks. She was starting to wonder if he was going to answer. This was the treatment she was used to having from him, after all. She had known it would be too good to be true for him to start telling her everything like he had promised. He was used to his secrets. Perhaps he had too many to divulge them all.

"Yes," he finally said. "Your blood smells… I don't know. It's hard to describe. Sweet. But not sweet. Powerful and enticing. It draws you in."

"So, I smell like a steak?"

Beckham laughed the most beautiful laugh. "I suppose you do, but a hundred times more desirable."

"Is that uncommon? I mean, doesn't other blood smell good? I don't think all our food smells the same. I really don't know how any of this works."

"It does all smell different. Some is more or less potent. If it's tainted by drugs, alcohol, disease, death, each has its own smell, besides the human pheromones attached to it. But you—" His eyes cut over to her, and she saw hunger written all through them. "You have the most amazing smell in the world. It's alluring and hypnotic. Which is exactly why we need to burn this handkerchief and get you cleaned up. I don't want anyone else to smell you. If they smell you, they will want to taste you."

"But not you?" she asked, thinking of all the times he had smelled her blood and not been tempted.

He inhaled deeply. "I couldn't imagine what you taste like."

Reyna tried to hide her smile but failed. "You could, if you wanted."

"Don't dangle temptations in front of me, Reyna. I have very little control."

She snorted. "I disagree."

"I lost count of the number of lives I took because I succumbed to my nature and didn't want to stop."

"Those two things are really different," she told him. "Before the cure, you didn't want to stop. That was the animal in you. Now you have control in spades, I might add, and you wouldn't do it again. I'd bet you haven't done it since the cure."

He shrugged. "I don't like to take chances. It's easier."

"Well, you're taking a chance with me, and I trust that you won't lose control."

He didn't respond, but he didn't have to. She wasn't frightened, because he wouldn't hurt her. He was doing everything he could to protect her at this point. If he ever drank from her, she was sure he would find this control he claimed to lack.

She was totally lost when Beckham stopped in front of a boarded-up store on a random street corner.

"Come in here."

"In where?" she asked, sizing up the building.

He opened a black gate and gestured her inside. They went up a flight of stairs and into an empty one-bedroom apartment. The only objects inside were a mattress on the floor and a safe in the corner. Beckham pushed Reyna toward the bathroom while he found a lighter in one of the kitchen drawers. He lit the handkerchief on fire and then threw it in a metal trash can on the floor.

Reyna stood there, wide-eyed, wondering if he'd done something like this before. He was so precise. "What is this place?"

He shrugged. "Safe house."

"Safe for who?"

"Right now? You." He rummaged through the medicine cabinet over the toilet.

He tilted her chin up, and she stared into those bottomless onyx eyes, lost to his touch. How gentle he was when he swabbed the cut clean, how precise he was in all of his movements, how much he cared for her pain and discomfort.

When he finished, his eyes found Reyna's. They locked on each other for a split second, understanding passing between them. This was the real Beckham Anderson. This man was hers.

It took all of five minutes from the time they busted into the safe house to when they were back on the streets, but everything had changed.

...

A short cab ride later, Reyna and Beckham were standing in front of the enormous skyscraper for the Visage Incorporated headquarters.

They hurried past the polished floors, people clad in pressed suits, and the body scanners at a fast clip. This place was terrifying in and of itself, but add in the fact that she was about to meet with the most powerful vampire in the company, and it was all the scarier. But she kept her chin up and stuck close to Beckham.

"What exactly are we walking into?" Reyna asked once they were safely out of earshot.

"Well, I have to find out why I wasn't informed of everything going on. In particular, I want to set Roland straight about goading me. He knew what this was about, and he knew what the crowd would look like."

"I don't understand what his motives are. Aren't you working toward the same goal for the company?"

She despised Roland, but he was cunning. He had planned for Penelope to show up that night of the fire in the hopes of getting Reyna alone. And he had planned for Beckham to get caught up in the crowd today. There was more to the big picture than what they were glimpsing.

"Obviously, this is personal. He's upset because I got the better of him in the club...probably because you turned him down."

They stepped into the elevators, and the doors closed behind them.

"Well, he was out of line and deserved everything that happened to him."

Beckham turned toward Reyna and cupped her cheeks in his hands. "You know I agree with you, but you're going to have to stay very tightly coiled through all of this. You can't react to anything. He's made it personal, but you have to stay professional even when you don't want to. He will be expecting you to act out."

"Becks, we need to get out in the open so we can move forward."

"That isn't the way this works. It's politics. You'll have to trust me. Do you trust me?" he asked. His eyes pleaded with her, but she wasn't sure if he wanted her to agree or disagree. It showed how much he was still warring with himself.

"Of course I trust you."

He nodded, kissed her once on the lips, and then released her just before the doors opened. She took a deep breath, allowing the feel of his lips to give her strength to move forward. She could do this.

They walked through glass double doors, and a receptionist awaited them. "Hello, Mr. Anderson."

"I need to speak with Harrington," Beckham said. "Is he in?"

"Yes. He arrived back in his office. I'll let him know you're here." The woman picked up the phone and pressed a button. "Yes. Mr. Harrington, Mr. Anderson is here to see you." She waited a second with a demure smile on her face. "Of course." She hung up the phone. "He will see you now."

"Thank you," Beckham said courteously.

Reyna followed Beckham into Harrington's massive corner office, straight into the lion's den. Seated behind a hulking desk was the frail, waxy leader of the vampire world and CEO of Visage. Harrington greeted Beckham with a smile, which would have been more reassuring if Roland and Cassandra weren't likewise seated to either side of him.

She drew up short, not wanting to get any closer to the intimidating trio. Beckham stood two steps ahead of her, and she tried to remember to heed his advice.

"Hello, Beckham," Harrington said.

"Harrington," Beckham acknowledged.

Harrington steepled his fingers in front of him and leaned forward slightly in his chair. "I'm glad you're here. How fares your dear Penelope?"

"She's stable, but she will never be the same. She will begin reconstructive surgery on her face as soon as she is able. The mayor has already said he will take every measure."

"How unfortunate," Harrington said.

"Yes," Cassandra agreed. "We always love a pretty face."

Beckham bristled at the trite tone and the implied meaning that they liked their food to be pretty. "Yes, it is very unfortunate, but we're all glad that she is alive."

"Undoubtedly."

Until now, Roland had remained silent, but Reyna felt his gaze on her. She refused to make eye contact with him. She would not give in to his ruthless and ridiculous behavior.

"At least Reyna wasn't harmed," Roland spoke up finally.

"Yes. Luckily, we were outside before the fires began," Beckham said, staring Roland down hard.

"I wouldn't exactly say she wasn't harmed," Cassandra singsonged. She sniffed and turned her nose up. "She looks as if she has rolled around in the dirt, and honestly, what is that outfit?"

"We were in the midst of the crowd at city hall," Beckham said as explanation.

Reyna should have known someone would say something about her state of dress. They were so bent on dressing their Permanent subjects up like dolls. The whole thing sat with her wrong. At least Beckham didn't try to justify anything. He gave a reason for her state of dress and nothing more.

"So, you did make it," Roland said, seemingly pleased with himself.

Beckham didn't bat an eyelash. "That was a brilliant performance out there. It's nice to know we're finally getting somewhere with the government."

Reyna reined in her frustration. This was politics, but it was the opposite of how she felt about the situation. Granted, she didn't know how Beckham felt about the whole thing. She couldn't believe that he would be okay with it all. He hadn't *seemed* okay with it, anyway.

"I told you he would think so," Harrington said to Roland.

"Why wouldn't I?" Beckham asked. "It's exactly what we wanted. Glad the fires made it so you could push it through."

"Indeed," Harrington said. "Unfortunately, we have some unpleasant news to discuss now that you're here."

"What unpleasant news?"

"I knew you were busy with Penelope this weekend, which is why we didn't include you in the discussions ahead of time, but you should know, Beckham, I trust you implicitly," Harrington said.

Beckham tensed. "As you should."

"However," Harrington said, "we cannot overlook Reyna."

"Me?" she asked, confused.

Beckham gave her a fierce look, and she clamped her mouth shut.

"What unpleasantness is there regarding Reyna?"

"Show him," Harrington directed.

Roland reached down and retrieved a large black camera out of a bag. "Can you explain this?"

"That's my camera," she said. She couldn't help herself. How had he gotten her camera?

"Well, there's her admission," Roland drawled.

"Admission?" she asked. "Admission to what?"

Beckham placed his hand on her arm. "For what, exactly? What is she being accused of?"

"Isn't it obvious?" Roland asked. He stood smoothly from his chair and walked around the desk. He still held the camera in his hand. "She's part of Elle."

"What?" she asked.

They thought she was a rebel.

When was the last time she'd had her camera? It had been a tumultuous weekend, to say the least, and she hadn't had time to work with her images since…the rooftop? No, the park.

Oh, Roland had filched the camera from her when they had left the restaurant for lunch. That was the only explanation. She was certain that she had removed all the images from her camera that were on her website. Nothing on there should have connected them to her or incriminated her.

"She's been feeding the rebels information about us since she arrived. She's a plant."

"That's absurd," Reyna said.

"I'd have to agree with Reyna," Beckham said, sticking up for her. "I'm with her all the time. I've even been with her while she's been out shooting. What images make you think she's part of Elle?"

"The images themselves don't show rebel activity," Roland said carefully. "However, the style of the pictures taken match an Elle website we've been monitoring."

"The one that has been causing all the trouble in the news? *Perspective*?" Beckham asked.

"Yes," Roland said.

"And you're sure they match them. You have exact matches?" Beckham asked.

"Stylistically, yes."

She couldn't hold back any longer. Even if the images were hers, there was no way she was going down as a rebel. She could be a voice without being part of the Elle alliance.

"My images are my own. They're not on some website. If there's no exact matches between them, then you have nothing but speculation."

Roland glared at her, but it was Cassandra who spoke up. She furiously stood. "How dare you speak to us like that."

"Cassie," Beckham said soothingly.

"There is more proof, Beckham. Felix confirmed that she was one of the Elle rebels. He said he had been in contact with her about the organization."

Reyna's mouth dropped open. Felix had told them that she was an Elle contact? If Felix was a rebel, then he was likely a horrible one. The only time she hadn't seen him look completely drugged was at their very first introduction.

Beckham stood very still. He refused to look at her. "And where is Felix now to give this testimony?"

Cassandra glanced away from him. "He's no longer with us."

"He died in the fires," Harrington confirmed.

Reyna gasped softly. She couldn't believe he was one of the ones who had died. She didn't even really know him, and it was a tragedy.

"And when did he tell you this?" Beckham probed.

"Before he died."

"So, we're supposed to believe the word of a dead man?"

"What more proof would you like before you believe that she is working against us?" Roland demanded.

Beckham was pissed. She could see it all over his face. He knew what was happening. Roland was upset and had worked against him to get rid of Reyna. Perhaps he would even try to claim her as the prize. No, they couldn't allow this.

"So, by questioning Reyna's allegiance, are you also questioning *my* allegiance?" he growled.

"I already said I trust you, Beckham," Harrington said. The old man looked as if he wanted Beckham to believe him, but there was something hard and fierce in his eyes that said he would burn everyone to the ground before letting them beat him.

"I've done nothing but serve Visage and the company's interests faithfully for *years*. I was one of the loudest voices for Visage in the early years. I helped the company get on its feet during the trying times of the initial wave of blood type matches. I've done everything for you, and now this?" he asked. "I vouch for Reyna, and since when is my word questioned?"

"I don't question your loyalty, Beckham," Harrington said. "You know I think of you as a son. You've proven yourself, but the evidence is incriminating and I won't take the chance."

Beckham laughed humorlessly. "A few pictures that you think match a website yet unconfirmed as an Elle sympathizer let alone part of Elle itself. *No* matching images, and I was *there* when they were all taken. Plus, the word of a dead man that Cassandra probably drained for fun."

Cassandra looked indignant, but Reyna could see he had struck a chord.

"Don't try to deny it," Beckham said. "We all know it's not the first time."

Cassandra shrugged her lithe shoulders and sat back down demurely.

"Your evidence is circumstantial at best. Let's lay it out there and say what all this is really about. Roland is pissed that I kept him from Reyna at the Vault and then beat him at his own game. He thought he could get back at me through Reyna, through this ruse, and he used *you*, Harrington, to do it. Let's discuss his actions if we're going to throw out accusations."

Roland's eyes blazed. She could see that he was losing ground with Beckham's speech. "I would never come forth without a real belief that she has been working against us."

"You're a liar and a cheat," Beckham said. "You wanted to sleep with her and you wanted to drink from her, but she's not your Permanent. She's not a fucking toy or a goddamn pet. She's a human being, and she's *mine*."

Everyone in the room was silent after Beckham's declaration. Reyna's heart was beating wildly in her chest. He had just defended her to everyone.

"Roland, is all of this true?" Harrington finally asked. Roland's silence was answer enough. "I don't want fighting within my upper rank. We should be pleased with the results of today, not bickering over a human. Unless you can bring forward more evidence, I'll have to defer to Beckham's judgment, as I always do. I want to find a matching blood type and get my full strength back. Then we can really move forward with our plans."

Harrington gave Reyna a deadly look, and it took everything in her to hold that gaze. Even though she was safe for now, fear clawed at her.

CHAPTER THIRTY-TWO

Reyna and Beckham left Harrington's office. Reyna had her camera back in hand. She had retrieved it from a sullen Roland. The look on his face told her that this wasn't over.

They made it down the elevators and back outside in complete silence. Reyna held the camera close to her chest as Beckham's driver appeared. She stepped inside first, and Beckham followed. The car started on the familiar drive back to Beckham's penthouse, and Reyna released a big breath.

"That was awful," she whispered.

Beckham nodded tensely. "It could have been so much worse."

She agreed with that. Harrington's trust of Beckham went so deep that he had let them go—though she was sure he was going to have them both watched more closely. She couldn't gallivant around at night anymore. Not that she was going to break the new curfew anyway.

Reyna felt as if she were coming down from a buzz. After the rally, the near-death encounter, and the accusations at Visage, she was drained. The only good part was that Beckham had chosen her and now they were going back to his place together as a couple. It almost made everything else worth it.

Once they made it to his penthouse, Reyna finally let herself think about what this meant going forward. She was here now not as an employee or an investment. He wanted her here. They had made it. Now what?

"How are you feeling?" Beckham asked cautiously.

"Shaken up," she admitted, "but I'm okay."

"I'm sorry that Roland dragged you through all of that. I should have been paying more attention from the start. Then I would have noticed what his endgame was."

"It's really my fault. I should have told you when Roland was advancing on me. Then we wouldn't be here and they never would have taken my camera." She sighed and rubbed her eyes with the palms of her hands. "I can't believe he stole it at the restaurant and I didn't even know."

"You were angry at me. It's not your fault that he was trying to blame you," Beckham told her.

"Well, I guess I should delete the website. It's too risky at this point." The thought of deleting it made her sick. She had put so much time and energy into that thing. The pictures would still be on her computer, but it was different. It didn't seem to have as much life to her.

"No," he said automatically. He reached forward and cupped her cheek. "If you delete it now, they'll know that it was your website. I don't want to do anything that might draw their attention. For now, the images are safe where they are. I programmed them so they are practically impenetrable."

"Oh. Right. That makes sense."

"You know I agree with your images, right?" he asked. His dark eyes were saying so much more than his words in that moment. She stopped fidgeting and got lost in their depths.

"You agree with them?" she whispered.

"Their message. I agree with the message you were trying to send. That there are people out there who need help. That equality is possible. We need to tackle the core issue of prejudice. That the rich sit on high when there are those that suffer. That was what I tried to capture in my work, too." He gestured to the framed pictures on the walls of the penthouse. "I could only hang these, but I think you can still see the influence in them."

"These are yours?" she asked in disbelief. "I admired them the first day I came here."

"I know. It's what made me think to give you the camera. No one notices the pictures. You have an eye for it."

"Thank you. Your images really are amazing."

"I appreciate that."

Beckham watched her closely as she examined the pictures again and tried to detect the hidden meaning. What was he thinking when he was shooting landscapes? Who was the woman in the café?

"I agree with you about everything. How people deserve to be treated. The direction our world is headed. How we need to do more to correct the problem, not rely on a path of dependence that is spiraling out of control."

Reyna smiled. It was nice to finally hear someone agree with her. It was wrong that ninety-plus percent of people lived in poverty and that the top one percent owned and controlled everything.

"Be careful," she teased. "They might accuse *you* of being part of Elle."

"I know. It's why I'm very careful."

Reyna paused. "Wait, what?"

He gave her a pointed look, and her mouth dropped open. What was Beckham trying to say here? Had he just said what she thought he'd said? No, no way. That couldn't be right. It made no sense, but she had to ask it anyway.

"You're a...rebel?"

"Yes."

Reyna felt her world tilt upside down. Everything from her time living with Beckham was a lie. He was part of Elle. He disagreed with everything he was doing working for Visage. How was that even possible? How could he keep up the double life? And at that, how was he so damn good at it?

She never in a million years would have guessed that Beckham had ties to the people who wanted to stop Visage's infinite growth.

"How?" she stammered.

Beckham gestured for her to take a seat on the couch and began to tell his story. "I decided a year ago that I couldn't sit back and let the world keep heading down this path. It was destructive for both humans and vampires. If Visage takes over the world, subjugates humans, reverts back to animals, then what? There is nothing left? Humans will die, and thus vampires will die. There is a balance in this world, and we need to find a way to achieve it. So, I set out to find a way to help in secret."

Reyna found it all hard to process. "But you staked your entire reputation on me in Harrington's office. What if they suspected?"

"No one suspects, and I did it because I knew it would work. Only a few Elle members even know that I work with them. And now you," he said.

"Then why are you telling me?"

He smirked. "No more secrets, right?"

"Right." She had already forgotten. "So, how did you get involved?"

"Penny, actually."

"Wait," Reyna snapped. "Penelope is in Elle?"

Beckham cringed. "Yes, she is. She has been my cover this whole time."

Reyna pitched forward in her seat. "You weren't dating Penelope?"

"No," he admitted sheepishly. "But I had to maintain appearances so that I had an excuse to go to meetings. I'm afraid they want me to continue to do just that."

"Wait, back up. You aren't with Penelope?"

Beckham reached out for her and planted a soft kiss on her lips in response. "No. Isn't it obvious? I only want to be with you."

Reyna felt her head spin at his declaration. She couldn't comprehend all this new information at once. First, Beckham and Penelope were never even an item, and now…now, he wanted her and only her. Reyna's breath came out in soft sputters, and her eyes rounded.

"It's okay," he said. "You don't have to say anything back. I've lived longer than you. I know that I've never felt this way about anyone."

"Oh, Becks, I left my family to be with you," she said with a sigh. "Of course I want to be with you."

His smile was spectacular. It was a smile that could block out the sun with its radiance. He had doubted her feelings for him even though she had been the one to push him toward it all along. She hadn't been sure of her own feelings until she had said the words to him. All this time, he had been pushing her away and she had been denying her true affections. Now with it out in the open between them, it felt absolutely right.

Their lips crashed together, desperate to feel the other's touch. None of the reluctance that she normally felt in his kiss was there. It was primal and addicting. This was all she wanted, all she had ever wanted. Beckham was hers.

He seemed to have the same idea as he hoisted her into his arms and carried her across the room. A dim light at the back of her mind realized that he was taking her into his bedroom, a place where she had been expressly forbidden.

Her heart soared with the barriers that had been cleaved this evening. He had been true to his word about her seeing only the man from the rooftop. She had been hesitant about it before, but now he truly trusted her with his deepest, darkest secret. A secret that both shocked and thrilled her.

Beckham pushed open the door to his bedroom, and Reyna stared in awe. His room was more like a wing of a house. It was all glass everywhere, and it was clear that this side of the penthouse had been redesigned to his specifications. There was a separate room to the left for his home office and a sprawling bathroom next to a massive walk-in closet full of expensive designer suits and ties. His room faced the city, and he had the most spectacular view, with a large open patio balcony. In the center of the room, where she couldn't keep her eyes from being drawn, was a colossal all-white king-size bed.

"Wow," she breathed, taking it all in.

Beckham laid her body out on his bed and ran his hands down her sides. "Welcome to my sanctuary."

"Why do you never let anyone in here?"

He lifted her shirt and kissed his way from her stomach upward, dragging her shirt over her head. "I like my privacy."

"Says the man with an all-glass view."

"Who lives on the top floor."

"True. Well, I think it's beautiful."

He leaned down and claimed her lips. "It's yours."

Their kiss was explosive. So much pent-up energy from the month came crashing down all at once. And it took everything in her not to rush him. She was desperate to feel him and know that he was hers and no one else's. It wasn't enough to know it in her mind. She wanted to feel it with her body and connect their souls.

She had never known anyone like this. All-consuming. The very thought of leaving him had been horrible. The idea that he didn't want her…even worse. Now she was here and their lips were pressed together and everything was right in the world.

Reyna forced his suit jacket off of his broad shoulders, and it dropped heavily onto the floor below them. He sat up, wrenched the tie from around his neck, and tore his shirt open. Buttons pinged against the wall as his impatience won out. She reached forward and ran her nails down the front of his chest.

He was perfection. Toned and tight with the muscular physique of a god. She was used to the men back in the warehouses, and not one of them held a candle to Beckham.

"God, I've wanted to do this for so long," he groaned as he flicked open the button of her jeans and dragged them off of her legs. "You have no idea how difficult it was when you came out dressed in nothing but lingerie."

He reached for her leg and kissed up her calf. He hit her knee and let her leg rest on his shoulder as he trailed his lips along her inner thigh. Once he touched her underwear, she squirmed underneath him, ready for him to take her again, but he didn't oblige her as he worked his lips down the other leg.

"Becks," she moaned. "You weren't the only one who found it hard to hold out. I was practically throwing myself at you."

"Oh yes, I remember."

He pulled her down roughly until her ass was resting on the end of the bed. Then he buried his face in her crotch.

"This in particular," he said, breathing hot against her underwear and moving to flick his tongue over the vein in her leg.

Her moans grew louder, and she wasn't sure she was going to be able to wait any longer. "Taste me. I know you want to." Beckham tensed, but she met his eyes. "I trust you."

"I don't trust myself."

"Please," she begged. She wasn't above begging for anything at this point.

She felt the smallest prick at her inner thigh, and then a flood of endorphins rushed her body. She shuddered. All of the blood flowed through her system, and everything was a total rush. Lying on the bed staring at the ceiling was a high. The feel of his coarse hands on her legs made her ache all over for him. Her head was both fuzzy and clearer than it had ever been before.

Then Beckham pulled back harshly. He stood a short distance away, breathing heavily and looking like he was torn between devouring her and running out of the room.

"That was heaven," she breathed.

"Reyna, I can't," he stuttered. "It's too dangerous."

She was floating in a sea of desire, and everything felt right with the world. It had only been a couple of seconds, but it had been bliss. She felt herself coming back to reality. The shot of endorphins was wearing off so quickly.

Jesus Christ, no wonder people got addicted to this.

"Is it always this wonderful?" she murmured softly.

He inhaled deeply. "No. It's stronger when it's emotionally charged."

She sat up on her elbows and smiled at him. "Come here."

"It's not safe."

"Then don't bite me."

"What if I can't stop?"

"You will," she told him. "We'll take it slow."

He cleared the distance between them. "The last thing I want is to take this slow."

His lips claimed hers once more with a fiery passion that she matched. With their lips still pressed together, she hurried backward on the bed, grasping his shoulders and drawing him back with her. He covered her body, and she grinded against him. So little clothing remained between them, and she pushed at his pants in earnest. He swiftly followed her command and removed them, and she rushed out of her underwear.

Pressing her legs farther apart, he slipped his fingers down in between her lips and massaged the wetness over her clit. She sighed and tilted her head back. Her body was so sensitive and heightened even from the smallest bite earlier. She could feel how easily her body responded to his touch and how attuned to him she really was.

Suddenly, the head of his cock replaced his fingers, and she arched off the bed, pushing him farther into her. She reached out and grabbed his arm for leverage, but he had other ideas. His hand snatched up her wrists and pushed them over her head. Then his dick thrust deep inside of her. She cried out as he stretched her to full.

Her eyes fluttered open and stared up at the deep, dark orbs. He looked not a bit hesitant. He was all man. Primal. Taking what was his in that moment. She could read it all over his face.

Mine.

Then he pumped in and out, faster and faster. Her body moved in time with him, and even when her heart felt as if it might beat out of her chest, she didn't ask him to stop. This was fierce and rough. Bodies slapping against each other. Heat building between them. Climax waiting on the brink.

Beckham was fucking her, and she loved it. Every minute of it. She poured her heart and soul into each movement.

He leaned forward on his forearms, capturing her lips in a searing kiss. She never wanted this moment to end. But she felt herself so near to her max. And by the way he grunted and fell forward into her neck, he was almost there, too.

"Oh God," she cried. She clenched tight all around him, her body seizing up as waves of pleasure rocked through her.

Then she felt something else. A prick at her neck. Two pricks. Two very distinct pricks.

Beckham shuddered into her body as his orgasm took over him, but his lips stayed glued to her throat. This time, it wasn't a flood. It was a hurricane. A violent rush that knocked the climax she had experienced out of the water. Endorphins took over. Her body didn't just feel fuzzy; it was starting to feel numb. The adrenaline was coursing through her system and attempting to revitalize her, but her fight-or-flight response wasn't working.

She wanted this. She wanted him to keep drinking. She wanted to feel this eternal paradise. She was trapped in the current and forgetting that she even wanted to swim out of it.

Then it was as if Beckham went deeper into her throat. She felt another prick, and it jolted her out of her daze. He wasn't stopping. Shit! He wasn't stopping. He had said it was hard to stop. He had said that he was struggling with it. Why had she tempted him? God, she wanted this, but not like this.

"Beckham," she cried. She slapped him as hard as she could on the shoulder. He didn't move. She screamed his name again and shook him. She didn't know how much he had taken, but if he kept drinking, he would kill her.

She rocked her body around and then screamed at the top of her lungs. The sound of the scream made him wrench his head up to look at her. His eyes were dark and empty. Her blood dripped down his fangs, over his chin, and fell down onto her chest. He was a predator, an animal, and the sight terrified her more than she ever thought it would.

Reyna scrambled away from him and off the bed. She grabbed for her clothes and put them on before she even thought another second about what she was doing.

She was dizzy and delirious. She didn't know what to think. All she knew was that he was going to kill her. He hadn't stopped, and he was going to kill her.

He came back to himself for a split second when he saw her rushing into clothes.

"Reyna?" he said, his voice low and dangerous.

She was shaking from head to toe. "You were going to kill me."

"I wasn't…"

"I trusted you," she whispered, her voice breathy.

She wanted to believe him in that moment, that the monster was gone, that her Beckham was back. She wanted to trust that this was a mistake and all would be right, but how could she forget that he had been feeding off of her like food, like his prey? He hadn't wanted her for anything more than food. She had sworn to herself she trusted him to stop, but he wasn't going to. Only her screams had jolted him back to reality, and even then, the monster was still brimming under the surface.

CHAPTER THIRTY-THREE

Reyna stumbled out of Beckham's room and toward the elevator. She had no plan in mind. Terror pricked at her, and it was the only thing fueling her forward. She was shaky. Her body disagreed with every movement. She felt like she could sleep for days, but the desire to run, run far away kept urging her on.

The elevator door was closing just as she saw Beckham's face appear. He slammed his hand in the slit before the doors closed, and they wrenched back open. She screamed at his appearance. Still completely nude, blood running down his chin and chest. He looked ferocious and deadly.

"Beckham, please," she muttered.

"I wasn't going to hurt you. You have to know," he said.

"I don't know." Her body trembled. "You weren't going to stop. You could have killed me."

"It was a mistake. Reyna, forgive me," he ground out, reaching for her.

She stepped back into the elevator wall and shrank from his touch. "You were right. You are a monster."

Beckham recoiled at that word and removed his hand. They closed on his hurt face, and she heard his fist slam on the closed doors. Her heart rate picked up, and she had to hold on to the railing to keep herself steady.

When the elevator opened, she lurched forward through the lobby. She tottered and floundered until she made it through the glass sliding doors. Some part of her mind realized she was making a spectacle of herself, but she couldn't seem to care.

As she stepped out into the daylight, she blinked back tears from the intense sun. She needed somewhere to go and collect her thoughts. God, this moving thing was horrible. So much of her body was screaming to slow down, but the other part was telling her to run. It made her head throb.

"Reyna," Everett called.

She turned toward the voice and blundered forward into him. "Everett."

He caught her easily. "Hey, are you all right?"

"Yeah, I guess," she slurred.

"You're bleeding." He touched her neck tenderly, and she winced. She hadn't even realized she was still bleeding. Everett's face darkened as he pieced everything together. "Did he do this?"

"Oh," she mumbled. She placed her hand on her throat, and when she pulled it away, it came back red. "Yeah."

"I've never seen you like this," he said softly, concerned. "You're really out of it, Reyna. Does it normally work this way?"

She shrugged and teetered forward. "I don't know."

He furrowed his brow at her answer but let it go. "You look fucked out of your mind. Where the hell were you going in your condition?"

Reyna shrugged again. "Away. I need to think…"

"You're not going to think doped up on a vamp bite. Christ, how much did he take?"

"More than he should have," she said with an uncontrollable giggle.

"Look, we need to get you cleaned up and somewhere where you can come down from this shit. Come with me. My shift is almost over. I can leave now," he told her.

Everett put a comforting arm around her waist and helped her to his Mustang. He ran back to the front to tell his manager that he had to head out early, and then they were zipping through the city. They reached his apartment a short while later. Reyna's head was drooping forward into her chest by the time they arrived. She could barely keep her eyes open. Her mind was muddled as if she was trudging through a swamp.

He unlocked the front door, and she sprawled onto the floor in a heap. She opened her mouth to say something, but she felt herself slipping toward unconsciousness.

"It's okay," she heard someone say to her through the murkiness in her mind. "I've got you."

Then it all went dark.

...

Reyna woke up in a daze. When she reached out, all she felt was some kind of scratchy surface. She opened her eyes and groaned as she hoisted herself into a sitting position. She stared around at her surroundings. It was dark outside, so she couldn't make out much in the room, but she was on a couch in a very strange place. Definitely not Beckham's penthouse.

She placed her head in her hands and tried to remember what the hell had happened. Everything was fuzzy, and she struggled to recall anything. Or where the hell she was.

"You're awake," Everett said, walking into the room.

She glanced up at him and sighed. At least she was in a safe place. "What happened?"

"I hoped you'd tell me."

Reyna shook her head. "I don't know. Why am I here?"

Everett frowned. "You came out of the apartment building high as a kite from a vampire bite, with blood running down your neck. I stanched the blood and put a bandage on for you after you passed out."

She gasped and touched the bandage on her neck. Everything slowly came back to her. The rally, the accusation at Visage, Beckham admitting he was a rebel and that he had used Penelope as a cover story, sex, the bite—

The bite.

"He bit me," she whispered.

"I gathered that much."

"He lost control when we were—" She stopped that sentence and flushed. Sex with Beckham had been incredible. Just thinking about it made her heat up at the remembered feeling of his body on hers.

"Right," Everett said, looking away. "Doesn't he do that all the time? Isn't that your job, after all? I always thought it was supposed to be safe and controlled for Visage employees."

Reyna stared down at the beige carpet and sighed. "That was the first time."

"Doing what? Having sex?" he asked.

She shook her head. "No. Well, yes. That, too. But it was the first time he bit me." She laughed humorlessly. "I guess technically the second time."

"You've been here for a month."

"I know."

"What the hell have you been doing?"

She shrugged. "Nothing. Today was the first day."

She felt weird telling him this. She hadn't told anyone but her brothers that Beckham hadn't ever drank from her. It felt like a secret he liked to keep hidden, so she didn't flaunt it. She had assumed he was drinking from Penelope this whole time, and he probably had been, to quell his cravings. That was probably why he'd bitten her at the Vault in the first place.

"Why wouldn't he drink from you? You're the same blood type, right?"

"Yeah," she agreed. "O negative. I guess he was afraid something like this would happen."

She gestured to her neck, and waves of remorse washed over her. She shouldn't have run out like that. It had been as if she couldn't help it. Her first instinct had been to run, and that was exactly what she had done.

"Did he come after me, by any chance?" she asked softly.

Everett shrugged. "I don't know. We left as soon as you came downstairs."

"He's probably beating himself up right now."

Fuck, the elevator. She was just remembering what had happened. Had she called him a monster? How could she do that? He wasn't a monster. She needed to make this right. She stood on wobbly legs. She was feeling better after sleeping for however long she had been out, but she needed to get back to Beckham now.

"He probably should be."

"No," she disagreed. "I trusted him to not go further, and I told him I trusted him. But he had trouble stopping. He told me ahead of time that my blood smelled too good. That's what the vampire we met in the alley said, too."

"Really?" Everett asked. He furrowed his brow. "I've never heard of that before."

"Yeah. It made it hard for him to stop."

"So, just like that, you're going to go back? After he almost killed you?"

Everett's voice was low and pained. He clearly hated this line of discussion. He wouldn't even look at her. He was staring down at his phone. She could never make him understand.

"He didn't mean any of that," she insisted. "He lost control. He wasn't trying to hurt me. My fight-or-flight reaction kicked in, and I ran without thinking. He followed me to the elevator and said it was a mistake. Now that I've come down from what happened, I know he was right. I actually said some pretty horrible things." She winced as the memory hit her fresh again. A monster. Christ.

"You should stay here a little longer, Reyna," Everett said. His eyes finally met hers, and he looked sad. "I'm not trying to push you, but what you went through was traumatic. Maybe you should give yourself time to heal and process."

Did she need time to process? Sure, having Beckham lose control had been scary. It had made her freak out. But he had said it was a mistake, and she believed him. She had been too freaked out to see beyond her own fear to his sincerity. She shouldn't have let Everett lead her away. She should have gone to the park and then come back a couple of minutes later to discuss what had happened. Instead, she had barely made it inside Everett's apartment before passing out.

"I'm fine," she said finally. She started toward the door, finding her balance along the way.

"You might be," he conceded. "Physically, at least, but that doesn't mean your mind is. I remember my bite. My body recovered, but I was still fucked up in here." He reached out and touched her temple.

"I'm fine," she repeated. "Really. I know Beckham isn't going to hurt me, and I want to let him know that I know that."

"I hate to say this, Reyna. I really do. But have you considered the fact that you have Stockholm syndrome?"

Reyna's mouth dropped open. He thought that she cared for Beckham because she was his prisoner? "I do *not* have Stockholm syndrome."

"Come on. Isn't it worth considering? It's the same kind of situation. He takes you off the streets, gives you everything you could want except your freedom. Then the first time he hurts you, you go running back to your cage, hoping he'll forgive you for leaving and wanting to make sure *he's* okay?"

"No, I'm not considering that." She refused. This was ridiculous. She had left. She had walked out of his apartment. She didn't feel like his prisoner, and she hadn't in a long time.

"He took you in, almost killed you, and now you want to go back without even stopping to think about it?"

Reyna narrowed her eyes. "Beckham isn't a bad guy. He lost control this one time."

"What happens the next time he loses control?" he asked, staring her down. "Do you wind up dead instead of drugged?"

"No. He would never do that."

Reyna crossed her arms. She didn't have to listen to this. All she wanted to do was get back to Beckham. Everett's words were laced with jealousy or prejudice or whatever the hell his problem was. But he didn't know Beckham. He wasn't like all the other vampires she had met. One bad action didn't make him bad.

"I hope you're right." Everett rested his hand on her shoulder comfortingly. "I don't want to argue with you. I want you to be safe. I'm not sure Beckham is going to keep you safe."

"Well, you don't know him."

Reyna pushed his arm away and walked toward the door. His time was up. The panic in his eyes about her leaving wasn't helping anything. She was going to leave whether he thought it was a good idea or not.

Everett stepped in front of her. "Reyna…"

"Take me back to Beckham's or get out of my way."

"You can't leave."

She glared at him. "Like hell I can't."

She pushed past him, but he grabbed her hands in his and shoved her backward. She stumbled a few steps. Her feet nearly left the floor, but she righted herself. Her eyes rose to Everett's. He had pushed her!

"Reyna, I'm sorry. I want you to stop and think about this."

"I appreciate you taking care of me. I do. But I won't let Beckham think I'm angry when I'm not. And you can't stand in my way of doing that."

"I understand," he said. His shoulders slumped, and he looked resolved. "But it's almost curfew."

"Why are you stalling?" she asked.

"Stalling?"

"If you're not stalling, then let me *leave*."

As the words left her mouth, the door burst open. Reyna screamed as a group of men in all black stormed the apartment. Everett lay sprawled on the carpet, but they paid him no mind at all. Two of them rushed straight toward Reyna. She screamed again and ran away from them, but she was both uncoordinated and slow with the aftereffect of the bite still in her system. She fought the guys off, but she had no luck.

"Everett," she cried. Tears streamed down her face in a panic.

One of the guys addressed Everett. "This her?"

He stood smoothly from the floor and dusted off his black shirt. He nodded once. "That's her."

"What the hell? Everett?" she asked, shocked and confused. What the hell was happening? Were they speaking to him? Why were they holding her?

"Reyna, I'm sorry," Everett said softly.

Her arms were jerked behind her and knotted in place with a heavy black cord.

"Everett, please," she pleaded. Tears streamed down her face. She couldn't believe this was happening. "Did you do this? Who are these people? What are they going to do with me?"

He stepped in front of her, and their eyes met. "I regret that you had to be involved, Reyna. But it's for the benefit of everyone."

"What is? Please, no. No. You can't do this. Let me go," she screamed.

"Take her out, guys," Everett said.

Reyna let loose a bloodcurdling scream. It was cut off as one of the guys behind her landed a swift blow to the back of her head. Her mind went hazy again.

"Beckham," she whispered before she blacked out.

CHAPTER THIRTY-FOUR

*D*rip. *Drip. Drip.*
      What was that noise?
      Beep. Beep. Beep.

Reyna took in a shuddering breath, but it made her head pound. Everything made her head hurt. In fact, her whole body ached.

She tilted her head back and rested it on a cushion. Slowly, she dragged her eyes open. It felt like only seconds ago when she'd had to force herself to open her eyes in a strange place, but she was certain she had never been here. Wherever here was.

It was a white room. In fact, it reminded her of the Visage hospital she had first walked into when this nightmare had begun. Her pulse quickened with her anxiety, and the beeping next to her increased in tempo.

Yes. This felt like a hospital.

The beeping was her heartbeat.

The drip…

She glanced over and realized that an IV was hooked into her arm. At least she had been asleep for that. She gagged at the sight of it and turned away. Her fear of needles hadn't abated even with her recent bites.

She forced herself to look back at the IV, and she tried to claw it out of her arm. She doubled over at the sight of the thing. It was too much.

Where the hell was she? Who had taken her? Why was she here? When would she see Beckham again? She had an endless array of questions.

The sound of the door handle turning pulled her from her depressing thoughts. The person who stepped into the room made her start. She never would have guessed.

"Mr. Harrington?" she asked.

She wanted to feel relaxed in his presence, but she remembered the evil glint in his eye. The thirst for power. The need to be in charge. He was a man not to be reckoned with, and she had no idea why she had drawn his attention.

"Hello, my dear."

"What am I doing here? Please, let me go," she stammered.

"Ah, ah, ah. I believe you have something of mine."

She was too stunned to say anything but, "I don't have anything."

"Now, we both know that's not true. Don't we?"

He walked carefully across the room with his slight build and took a seat next to her hospital bed.

"I've no idea what you're talking about," she told him truthfully.

He smiled deviously. "We ran a few tests after Everett reported suspicious activity regarding you when you passed out in his apartment. A remarkable young man, I might add. He told us later that he found it odd that Mr. Anderson never drank your blood when you were a clear blood type match, and even more odd that he couldn't seem to stop. Everything we know about Beckham is that he is a man of control if nothing else."

Reyna was shaking at this point. She didn't know where he was going with this. She had thought it all strange, but she hadn't thought it *important*.

"And so it seems we have our answer. Your blood type was filed incorrectly at the hospital."

"What?" she asked, perplexed.

"You're not O negative. You are much, much rarer than that, my dear sweet Reyna. You are in fact Rh null, and you match *me*."

TO BE CONTINUED

THIRSTY FOR MORE?
TURN THE PAGE TO READ WHAT BECKHAM
THOUGHT OF MEETING REYNA FOR THE FIRST TIME!

BECKHAM

The call came while Beckham was still at the office.

A sigh escaped his lips at the name that appeared in his contacts. Something sufficiently generic, but only he would know who was really calling. Fuck.

He closed his eyes and answered, "Anderson speaking."

"We found it," the voice said, smooth and silky.

"You're sure."

"He just called from the hospital. It popped up into their system only seconds ago. The flag came through. He's already changing her information. Should I give him the go-ahead?"

Beckham hesitated. He knew what this meant. It would upend his life. Change everything. But it was what he was working for, why he was risking his job, lifestyle, and literal life in the upper echelon of Visage.

Plus, it would subdue some other complaints he'd had from Harrington recently. Complaints he could manage, but dissension was another thing. Not when the rebellion hung in the balance.

"Do it," he said with resignation. "Make the match for me."

"Done. Her name is Reyna. Go pick her up."

"Understood."

Beckham hung up and let the silence linger. He'd thought that he would feel more concerned that he was about to betray the only life he ever knew. The vampire world he had reigned over for decades, the friends and colleagues he'd risen up through the ranks with.

He felt mostly annoyed.

He dusted off his button-up, rolled down the sleeves, and slid his arms into his bespoke suit jacket. His assistant appeared frantic as he swept past her with a dismissive, "I'm going out."

Most of his assistants acted that way. They feared him. They had every right to fear him.

"Anderson," Roland called as he passed him on his way to Harrington's office. The obnoxious, meddling vampire leaned against his assistant's desk—a new blond, since he kept going through them like feeder stock. "Give my regard to Penelope."

Beckham waved his hand at the man as he continued down the hallway. He knocked once on Harrington's closed door, ignoring Harrington's own assistant before stepping inside. The vampire seated behind the desk was frail. As frail as a vampire could get. But no one should underestimate him.

He was easily the most fearsome, brilliant man Beckham had ever known. It was why he had followed him out of his blood craze into this new horizon. To the blood cure. Where he was no longer just a savage beast and could retain some of his faculties. It was only when he was in far too deep that he realized his error.

"Beckham," Harrington said with a genial smile. "Come in, my boy."

"I just wanted to stop in to let you know they found a match."

Harrington's eyes lit up. As if he thought that he meant a match for Harrington—the one thing he had been searching for all these long years. And they had...but Beckham was taking her for himself. Protecting her.

"For me," he added as if it were an afterthought.

"I see," Harrington said with a soft sigh. "And?"

"I'm going to collect her. I'll be out of the office the rest of the afternoon."

"Is this a change of heart?"

Beckham smirked. He knew he couldn't lay it on thick. He'd been too opposed to the idea of having Permanent subjects in their homes for Harrington to be fooled by a flip-flop in position. Not only was it going to wreck Beckham's life to have a Permanent subject, but it was certainly going to end up with a lot more people killed by the entitled vampire elite. But he had to give in just a little.

"I can see the appeal," Beckham said. "You know how I am about privacy."

"It will be for the better. Just wait and see."

Beckham nodded. "I believe you, sir."

"We'll have a meeting after you return. Talk it over!"

"As you wish."

Beckham backed out of the office. That was as obsequious as he could manage. He wasn't much for pandering even before he'd been turned. He certainly didn't fucking care for it now.

He exited the Visage building downtown and hopped into an awaiting town car. His driver pulled away without incident, and they were meandering through the heavy midtown traffic. It would take an hour to get to the hospital. A fucking hour.

"The goddamn warehouses," he grumbled.

He spent the hour on his phone, alternating between acquiescence to what he was about to walk into and abject fury. He was caught between a rock and a hard place. And every thought about it made him more and more angry. Yet there wasn't a thing that he could do about it.

He was proverbially fucked.

Visage ran the world. Beckham was a senior executive for the company that employed more people than any other company in the world. They employed them as blood donors. Because of the cure, each vampire was matched with the blood type that they had when they were human. Drinking exclusively that blood reduced vampires' bestiality. They were still animals. Beckham didn't believe they could ever be anything else. But it also let him function in society, hide in plain sight.

And on the other hand, there was Elle. The rebellion that wanted the end of Visage. That believed that the humans who were employed were little more than chattel. They were food. Nothing more. Nothing less. And they all deserved *more.* A voice of reason in the depressing, deafening din that said that Visage would rule all and humans would fall under vampire rule.

He believed them.

Believed in them.

Which was why when they had asked him if they found a match for Harrington, if he would take the person in, he'd said yes. He could protect her, keep her out of reach.

There was no way to delete an entry in the system. If the match was found, then that person would inevitably find their way to Harrington. But they could change that match, and that was what had been done today.

So now, there were multiple problems.

First, he had to agree to terms he'd previously disagreed with Visage on. Giving just an inch more to the company that was determined to take a pound.

Next, he had to take this woman in without letting her know that he was leading a double life. He'd have to live with her in his space and no longer be able to come and go as he pleased. It would fuck up everything.

And finally, the worst of all, he couldn't drink from her. She would be living in his house as the person he was supposed to drink from. She was the wrong blood type, and *she couldn't know that.*

If he fucked up, if he drank from her, then he'd lose himself.

Lose the man he had been building underneath the monster that he knew he was.

"Fuck," he snarled again. "Back to anger I swing."

He threw his phone across the car and put his head in his hands. This was an error. There was a calculated error in here somewhere. He had to figure it out. He had to shore up all possibilities.

Penny.

Maybe Penny would know.

He grasped his phone again and rang his main undercover contact, the woman he had been pretending to have a relationship with.

"Hey, Beckham. Miss me?" she teased. "You want dinner after work?"

Penelope Sky was the mayor's daughter and conveniently Beckham's blood type. That had been the easiest cover he'd ever had. Even if he and Penny didn't exactly agree on the state of their relationship at any given time. Like the fact that it was off.

"I'm on my way to pick up a Permanent blood donor," he said.

Penny breathed out softly. "Really? Unlike you."

She knew what this meant. She'd been in the Elle meeting when it had been discussed.

"Decided to go through with it."

"Well, you can always drink from me if you want."

It sounded flirtatious, but it was a legitimate offer. He wouldn't be able to drink from this person—Reyna. He'd need a backup. He'd need a way to survive. He couldn't be around her starving, either.

"That sounds appealing," he said in lieu of yes.

"Do you know who it is?"

"Her name is Reyna. That's all the information I got from the hospital."

"A girl, then," Penny said, a little petulant.

"Woman," he corrected. "Visage doesn't employ children."

"Yet," she grumbled.

"Penny."

He never could tell if this phone was tapped. He had a burner, but only calling Penny on it was suspicious as well. His entire life was this bullshit facade. He loathed it at every turn.

"Well, tell me what she's like. I'll have to meet her at some point."

"I can't just stash her in the penthouse and leave her there?"

Penny chuckled. "She's a person, Beckham. You should treat her like one."

"Excellent reminder."

The silence stretched. He wanted to say so much more. Wanted her reassurance that he was making the right choices even as he felt all the roads closing to him.

"Call me later," she said. "I want to hear all about it."

"Maybe I'll come to you."

It sounded inviting, but it meant somewhere they couldn't be overheard discussing Elle.

"Looking forward to it."

Beckham hung up, more resigned than ever about what was coming. He would meet this Reyna. He'd stash her in the penthouse. He didn't need a reason to not drink from her. She was his employee. He could do what he wanted.

With that, his driver pulled to the side entrance of the hospital. He stepped out of the car and through the back door. Hospital employees cowered when they saw him. He gave off that impression. A waft of fear that lingered as he past. It was what had made him a lord. It was what had made them worship him.

He reached the door and knocked twice, straightening to his considerable height, which took up much of the doorframe.

The door opened, and Dr. Washington stood in the frame. He nodded his head at the doctor.

"Reyna, allow me to introduce you to your Sponsor. This is Beckham Anderson, senior vice president of Visage Incorporated."

Washington moved out of the way, and the woman stepped off of the hospital bed. He stilled under her dark gaze. She was, on all counts, nothing special. Under a layer of grime, she wore plain jeans and a T-shirt, tennis shoes, and had a baseball cap in her pocket.

No one should have noticed her. And yet, he could do nothing else.

He just stared at her. The pale, angular face that carved out her cheekbones and cut her jawline to a razor's edge. Her lips a full pink pout with a notch in the middle of her bottom lip. Her dark hair was long and lush, falling like a curtain down her back even in a high ponytail. He had no idea what it would look like around her shoulders after a long and thorough wash.

But it was her eyes that first captivated him. A brown so depthless that he felt instantly lost in them. As if they were not a mirror but a portal to another world. She trapped him in that gaze and let him burrow down deep, falling into an alternate timeline where they did not meet like this as Sponsor and subject but as man and woman. As two people on the streets who found each other.

That wasn't reality. She wasn't a portal. Nor a siren.

She was just a woman.

Albeit possibly the most beautiful woman he'd ever seen.

When neither of them said anything, Dr. Washington cleared his throat and continued. "Mr. Anderson, your new subject, Miss Reyna Carpenter."

He still didn't respond. Their staring contest was prolonged, and he couldn't look away. Felt it in his bones that all those other problems he'd been worried about on his way over here meant nothing.

Because it hardly mattered that both of his bosses wanted this or that he couldn't drink from this woman. All that mattered was that he was beyond fucked.

Her scent, her poise, her lifted defiant chin.

As if she wasn't scared of him. As if she could stand there and act as if he did not frighten her, when everyone else in the hospital had recoiled at the sight of him.

No, the worst part was that he wanted her.

He *wanted* her.

"Well," Dr. Washington said uncomfortably, "what do you think?"

He was soooo fucked.

Beckham broke her gaze to turn to the doctor. He had to remain himself. No one could know. They'd put her with someone else. They'd find another way.

He could never have her.

He *would* never have her.

"Yes. Fine," he forced out. "She'll do. I have a car waiting and a meeting to attend. Get her ready to leave immediately."

Her eyebrows hiked up at his cold demeanor.

Good. Look away. Don't show interest. Don't make me hunt you.

"I believe she is ready to leave," the doctor said. "We need your approval signature, and then she can be discharged."

The doctor handed over a piece of paper, and Beckham scrawled his name across the line with a flourish.

"Great. She's mine," Beckham said, relishing the way *mine* slipped off his tongue. "Can we go now?"

"Yes. Yes, of course. Reyna, come along."

Reyna took a step toward him, her insolence still fully on display. Then she leaned over to the doctor, never taking her eyes off Beckham, and asked, "He's not going to hurt me, right?"

His nostrils flared. So she *was* afraid, and she masked it that well. Oh, fuck. He would not just claim her; he would break her.

No. He had to slow himself down.

It had been a long time since he'd broken someone.

Since he'd craved it.

He wasn't that monster anymore. He had to remember who he was. Even if the sight of her made him want to lose all control.

"I am not here to hurt you. You are my employee. I will treat you like an employee," he said, forcing impatience into his voice. "And as my employee, we are in a bit of a hurry, so anything else you might wish to discuss with the doctor will have to wait. If everything is in order, we will leave."

Reyna looked up at him as if she were drowning and he were a life raft. Oh, how he would revel in that look. She might hate him. That was better. For her to hate him. Then he would never get close enough for her to learn about his life. For her to invade anything more than his penthouse.

She was the most dangerous creature he had ever known.

She could ruin *everything*.

And a part of him wondered if he'd enjoy it when she did.

Acknowledgments

Thank you, thank you, thank you for coming on this incredible journey with me. *The Monster and the Last Blood Match* is the book I never compromised on. From day one, I knew exactly who Beckham and Reyna were and how I wanted them to come alive on the page. It's been a hard-fought battle and a decade of love, but they're finally here!

I have so many people to thank for making this happen. First, my agent Kimberly, who fell in love with Beckham and Reyna's story and knew that she could sell it. You've been my champion in this from the start. You never stopped fighting for them. You never gave up. If I have one person in my corner, it's you.

To the team at Red Tower, who loved Graves so much that they never wanted to leave his world. Here's my lovely pre–Monster War story for you. I will never get over the gorgeous cover you created or the way you championed this book. To Tantor, who got the incredible Caitlin Elizabeth to narrate these books. I adore it so very much. And to all the foreign publishers who have translated this series. I'll never forget when I was in Paris and readers couldn't speak the language and were arguing with me over the ending by throwing the end of the book in my face. I see you. I'm not sorry that I love cliffhangers. I promise to make it better…eventually.

And of course to all the authors who helped me from the start and stuck it out for the decade it took for this story to find its place — Rebecca Yarros, Diana Peterfreund, Mari Mancusi, and Staci Hart. Sierra Simone — who always makes me think deeply about the relationship between power, money, and sex, and in this book in particular, sex work. Also those author friends who read, blurbed, and championed this book — Rachel Van Dyken, Wendy Higgins, Corinne Michaels, Nana Malone, Jessica Prince, Ava Harrison, Erin Noelle, Carrie Ann Ryans, and S.C. Stephens. I could not be here without all of you. This is a very isolating job, and you all make it worthwhile.

Thank you to Dani, who died a thousand deaths when I finally put this book into her hands. You're the best! To my assistant, Devin, for keeping me sane all these long months of edits. Thank you to my early readers, who suffered through reading it chapter by chapter and never gave up on the book through its many iterations. I love you: Anjee, Katie, Sharon, Becky, Lori, Christy, Polly, and Amy.

Thank you to my wonderful family and their enthusiasm for my writing and acceptance of my bizarre schedule. Plus, dealing with my desperate love for supernatural television shows my entire life. This book simply wouldn't exist without *Buffy the Vampire Slayer*. She's the hallmark of my childhood and the reason I fell in love with fantasy. Team Angel forever! (No fear, Spuffy fans. I adore Spike, too.)

And as always, my husband, Joel. You make this writer life easier and more worthwhile. And for taking care of our son when I have to spend the weekends editing and hours typing away on the computer or taking videos of me in the store signing books. You are the light of my life. You're my perspective.

Finally, YOU! Yes, you! You wonderful reader! Thank you for giving Beckham and Reyna a chance. For loving my alpha broody vampire and his stubborn, strong-willed girl. I can't wait for you to find out what happens next!

SHIELD OF SPARROWS IS A SLOW-BURN, HIGH-STAKES ROMANTASY PERFECT FOR FANS OF SARAH J MAAS AND EMILY THIEDE — WHERE ENEMIES BECOME LOVERS, MONSTERS WEAR CROWNS, AND A FORGOTTEN PRINCESS FINDS THE POWER TO BURN A KINGDOM DOWN.

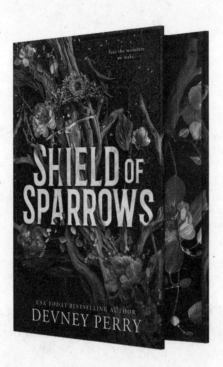

The gods sent monsters to remind mortals to kneel.

I've been kneeling my whole life — and I'm done.

As the overlooked second daughter of the kingdom's royal line, I was never meant to rule. Never meant to fight. And definitely never meant to marry the kingdom's deadliest monster hunter to seal a treaty soaked in blood.

But the day he walked into my father's court, everything changed.

Now I'm crossing cursed lands beside a stranger who sees me as a burden, bound to a future I never asked for, and watched by gods who delight in human ruin.

Everyone wants me to be something I'm not — a warrior, a symbol, a sacrifice.

But being invisible my whole life has taught me one thing: *there is power in the shadows.*

I just need to find the strength to take it.

CONNECT WITH US ONLINE

@REDTOWERBOOKS

@REDTOWERBOOKS

@REDTOWERBOOKS

JOIN THE ENTANGLED INSIDERS FOR EARLY ACCESS TO ARCS, EXCLUSIVE CONTENT, AND INSIDER NEWS! SCAN THE QR CODE TO BECOME PART OF THE ULTIMATE READER COMMUNITY.

RED TOWER
BOOKS™